The Garden of Eden All Over Again

Jude Collins is a senior lecturer in education at the University of Ulster. He is also a columnist with the *Irish News*, contributes regularly to BBC Radio Ulster and BBC 5 Live and has written two collections of short stories.

The Garden of Eden
All Over Again

Jude Collins

POCKET BOOKS

TownHouse

First published in Great Britain and Ireland by Pocket/TownHouse, 2002
An imprint of Simon & Schuster UK Ltd, and TownHouse and CountryHouse Ltd,
Dublin

Simon & Schuster UK is a Viacom company

1 3 5 7 9 10 8 6 4 2

Simon & Schuster UK Ltd
Africa House
64–78 Kingsway
London WC2B 6AH

Simon & Schuster Australia
Sydney

TownHouse and CountryHouse Ltd
Trinity House
Charleston Road
Ranelagh
Dublin 6
Ireland

A CIP catalogue record for this book is available from the British Library

ISBN 1 903 65023 2

Typeset by SX Composing DTP, Rayleigh, Essex
Printed and bound in Great Britain by
Omnia Books Limited, Glasgow

In memory of
Paddy and Minnie
Loving parents

CHAPTER 1

There was a clock crawling across the kitchen floor. He had come powering out from under the Aga, little black-purple back gleaming. Checked, made a feint left, turned right, and was now heading for where Maeve was kneeling. Past her stockinged feet, under her ankles, under the spread of her skirt. Warm in there, like a tent with no ventilation. Maybe he'd hook his little feet on to her school stocking, pull himself up like a climber mounting a cliff face. Pause at navy knickers. Mmm-hmm. These don't belong to Cait Cooley with the beaky nose, they belong to Maeve McGrath with the nice fat chest. Ho-kay. Then limbo under the elastic, make his presence felt, send her shrieking from the room. Family members smile quietly – *such* an emotional child.

'Exert thy mercy on the people of China,' Our Father said, 'who still sit in darkness and in the shadow of death.' Missionaries, having their fingernails pulled out, refusing to spit on the crucifix. That's what I should be thinking about, not girls' knickers, even if it was just my sister inside them. Especially if it was my sister. I pressed my forehead hard against the back of the chair, rubbed the skin of my right cheek. Poor wee face . . . Concentrate, you bugger. Think of China's darkness, with a smell of boiled rice. Only I can't because ting-tong Chinese darkness is lifting and instead Bernie Dunne is sitting on the edge of a bath, taking off her socks. Her feet are small and her toenails like tiny shells. This time tomorrow her birthday will be over.

'Father, Son, Holy Ghost.' Chairs scraped on the tiled floor as we rose from our knees. Our Father stayed kneeling, going over his trimmings in a loud whisper, burping occasionally.

Maeve was standing with her arm around Mammy's neck, whispering. Eyes rolling like a mare. Pss-wsss. Mammy elbowed her away, put a saucepan of milk on the cooker. 'Ask Our Father and don't be annoying me. Have you clean knickers for the morning?'

'Mamm-ee!' Maeve covered her mouth, stared at me.

Our Father blessed himself again and rose from his knees. Sat back in his armchair, loosened the top button of his trousers. 'Now what is she looking?'

'A céilí.' Mammy passed him his mug of Ovaltine. 'What need there is for running, I. Do. Not. Know. To dumps and dives. Isn't the new hall opening on Sunday?'

'I don't want to go the new hall.' Maeve's voice was like nails on a blackboard. 'I want to go to the céilí.'

'Are they charging for this céilí?' Our Father asked, rubbing the little bit of forehead between his wavy grey hair and exploding black eyebrows. Maeve claimed she saw him shaving across the forehead wrinkles one morning to leave a bit more space.

'One and sixpence,' Mammy said. 'To mix with the tramps of the country.' Maeve turned down the corners of her mouth, myaah, boohoo, girn, and went pounding up the stairs.

Our Father took off his slippers, tucked his chin into his chest and stared at his feet. Then twisted each foot in turn – left one this way, that way; right one this way, that way. To avoid arthritis. Mammy, humming in the scullery, mopping the floor. *Semper labor*. Out now, before you choke on the boredom.

'I think I'll go for a walk.'

Mammy stopped mopping. 'A walk?' Red blotches on her neck were the shape of maps of Europe.

Our Father leaned forward and pulled at his big toe, as if trying to remove it. 'Now what's he looking?'

'Looking nothing. Just said I might go for a walk.'

'Where are you going to walk?'

'Nowhere. All I said was, I'm going for a walk. A walk. A short walk.'

'Where to?' Mammy's jaw stuck out above the brush shaft and the light caught her gold filling.

'Cripes almighty. You don't decide walks in advance. You just do them. Without thinking.' Liar.

'You must be going somewhere.'

'Funny sort of place to go, nowhere. And it dark,' Our Father said. After two unsuccessful tries he cleared his throat and spat in the fire. Sizzle.

'All right,' I said. 'I'm going to Foxy's.'

'What're you going there for?' Mammy said.

'If that's where you're headed, you could get the *Herald* and *Con*,' Our Father said. 'And I'd have them tonight, not have to wait for Foxy to bring them tomorrow.'

'Need money if I was to.'

Mammy sighed and got her handbag from the drawer in the hall. Groped in it until she found a ten shilling note.

'Ask her for the change,' Debbie Reynolds said, putting her chin on my shoulder and pushing her front against my back. 'Say you're thinking of buying a Catholic Truth Society pamphlet about Maria Goretti, the famous Virgin and Martyr. Second cousin of Gina Lollobrigida.'

'And bring me back the change,' Mammy said. 'There could be a collection at the chapel tomorrow for the Holy Souls.'

'They're never done collecting,' Our Father said, leaning back and lifting his foot in the air.

There was a thud from upstairs, then the sound of Maeve crying. 'Aggghhh-hannnnghhh.'

Mammy stood listening, her head to one side. As the sobs faded she took the two tortoiseshell combs from her bun, allowing it to collapse down her back. In the pictures, women looked great when they let their hair down. Mammy looked a bit mad, staring after me.

'Don't you be long out in that wind. God knows what could blow down on top of you.'

I ducked out the back door, the ten shillings balled tight in my fist. The noise of Our Father burping followed me into the yard.

It had stopped raining but the wind was stronger. It pushed through the holes in the gable end of the boiler house, rattled the sheets of corrugated iron that formed its roof. Mammy kept on saying they should be nailed down, that some night they would fly off and cleave someone. Our Father kept on pretending not to hear. He hated spending money on things like that. I pictured him standing, pockets bulging with fivers, the point of a corrugated sheet, quivering gently, lodged in his skull.

Keeping my eye fixed on the square of light that was Foxy's shop I crunched towards the end of the lane, my lips moving in time to my footsteps.

Bernie my love, hear the thunder of my heart. Let me suck the bits of food from between your teeth.

*

Foxy's boots, spattered in cow dung, were at eye-level when I opened the shop door. He was standing on the counter, arranging tins along the back shelf. The tilly lamp threw a huge shadow on the back wall.

'Holy mulloley,' he said, positioning a tin of fruit cocktail and jumping down. He wiped his hands on his brown coat, the lamp catching the ginger hair peeping from his nose. 'You caught me three steps from heaven, as the boy on the wireless says. Doo-doo dee-doo doo doo-doo-doo-doo. Now. I have your business here.' He ducked below the counter and surfaced with a copy of the *Con* and the *Herald*. 'McGrath' was scrawled across the top. Con for Constitution, not conning, God's truth. Ulster not to include Donegal or Cavan or Monaghan, a Herald for Six Counties.

Foxy leaned his elbows on the counter, rear stuck out behind. 'Do you know what I was wondering – what way is it that some things happen and others don't? There's a question for you.'

'You asked me that last week.'

'I know I did. And what's this you said?'

I shrugged my shoulders. 'Fate, probably. Or predestination.'

He gripped the end of his nose between his finger and thumb for a few seconds. Exhaled. 'Pre. Dest. Ination. So. Did I tell you I met a man in the town this morning?'

Three boxes of Roses sweets. Side by side on the counter, six inches from my hand. 'No, I don't think you did.'

'Man by the name of Traynor – Councillor Neil Traynor, the very man. Has the electric shop in Market Street, drives a big giant of a motor car. Young lad about your age.' He held up his first and second finger, squeezed against each other. 'Here's me, passing Gormley's sweetie shop, and here's him pulling up at it. That close.' He put a little finger in his ear and wiggled it, checked what he'd brought out. 'Now. Supposing I'd been in John Street instead of Castle Street. Or if I'd stopped to tie my bootlace or light a cigarette. I wouldn't have met him, would I?'

Roses, two shillings. There'd still be change. A prick brings roses to a flower. 'Probably not. What difference did it make?'

Foxy scratched his Adam's apple. 'Well maybe not a pile. But at the same time I was wondering. The way you could miss somebody.'

'Or something. You could miss some thing as well.'

'Thing?'

It wouldn't have to be wrapped. 'Like, say, the time of a train. You could miss that. Or the water when the well runs dry.'

'You'd soon feel the loss of that, right enough.' Foxy straightened up, nodding and rubbing his hands together. 'For want of a nail, the shoe was lost. For want of a drink, the horse died of thirst.'

Bernie on the stage at the feis, in her costume. Arms straight by her side, knees pumping suddenly, the green flap of her costume bouncing off her thigh as her foot shoots out. Eyes fixed, her mouth a rosebud of concentration.

'. . . "Queer the way things works out," says I to Councillor Traynor. "There's you in your grand shop with gramophones and vacuum cleaners and the Lord Harry knows what, and here's me out in my wee huxter place."' Foxy wiped the counter with a cloth, then turned and ran it along the row of cans on the bottom shelf. '"If I'd gone working in Scotland one time I had a chance to work in a steel mine there, I could be a millionaire now. For all we know."'

Roses. With a little window to show the purple shiny paper and the green paper and the blue paper on the different sweets. Slip a note in with it: 'From your secret admirer'. A secret low-down prick, more like. She wouldn't know but she might guess.

'. . . "Nothing fancy. Just a tilly lamp and a wee chair for sitting on behind the counter, and a wee hut out the back for doing our business, not much but it does the wife and me."'

In a room with glass walls through which I can see the sea but not hear it, Bernie comes shimmering across the wooden floor that's the colour of honey. She's got on a white dress that flares out when she spins round, and her hair goes out from her head too, and then she stops, panting. Falls into my arms laughing. Here you are, Bernie, and here's a birthday kiss for you and well yes, if you like, give me one back on my ploughed-field face.

'. . . "The smell isn't a problem, we have Mr Smell under control rightly, Councillor," says I. "Shake a taste of Dettol every time I'm finished my business, that's my practice. And if the wife was in the shop for a day, she'd do the same thing. After her business."'

Right then. Just go up to her, maybe after Mass on Sunday. Here's a birthday present, as a token of my . . . So what if Maeve and Cait Cooley were watching? Cait's watery little red-ringed eyes following everything, whispering her report to Maeve. To hell with Cait.

'. . . transport is all is wrong with me. So he said he'd see what he could do. "I'll promise nothing but I'll do my best," sez he.' Foxy straightened up and blew hard into a hanky. The hair on his wrists the same colour as his shop coat. 'A brave decent man, Councillor Traynor. No difference with him who or what you are.' He put a Biro in his breast pocket, adding another mark to the forty-nine scores already there. 'Mind you, if I had a pony and cart, it wouldn't take me an hour to red the whole handling, leave her clean as a new pin. I'd have that pit dug out and me drove up to that new sewage place they have opened in the field behind your house, you know the place rightly. The Sewage Plant, they call it. Where they do bring the business of every lav in the town.'

In a year's time, all this might be beyond me. Dancing and girls and ordinary things like the sewage plant in our back field, a concrete bunker stuffed with dung. I'd be above all that, on higher ground. A life of the spirit. Or maybe not. More crack if I could keep my feet on the ground with everybody else, able to dance and laugh and catch people when they finished a swirl. Bernie was so thin she'd be easy to catch.

'. . . Your daddy knows himself, I'd have that cart spick and span after. Clean as your plate after licking.'

Foxy wanted the loan of our pony and cart. To move his shite.

'That's the kind of workman I am – scraped and shining. For if things were any other road, it'd only have me annoyed.'

I nodded. Right.

'"Do you know what I'm going to tell you," says I to Councillor Traynor. "Them regulations has me tortured. Boys from the Health hiding in the bushes for to catch me, over the head of a couple of cartloads of business." You'll mention it to your daddy, now? All it would take would be an hour, that wee pony of yours and the cart. See in the summer? Flies has us tortured. Coming burring and buzzing the size of your fist, in and out that lav door.' He paused, picked up a tin of fruit cocktail in his right hand, scratched his behind with his left. 'Fate, surely to God. That's what does it.'

'I'll take a box of Roses too, Mr Johnston.'

I stood outside Foxy Johnston's shop, the newspapers in one hand, the box of Roses in a white paper bag in the other. Bring them up to her, Porridge-face – she'll not eat you. Quick, before you start thinking about it.

Turning right and leaning against the wind, I climbed the hill towards Knockbeg Park. In five minutes my feet, passing each other in turn, would carry me to the door of Bernie's house. Rat-a-tat-tat. Hello, Bernie, smile in places, eyebrows up. I just happened to be passing and . . . Shut up. SHUT UP. Start again. Hello, Bernie. Heard it was your birthday – oh indeed, wee birdie told me, ha ha – so thought you might like this. Reach inside your trousers pocket . . . NO. Have it in your hand. Behind your back. Hope you like Roses, Bernie, ha ha. And by any chance would you be for that céilí tomorrow? Until last summer she had worn her hair in long plaits down her back. Presumer claimed that when she combed it out, she could sit on it. Then in August she'd got it cut. Styled so it swung round and framed her face like a bell, moving just a fraction after she did. You could see the little knobbly bones on her back and neck when she wore a summer dress. Make your own predestination.

When we were in High Infants in the convent, Bernie had been in the class. Her nose ran and when she got on the hobbyhorse, you could see her knickers. Pascal Brown said they were made out of sailor's shirt-tails, and we all laughed and a couple of us pushed her off the hobbyhorse.

She's changed a lot since then. Her hair was fairer now and she sometimes wore a blue ribbon in it. When she walked in to Mass on a Sunday morning, there was no sign of her knickers, although you knew they were under her yellow or red dress.

The front-room light was on. To the right of the fireplace her father was eating a bowl of cornflakes and reading a newspaper propped up against a milk jug. In between spoonfuls he spoke, shifting awkwardly in the chair, wagging the spoon and nodding his head in agreement with himself. His eyes never moved from the print.

Across the room her mother was polishing the mirror over the fireplace. Hawed her breath to mist a bit of it, then polished hard so that the sleeves of her dress shook. Finished at last, she went over beside her husband, took his spoon and ate two spoonfuls. Then tapped him gently on the head with the empty spoon and put it back into his bowl. Germs in the milk now. Swimming.

A light blinked on in the window above them. Bernie in her school uniform, a brown gymslip over a yellow blouse. For a moment she stood still; then rolled up a sleeve, scratched her right arm, and raised both arms above her head. Moved them in a flowing motion. Ballet. Stopped, began to pull a brush through her hair, grimacing with each stroke.

The grass whispered against my trouser-ends, then gravel pushed against the soles of my shoes, muttering. You're some boy. Looking for occasions of sin to wander into. What would St Bernadette think of such carry-on? Or Maria Goretti?

My breath began to come in little gasps. What if Bernie looked out, saw my face with the sour-milk cheek, curdled and scarred, staring up at her? Wuff-wuff, I'm a mongrel with a queer face, pat me or boot my arse, I'll be grateful for either . . . OK, count to five again slow-leee. Now. Let the gaze swivel casually. Look at the chimneypots, smoke being whipped away, swaying treetops. Finally, let the . . . Ohshiteshootmenow! Light out. She was gone. Trying not to moan, I forced myself to cross the street and stumble up the path to her door.

Press the bell. No sound. Bugger damn. I lift the letter slot and rattle it. As its echo fades, fear begins to bite. Won't know what to say to her. Her da may shout for me to go and boil my head, or throw a punch at me. Something has sucked the oxygen from my chest.

Listen. Above the noise of the wind, footsteps. Coming up the hallway in front of me, coming towards the other side of the door. In three seconds from now the door will open. Her ma or da will stand there and I'll have to ask can I see her. What the hell have I been dreaming of? Buying sweets, knocking at a door and it near the middle of the night. Stand or run. Fate is only feet away.

Turning, bent at the waist, I stride down the garden path. Now I'm on the footpath, sprinting towards the main road. Ram the box of Roses back into my pocket as I run. There's the sound of a front door opening behind me, but I'm not going to stop and check. A woman emerging from a phone box turns and looks in my direction. In the distance a banger goes off.

Down the hill again towards home, trotting now. Brain crackling like bacon. Damn, Ohshiteshootmenow. Why hadn't I stopped? Asked was Bernie in, talked to her. About? About anything, Uglymug. School, the weather, Chinese women getting their feet bound. Birthday. I'd bought the sweets, why not at least give them to her? I am in blood steeped so far, that should I wade no more/ Returning were as tedious as to go o'er.

Past Foxy's shop, into our lane. Cattle come lumbering through the darkness towards my footsteps. I draw back my arm and fling the box of Roses at the nearest one. It bounces off its nose. Eat chocs, you big dumb fucker.

Her da sitting there, spooning cornflakes into him. One night, years ago, he had pulled his trousers off, thrown them into the corner of the room and jumped into bed with her mother for the first time. Now he sits and eats cornflakes and wags his spoon. Or maybe it was all a front. Maybe that was why it had taken so long for the door to be answered. Maybe her mother and father had been . . . OhforGod'ssakeyoubuggershutup. Her father had been in the front room all the time. He'd probably forgotten how to wipe his arse by now, never mind try on the other.

In the kitchen Mammy's hands were in a bowl, the flour clinging to her arms. Maeve took the papers upstairs to Our Father. The armchair was still warm from his behind. A four-square arse, putting its weight where it felt like it, passing out heat to any surface it chose. While I hunkered about on the edges of life. Keep the coat buttoned across the front, leave the change quietly in the bowl on top of the chest of drawers.

'I met Maggie Ryan the other day at Hutton's, in leaving a skirt to get let out.' When she leaned on the dough her knuckles disappeared into it. 'She says you never wrote back to her Francie. He'll be home any day now, she says.'

Francie Ryan's letter with a Maynooth postmark four weeks ago, in early October. The lads were great, the Dean was great, the life of the seminary was great. They had football and singsongs. 'I have never been happier, Jim. God bless, Francie.' Who asked him to write to me? And if he did write, who asked him to write this bag of balls? No word of girls on bicycles with mud splashing the backs of their legs. No word of that day we walked home from primary school and he asked if I knew what riding meant. 'I was busy revising for exams,' I said, picking up the newspaper. '*Macmillan: You've Never Had It So Good.*' That's all you know, you moustachy bastard.

Mammy put the bowls away, wiped the tabletop with a grey dishcloth. 'Nice features on him, young Francie.' Right hand checked her bun of hair, squeezed one comb in tighter. 'Did I say I'll be heading to nine o'clock Mass in the morning?'

Well now. Glad to hear it. Because tomorrow is Saturday, Mammy, not Sunday, and I will stay in bed, Mammy. I'll waken at ten o'clock, stretch my legs, move them out of the warm bit and then back in again. I'll tilt my head to stare at the crack in the ceiling. Speak to Debbie Reynolds about that bit in *Singing In The Rain*, where she jumped over the couch and you saw the little cream knickers tight against her bum. Did she have to practise that an awful lot? Listen to the Buddy Holly EP, we-eh-he-he-hell. Maybe go down the field to the river, see is anybody fishing. Then head into town and meet Presumer. All of that, or some of it. But No Mass. Definitely.

And yet. Sixty years from now I'll be seventy-seven. Inches from eternity, if not already in it. See things a bit different then. Lying in a bed and realising you aren't going to get up off it. Ever. Or five minutes after you'd died. Think about that. All the people creeping out of the room, still alive, leaving you stretched there with cotton wool up your nose, God knows what up your other end and pennies on your eyes. No more dances or spitting. No more Roses. 'We have a deathday, the same way we have a birthday,' the missioner had said, gripping the velvet edge of the pulpit. 'Only we do not recognise its face.'

Mammy picked up a crumb and squeezed it between her finger and thumb. 'The Pope gets up at four in the morning and reads his breviary for an hour before saying Mass. Isn't that some going? Such a good holy wee man.' Then she carried the empty cups into the scullery. I left the kitchen, went upstairs quietly and quickly.

The fire in the bedroom grate had settled to orange. I put on the light. Jesus in place above the bed, his face light green, eyes rolling beneath the crown of thorns. Over from him, nice St Bernadette.

I opened the bottom of the chest of drawers. The syrupy smell of mothballs. At the back, on top of the yellowed newspaper, an eyeshade and an orange and white Penguin: *For Whom The Bell Tolls*. Underneath it, last Sunday's *Irish Independent*. 'Hoarse? Go suck a Zube.' Whores go suck a Zube, Presumer had said.

The hot-water bottle had been placed too low in the

bed – I had to wiggle lower, then reach down and position it between my knees. After three pages of reading, the print of *For Whom The Bell Tolls* started to wobble, sentences began repeating themselves. '*I am an old man old man old man who will live until I die,*' Anselmo said. '*And I am not afraid not afraid not afraid of foxes.*' But with the light out and my arms crossed on my chest (to show God I'd pray in my sleep if I could) things feel warm and safe.

Through half-open eyes I take in the dressing table, mirror, the hairbrushes and the silver box with the safety pins in it. The brass knobs of the bed catch the firelight, reflect its flames as bulges. St Bernadette, a brown blur, looks down from her picture. In the grotto beside the chapel, another St Bernadette kneels, never tiring, her hands raised in prayer to Our Lady. The wind thrashes the trees, a car in the distance struggles up a hill. The bark of a dog, then silence. God speaks, the missioner told us, in the silences. Use your lunch hour, with a chum or alone, to visit the one Person who is always glad to see you. Visit, lads. Kneel. He'll speak to you.

I turned over on my side, placed the hot-water bottle against my stomach. The warm milk inside me gurgled. Then I felt Debbie Reynolds snuggle up closer, her knees nudging the back of my thighs, her breath soft on my neck. 'Did I ever tell you your ears look gorgeous from the back?' she said.

This night as I lay down to sleep/ I pray to God my soul to keep/ And if I die before I wake/ I pray to God my soul to take.

CHAPTER 2

In the morning, I waited until I heard the van door slam, engine cough into life, the wheels crunch out the lane into silence. Our Father was gone. There were saucepans banging in the kitchen, which meant Mammy was back from Mass. In the bathroom I had a big pee out of my muscular mickey and splashed water on my face and neck. Then took the jar of yellow ointment from the press, scooped a glob and rubbed it into my right cheek the way the nurse had shown me. Start below the eye, make wee circles with your fingertips, on down and down to the edge of the chin. Not that it made any difference. Just as curdled when I finished as when I started.

'It was a funeral Mass,' Mammy said, pouring my tea. 'Some poor soul gone to their judgement. Will I get more toast?'

I ate another slice, propped up the previous day's *Irish News* against the milk jug. Stirling Moss was up in court for driving his new Austin Seven straight into a van and nearly killing a woman and her husband. His lawyer said he'd been trying out the braking system which had proved deficient. Tick, tick, tick, said the clock. Eleven o'clock. I'd visit Presumer. I slipped out the back door when Mammy was upstairs with Maeve making the beds.

The garage on the hill had two cars crouched beside it,

one with rust the shape of a map of Ireland in its passenger door. Past Gormley's shop, up Castle Street, turn in at the small lane halfway up. A row of white-washed houses, green and black stains where the wall met the ground. The Rat's Pad, linking Castle Street with the schoolyard.

I knocked at the fifth door along. Nothing. Its top and bottom half were closed. In summer Presumer's mother would open the top and lean out, elbows on the bottom half, staring towards the light and noise of Castle Street through the smoke from her Woodbine. I knocked again. There was a scuffling, like a dog or something bigger rubbing against the wood. The top half opened slowly.

She had one hand holding the front of her pink nightdress and the other pushing her teeth into place. Two lines ran from the corners of her mouth and collapsed into wrinkles on her chin.

'Jesus, Mary and Joseph – banging at this damn hour.' She cleared her throat. 'GER-ARD!' The shout ran through the house, came back again over her shoulder on to the street. 'Whatchumaycallhim's here. With the, you know, thing on his face.' A faint shouted response, coming maybe from under blankets some-where. She opened the bottom half of the door and indicated I should follow her. 'And stop you pulling my leg.'

This last was directed at Presumer's wee brother Sean, who was now revealed, fat cheek pressed against her thigh, watching me. She slid a sweet into his mouth and nudged him back into the house. 'Under the clothes and keep warm!' she yelled. We could hear him sucking and humming from the bedroom.

A wave of her arm told me to find a space on the couch, where several cats were sleeping on top of some old coats. Behind her the shadows of the Rat's Pad peeped through the dirt of the window.

'You'd never make me live here, would you?' Debbie Reynolds murmured in my ear. I shook my head without moving it.

'I should be in my bed too,' Mrs Livingstone said. 'Getting my beauty sleep.' She gave a half-laugh that ended in a cough.

A door in the corner opened and Presumer entered, wearing a grey shirt and black drainpipe trousers with what looked like a grease stain on the front. He lifted a bread knife and pointed it at me. 'Know what I dreamt last night? We were all in the concert hall and Dickey brought me up on stage to give me a medal for my English homework, only he couldn't pin it on because neither him nor me was wearing any clothes. He'd hair all over his arse, like a buffalo.' He cut a thick slice of bread.

'That's a nice way to talk about a Brother,' his mother said, lighting a half-cigarette.

'Only said he had a hairy arse.' Presumer cut a slice of bread, piled it with margarine and jam. 'Could have said about the way he used to go on at rehearsals in First Year, instead. Remember that, Jim?' I shook my head. Presumer wiped his mouth with the back of his hand. 'Do surely. Letting on he was measuring us for costumes. "Just let me check, son, hold still, son. Move your wee leg this way – 'at's it now".'

'What are you talking about?' his mother demanded. 'You're talking double Dutch.'

'Listen, Ma. The bastard has a hairy arse, OK?

Anybody could have a hairy arse – Oliver Plunkett, the Pope, Martin de Porres . . . Though the Pope couldn't be a bastard, could he? He could be bastardy but he couldn't be a real bastard. Real bastards can't become priests.' Presumer took a bite of bread, then made pointing motions in the air. 'Works the other way round as well. Francie Ryan has no arse and he thinks he's a saint, only he's really a bastard. A pain-in-the-arse bastard, not a hair-on-the-arse real-real bastard, because if he was a real-real bastard he couldn't be a priest.' Presumer turned to me. 'He's home, you know. Dressed in a black suit and hat.' Presumer showed his teeth in a clenched smile. 'Parading around with an arse in his trousers but no arse *inside* his trousers.'

'I should have whaled your arse when you were wee, put manners on you,' his mother said, sipping her tea.

Presumer tickled a ginger cat. 'Ma's powerful for manners. What about that Bridget Bardot nightie of hers – sexy cat, eh? And the way she puts her teeth in before she answered the door – class, eh?'

Before I could respond, the ginger cat leapt from under Presumer's hand to the dresser and sent a plastic bowl of sugar clattering to the ground.

'Lepping Jesus – look what you done, Gerard!' Mrs Livingstone stood and scooped the cat from the dresser, thumping it hard against the wall. The cat screeched and Sean appeared at the bedroom door, round eyes in a white face.

'Naughty Mummy,' Presumer said, stroking the cat. 'Some night, she sleep, pee in ear, OK?' He straightened, folded a slice of bread and jam and pushed it into his mouth. Turned, made the sign of the cross, pointed to his mouth. 'This is Mi-Wadi.' Then he began to cough, bits of food flying everywhere.

'May you choke, you bad bloody article,' his mother told him, wiping her front. 'No wonder you never have luck.'

Presumer took a drink from a jug of milk, burped loudly. 'Mother dearest, would you have something in the way of money? A bob or two.'

'One or two – which?'

'Two.'

'Have not.'

'All right, one then.'

She disappeared into the bedroom and came back with two sixpences. 'That's nearly half a night's work at the golf club, mind. I don't know what the hell I do be giving it to you for, anyway.'

Presumer knelt on the floor beside her, grabbed at her hand and tried to kiss it. 'You give like the pelican because your love is lodged deep in your breast. And one day, Mother, I promise, I shall take you from this drudgery. Before that, though, I need a new film for my camera.' Presumer had won the camera in a mouth organ competition the previous Christmas.

'Taking pictures of damn all. People thinking you're a halfwit.'

'Not damn all, Mother. The world, the universe.' He turned to me. 'Did you hear Mary O'Kane is for singing at the opening of the new hall on Sunday?'

'I heard they were doing a play,' I said.

'Mary'll be singing before it.' Presumer crouched, made camera movements with his fingers. 'Local star enchants Omagh – Livingstone catches moment. Click-click. Thousands in tears, Queen knights Livingstone, sword slips, cuts off pageboy's balls, click-click, Duke of Edinburgh breaks his royal arse laughing.' Then he clapped his hands above his head and did a sort of Spanish dance around the room.

'If you want exercise, take my bike to Baldwin's, get them to fix its puncture,' his mother said, throwing her cigarette butt in the fire.

Presumer swallowed the last of the bread and pointed at me again. 'Wait till I get my coat.' He disappeared into the back room and almost immediately re-emerged, his Brownie camera in one hand. 'Look at this – four shots still in her.' He pointed to the little window in the camera where a nine showed. 'One of your Maeve in there, standing outside the convent with, what's her name . . . Cait, right. Pokey red eyes, big nose. Honk-honk. Her and Maeve yapping and arguing about a céilí or something. I was hoping they'd start nipping each other's diddies.'

'Quet that bloody corner-boy talk,' Mrs Livingstone said in a high voice. 'And tell Baldwin I need that bike tomorrow.'

The main street was thick with shoppers, mostly country people. Into Omagh town for confession in the chapel. I'm sorry Father, OK daughter, three Hail Marys, job's a good one. Then down the hill to the shops to get tea and sugar and bacon and sausages, brandy balls for the wains.

'Is your ma mad?' Presumer asked, one eye shut and walking as if his knees didn't bend. 'I sometimes think mas are mad. They're always nyamping and fretting, they hate cats, they hate crack, and they're always saying they're tired. Though I suppose you'd be tired too if you'd eight pounds had come elbowing out between your legs. Imagine, eh? – a shite eight pounds weight!'

Halfway down the hill a policeman stood at the door of the barracks, his revolver black and heavy in its holster. Presumer did a little bow. 'What time do you have, please, officer?' His voice sounded ever so slightly foreign. The policeman eyed him, then slowly took a watch from his tunic pocket. Quarter past eleven. 'Thank you, officer,' Presumer said. 'I am obligated.' We moved down the street. 'RUC – Rough Ugly Cunts,' Presumer whispered out of the side of his mouth. 'Put their baton up your arse as soon as look at you.'

We passed Swann and Mitchell's, where Mammy always took me to get measured for new shoes. Bargaining with Mr Swann about the price. The mark on my cheek burning.

'My ma is never done fretting. She wants me to take Maeve to this céilí.'

Presumer stared. 'Holy shite – your sister to a céilí! Wouldn't fancy that. You could hardly court your own sister, could you?'

'I'm to see nothing happens to her. Or Cait. Cait Cooley's going with her.'

Presumer drew a huge beak-shaped nose in the air. 'Wonder what it'd be like riding someone with a nose the size of hers. Have to keep your head pushed back the whole time – put a right crick in your neck.' He kicked the pedal of the bicycle and made it spin backwards. 'Will you have to dance with her – the Cait one?'

'Hope not. Three-hand reel – her, me and the schnozz.' I felt a bit bad saying it, but Presumer laughed so hard it was worth it.

The inside of the bike shop was dark. Isaac Baldwin

emerged from a back room, scratched his moustache with an oily finger and took the bike by one handlebar. He was full up now but he'd fix the puncture tonight, and tomorrow morning he'd send the young Traynor lad out to the house with it. Almighty Traynor worked in his da's record shop across the street but helped out in Baldwin's when they were stuck. He'd been in the class at primary school with me and Presumer, but could never do the sums and left when he was fourteen. But that was all right because his da was rich and a town councillor. Maeve hated Almighty. He'd grin and wave when he saw her, even from the other side of the street. 'The ignorant skitter!' she'd mutter. Even Cait hated him. Maybe Almighty would get fed up with rejection and go to Maynooth. Not hard keeping your hands off women if none of them could stand you. Except they wouldn't have him because for Maynooth you had to be smart.

Now Presumer and I were going past the chapel, along John Street, up the steep incline of Gallows Hill. He pointed ahead. 'Tonto say climb holy mountain, Kemosabe – check for High Wire Girl.'

Standing at the low wall that ran round the Jail Square, we could see the Show Grounds laid out below. From the wall there was a straight drop of about thirty feet; then the ground sloped gradually down to the wall around the grounds. Today, most of the grass inside the wall was covered by a red and white tent with poles sticking through the top and flags attached. Caravans were parked close to the boundary with the Christian Brothers' Park, ponies the size of sheep grazing near them. Maybe Foxy would be able to persuade one of the circus people to lend him a pony and cart.

'Who's this girl we're supposed to be looking for?'

'High Wire Girl.' Presumer smiled a Jack Palance smile and climbed on top of the wall. Began walking along it, hands out to balance. 'Not see the posters? The Great Collette. She walks the high wire above the lions' cage.' He waggled his fingers, patted his thighs. 'Wears a wee frilly job that length . . . Say you were a lion, eyeing these two big soft legs above you, wishing she'd tumble down till you . . . Wheeeow!' He pretended to wobble, then jumped back safely on to the gravel path that ran alongside the wall, all round the Jail Square. 'Right. Let's mosey down, Tonto, and check out the terrain.'

We moved down the hill, leaning back slightly to balance against the slope. Prams sat outside the front doors of terraced houses, wee girls arguing as they played hopscotch on the pavement. Toddlers with sticky faces and damp noses stared up at us. At the bottom of the hill the Show Grounds were a hum of activity. People going in and out, the throb of engines, the smell of oil and animal dung. Somewhere a loudspeaker blared instructions.

Presumer took his camera from the paper bag, held it in front of him like the priest with the monstrance.

'Have you a pen?' he asked me out of the side of his mouth.

'I have.'

'Put it in your breast pocket. And stop for nobody until you get to the caravan at the end. If they ask, you're a reporter for the *Strabane Chronicle* and I'm your photographer.'

Nobody stopped us, nobody questioned us. We passed clattering generators, chrome caravans, men and women with watchful brown eyes. 'Keep going,' Presumer whispered. We walked between two rows of caravans until we reached a green patch near the Christian Brothers' Park wall.

As we did so the door of the second last caravan opened and a man came down the steps. He was carrying a bucket and scrubbing brush and his head was bent. He didn't appear to see us as he passed.

'What's so great about this High Wire Girl anyway?' I whispered. 'Loads of them do the high wire thing.'

Presumer breathed on the lens of his camera, wiped it with his shirt-front. Then rubbed his thumb and first two fingers together in front of my face. 'Mon-ee. The *Ulster Herald* is giving three guineas for the best picture sent in between now and next June – "A Farewell to the Fifties" picture. See if I get a decent snap of your woman? Those big horsey legs and that wee frilly thing over her bum – give the judges such a dose of the horn, they'll not even look at the other entries. Here, hold this.'

He passed me the camera, walked briskly up the caravan steps. Knocked hard.

No reply. Presumer made a zombie face, did an Elvis Presley move with his pelvis in my direction, then knocked again. 'Hi!' he called, his mouth to the door. 'Anybody in?'

The door opened two inches. 'Ess?'

'Is Collette about?'

'Iss what?' The woman's voice had a flat sound, as if something was stuck in the back of her throat.

'The Great Collette. The High Wire Girl. Where's she at?'

'Iss trespass. Circus, circus, circus.' The woman was standing at the door now, shouting. One bare arm emerged from a purple shawl to wave angrily towards the exit.

'Holy Jesus,' Presumer sighed and raised both hands. 'Hold your water, missus. All I'm looking is a snap of Collette in the yoke with the frills. No lions.' He rubbed the back of his neck thoughtfully. 'Good publicity for your circus if it gets in the newspaper, eh? Savvy what I'm saying?'

Before the woman could answer, the man who had been in the caravan appeared again, his bucket now filled with water. As soon as she saw him, the woman began to call to him in a foreign language, her words hitting the air like small black hammers. Then pointed towards Presumer and myself.

The man put down his bucket, so quickly some of the water slopped over its edge. Then, his face like stone, he began to stride towards Presumer, who turned to face him, shaking his head and smiling.

'Whoa, Dobbin boy, steady there. You see, the *Her*—'

In mid-word the man grabbed Presumer by the front of his shirt, pulled him down the steps and flung him towards the Show Grounds gate. Presumer's arms flailed as he tried to keep his balance.

'Caravan is privacy, sonbitch! No question!' the man shouted. He swung round to me. 'Also scarfiss bashtar! No question!'

I held the camera behind my back and moved nearer to the gates. Presumer began to speak very quickly.

'You've the wrong end of the stick, mister. It's not me wants the picture – what would I want a picture for? Under orders, you see. Sergeant Armstrong from the police barracks – doesn't mince his words, no fear. "A

nice photograph of Collette – that's what I'm looking" –
his exact words to me. Savvy-vous? Caw-lett. Beautiful
woman. Pretty girl. Me give Sergeant one photograph,
put other photograph into competition. Savvy? Sergeant
making identity list, I think.'

At the word 'identity' the man stopped shouting. He
turned, looked at the woman and said a quick couple of
words. She replied briefly, then stood with her hands
together as if in prayer. The man turned back to us, his
face twisting into a smile.

'Ah yes. Collette. Unfortunately, not here. On
personal business. I will tell her. Assist authorities where
possibly human.'

Presumer pulled his shirt back into position. Folded
his arms and nodded. 'Glad to hear it. Because Sergeant
Armstrong said if I didn't get a photograph, he'd have
my arse for breakfast.' He laughed and the man laughed
too. Then the woman joined in, her laughter bobbing
like a cork above that of Presumer and the man.

Outside the gate, the town sat looking down on us. The
spire of the Protestant church; to the right, the two taller
spires of the Catholic church; then the Courthouse. Not
speaking, we moved up Castle Street, past the Post
Office and Swann and Mitchell's Shoes, towards the
centre of town again. Presumer whistled softly between
clenched teeth.

'Munch, munch,' he said at last, jerking a thumb over
his shoulder. 'Definitely a munch-munch case.'

'How do you mean?'

'Your man. Something is chewing on his guts.
Squelch, crunch, munch.'

'He didn't like you trespassing on his property, is all.

He comes back and finds you quizzing his wife and trespassing on his property. What'd you expect?'

We were outside the Belfast Bank. Presumer stopped and glared at me. '*His* property? What are you talking about?' He stood close to me and tapped my chest. 'Let's say you're a circus person, right? And you're walking along with a bucket, and you see this guy who wants to get a picture. Would you start roaring and try pulling the balls off him?'

'I might.'

'All right, let's say you would. Next question: *why* would you start roaring and pulling his balls?'

'Because . . . Because when I came back you're tormenting my wife and she starts complaining to me about you . . . Anyway, what was that rubbish about Sergeant Armstrong asking you to take photographs?'

'I had to say something, didn't I? Worked too. See the way his big gob dropped?' He held out his hand. Drops of rain had begun to bounce off the footpath, darkening it in little island stains. 'Angels' piss.'

We both ducked into the doorway of Swann and Mitchell's. On both sides of the street people had begun to run for cover.

'That jibber-jabber balls-merchant was frothing at the mouth,' Presumer continued, raising his voice above the crackle of rain on pavement and roadway, 'because he's got something to hide. That's the way with guilty people. They get suspicious, get annoyed, because they're scared of their arse somebody will smell out their skulduggery. Somebody on the side of the angels, like us.'

A woman in a see-through plastic coat ducked into the doorway beside us.

'I declare to goodness,' she panted. 'I'm soaked to the skin. Every stitch on me.'

His back to her, Presumer rolled his eyes and put his mouth close to my ear. 'Kidnappers,' he breathed. 'Buggers have got a millionaire's son stuck in the back of that caravan. Handcuffed in a cage, shoving stale bread in to him to keep him alive.'

'There are no millionaires in Omagh,' I said. 'No kidnappers either.'

'Half-millionaires. Quarter-millionaires. Turkey cocks with big cars and big bank accounts that think the sun shines out of their arses and their wee dotes' arses too.'

The woman twisted her head round and glanced at us briefly.

'These people aren't kidnappers,' I said. 'They're in a circus.'

'They could be kidnappers in a circus. They could have started years ago. Joined the circus so they could move from town to town, one jump ahead of the law. Kidnapping as they go.'

The rain slackened, and the woman in the see-through coat tightened her scarf and headed out into the street again. We followed her.

'You don't have to photograph Collette,' I told Presumer. 'There are loads of people you could photograph. Babies in prams, your man Neil, your ma – you could photograph *her*, couldn't you?'

Presumer shook his head. 'She hates getting her picture took. Thinks it steals another bit of her soul every time. Anyway, this is personal *and* business, you see. I want the picture for the competition *and* I want the picture for me. To look at.' He clenched his fists together and stared at them. 'She's been everywhere, your woman

– you'd know looking at her. Hungary, Suez Canal, China, Philippines. Just looking at the picture I'll be able to sniff abroad off her – you dig, daddy-o? When the winter nights are cold and I'm so all alone, ba-ba-ba-boom-boom.' Presumer stopped and brought his right arm to shoulder level then whirled it forward, hinching an imaginary handball at an imaginary wall. 'Know what I dreamt the other night? I was in a circus and some bastard had put me in the lions' cage and locked the door. Next thing your woman Collette comes up and starts to slide between the bars to rescue me. Only they're so tight together she has to take all her clothes off and grease herself down with some oil. Should have seen the job she had getting her diddies through.'

'How did she get you out?'

'She bent the bars with her bare hands. Muscles all down her back and bum winking at me while she was pulling the bars apart. Yeeeooooh!' He put his hand on the front of his trousers and pretended to be pulling his thing.

'You're mad.'

'If I'm mad,' Presumer said, 'why did Jabberhole from the caravan change his tune? One minute he wants to barbecue my balls, next I'm his bosom buddy. I think,' he said, ducking his head to look over each shoulder in turn, 'at this very minute we could be being watched. In imminent danger.' Then he gripped my arm so tight it hurt. He was panting. 'Did you see that?'

'See what?'

'That. THAT. Down there. Your woman in the navy gaberdine.'

'For God's sake—'

'Your woman. Collette.'

I looked along the street at the tall figure standing outside Swann and Mitchell's.

'That's the Great Collette?'

'That's her!'

'Walks the high wire above the lions?'

'Makes them horny as be damned.'

The head at this moment was leant towards the window of Swann and Mitchell's, the part where the women's shoes were kept. A reflecting head looked back from the inside, two headscarves dipped forward to meet and merge. Siamese twins.

'Give us your pen.'

'What do you want a pen for?'

'And a bit of paper.' His voice was tense. 'Right. You take the camera.'

I stood and waited while Presumer walked back up the street towards the figure at the shop. The woman straightened.

'Excuse me. Are you Collette? The High Wire Girl?' He spoke slowly, like someone coaxing along a victim of memory loss.

'Ah. High Wire.' Her voice was more girlish than I'd expected from one so strong-looking. 'Ess. Am circusact Collette.'

Presumer's arms were in the air, fluttering. 'To walk like that – in your costume – above a crowd of lions. Whew.' He shook his head and laughed and the woman smiled slowly. 'Not for a million could I risk having a lion put his teeth round my leg.'

'You learn.' A soft little voice. 'Where will is strong, you learn.'

'Not me – you must have the nerves of a tiger . . . So here. Ask you a favour?'

'Fervour?'

'A – a compliment – no, not a compliment – a kind act. Not much.'

'Not much,' the woman said. She had dark brown eyes, with black eyelashes that seemed to curl more than those on other women. From the front her nose was long and straight, but from the side you could see that it had a little ridge just below the eyeline. Inside the blue gaberdine coat, her body pulled the material into spears of shadow and light.

'Would it be all right' – he turned and waved for me to approach – 'if I was to take your picture? You know, photograph. Maybe get your autograph too.'

'Autograph too?'

'Name. Signature. It's a custom here. Signature.'

'So. Two things are requested. Photograph, one, and signature. Autosign, two.'

'Right. A full-length, if that's OK – not an identity job.'

What was he talking about? This photograph, no matter what way he took it, would be pointless. Who cared about a dark-eyed woman standing in the street? The Collette in a frilly costume was what people wanted to see.

But now the atmosphere had changed. The Great Collette had stopped smiling and her lower teeth, hidden until now, showed. One tooth, on the right-hand side, stuck out a bit.

'You speak of identities, please?'

'Nothing. Slip of tongue. It's a full snap of you I've looking.'

Collette didn't reply – just stood still, eyeing us both. Something important was about to happen – I could feel it. I thought maybe she was thinking of stepping out of her coat right there in the middle of the street, revealing underneath the costume and the big long horse's legs that Presumer had talked about. But she didn't. Instead she took three swift steps and was beside me. Then the camera was out of my hand, she had found the clip, she had opened it.

'You have to keep the film in the dark!' I yelled. But it was too late.

'Oh dear,' the woman said, smiling. 'Oh the deario.' She gripped the edge of the film and pulled it free. 'What a mishap to have opened your camera. Is catastro-if.'

Presumer grabbed the camera from her and tried desperately to push the film back inside. It got crumpled. Little yellow wigwam corners jutted from the camera at all sorts of angles. Eventually he gave up and crammed the film into his pocket.

'Jesus. You've ruined the whole film. Twelve shots.' His face was white, except for a half-circle of darkness under his eyes.

'Oh my dear. To speak the Lord Host's name. Is ungentlemanly! But let us see.' She tapped her chin with a brown finger. 'In recompense, shall you perhaps visit the circus as my partial guest? At reduced fee, one shilling rather than one and sixpence.'

'That film cost two bob.' Presumer's voice sounded as if he had broken glass in his mouth.

'When you come, ask for me at the gate – the Great Collette. And condolences for the troubles of your camera.' She smiled, spread her hands in a gesture of helplessness.

Presumer stepped back a pace, his face crumpled. 'Bitch!' he said in a loud voice. 'Jabberwock bitch!'

Several people passing turned and stared. Presumer ignored them. Collette gave us a wave like the Queen and moved on down the street.

I led Presumer, who was swearing and blinking a lot faster than usual, towards Castle Street. He was still shaking when we came to the Rat's Pad turn-off. We stopped for a moment, and then he said he'd maybe better come out the road with me for a while or he might start punching a fucking wall and maybe his ma and wee fucking Sean as well. Even though it was only four o'clock in the afternoon the light had begun to fade. A wind had risen, making the canvas canopy flap above Gormley's shop.

'That's two bloody crimes inside five minutes – theft first and then aggravated assault. Can you believe it?' Presumer shouted above the swoosh of trees. 'She took my property and she assaulted it, and now those photographs are buggered. Circus hoor!' he shouted at the sky through cupped hands; then took a kick at some weeds growing along the base of the wall, behind which the Army had its barracks.

'Maybe it was an accident.' To be heard above the wind I had to half-shout. 'Maybe she didn't mean to wreck the film.'

'And maybe pee-the-beds and parsley grow out of my arse. There's something fishy going on in that circus.' He tried to kick a stone and missed it.

Two figures emerged from a house at the bottom of the hill. Brothers Dickey and Meehan. They moved towards us, fingers splayed over the crowns of their hats, coats whipped tight against their bodies.

'Gruesome twosome,' Presumer said. 'Legion of the rearguard. Can't go near a bit of fluff until the day they die. Imagine that – would it be worth waiting for, do you think?'

'Waiting for what?'

'Until the day you die for to get your hands on a bit of fluff.' He stopped walking backward and moved alongside me again. 'Can't get at a bit of fluff UNTIL – until the day they die. Get it? Until. Hand out from under the sheets for a last-minute feel.' He made his mouth the shape of a whistle and blew into the wind. 'Bet you that's what heaven's like – diddies galore, morning till night.'

He had to face forward again then because the Brothers were almost level with us. We both saluted. Brother Meehan nodded, but Brother Dickey turned away, as if to avoid looking at something unpleasant. Then they had passed.

Presumer looked back over his shoulder at them. 'Dickey's out to get me, you know.'

'Don't be stupid.'

'If he could kill me and not get caught, he would. Cut my body up and melt it down on a cooker.'

'No he wouldn't. He's a Christian Brother. That means he can't go around killing. Even thinking about it would be a sin for him.'

'He wouldn't let me join the recorder club – remember? Stupid big-arse bastard.'

I remembered it. We'd been in first year at grammar school and Dickey had started a recorder group, that would eventually play at the Christian Brothers' Concert. For the first two weeks of practice he'd let us use the recorders he kept in the classroom press. But then he said if we wanted to join the club, we'd have to bring ten shillings to buy the recorder. That way if we broke our recorder, he said, it'd be our loss, not his.

That Friday, ten of us First Years lined up at Dickey's desk after school, with our money. He took it from each of us in turn, wrote our names in his book, and gave us the recorder to take home. They were brown and shiny and beautiful. The last in the line was Presumer. Dickey didn't even look up. 'Go home, Livingstone,' he said, and went on adding up sums and writing in his book. 'But I have the money, Brother,' Presumer told him, putting a crumpled ten shilling note on the desk. 'Look.' Dickey straightened up and brushed the money off his desk, so Presumer had to pick it up off the floor. 'Go away home out of this, Livingstone, and out of my sight this minute.' Some of the other boys said they saw Presumer crying down the schoolyard, but that was a load of rubbish. I'd never seen Presumer crying in my life.

We passed the Army barracks wall. Lights showed behind a poster telling us to join the Army and see the world.

Change the subject. Stop him thinking about Dickey and Collette. I pointed to the wall of the base. 'I could never do that – could you? Jumping out of a trench with your bayonet. Dig, twist, open somebody up. They shoot you if they catch you deserting, you know. Sometimes torture you first.'

Presumer put an imaginary gun to his head and pulled the trigger. 'Ouch. Yaroo, that hurt, you fucking rotters. You rotting fuckers.' He paused. 'They have a good time in training though. They get lorry-loads of women, the first couple of months. Not know that? Boat them here from all over England. Three women for every soldier.' We walked for a while in silence. 'After, they send the women home and the soldiers have to go to Kenya and places like that. Buck niggers lepping out of the jungle with hook knives, cutting off their things. Big chopping block, stretch it out, then – ch-*hunk*.' He nodded slowly. 'England's where the money is. I'm for there myself this summer.'

I felt a thickening inside my throat. 'For the summer?'

He shook his head. 'For keeps. To Blackpool. Amusements and everything – like Bundoran only better. Down the road from Manchester. Manchester United, Preston North End, Blackpool. Stanley Matthews.'

'What the hell are you going there for?'

'Work in a factory. Or an office. Or . . .' He waited until we had passed another house, as if someone inside might be eavesdropping. The wind surged, plastering our trouser legs against our shin bones. 'Open my own photography place, have them queuing up. "Karsh of Ottawa? Pile of shite, matey. Gimme Livingstone of Omagh. Bleedin' genius, 'im." '

At McCauley's with its pretend-castle wall, Presumer stopped.

'Could she be smuggling cigarettes, do you think?'

'Doubt it.'

'Horses, then. Or crocodiles.'

'Hardly.'

'Christ, can you credit it? A whole roll of film – the fucking bitch.' He raised his hand to shoulder level, palm facing me. 'I solemnly swear, swear; by Almighty God, God; I'm going to get the Great Collette, Great Collette. So help me God, God.'

Then he brought his hand down in a looping US Cavalry salute and headed back to town. I leaned into the wind, towards home. It was getting dark.

Angel of God my guardian dear/ To whom God's love commits me here/ Ever this night be at my side/ To light and guard, to rule and guide. Amen.

CHAPTER 3

That night I woke and thought for a minute there was something in the room. An animal, maybe, a dog or even a cow, gasping beside my bed. The night was full of noises, one riding on top of the next. At the bottom the wind – hissing up the trees' skirts, thrashing their limbs, shaking with excitement. Above that, occasional clatterings. A bucket went bouncing along the yard outside, bashed against the wall of the shed, rolled to a stop. The corrugated roof of the boiler house lifted, rattled, slammed down again. And above that, the whistling sound. Sometimes it surged up until it was high and demented like those whistles they use to get admirals on board a ship. Other times it was like a tiny bird, faint and getting fainter.

I got up and went pad, pad, pad in my bare feet to the bathroom. The wind had invaded the water pipes, making them moan and rattle too. The bathroom window was being pelted by twigs and leaves.

Ten minutes after I got back to bed the rain started. Five or six slow drops, then a full raging downpour, thudding into the gravel and the grass and the trees, drumming on the roof. In the fireplace bits of ash and soot spat out on to the carpet. At one point I thought I heard thunder; and I could have sworn there was a flash of lightning. God, up above the darkness, pressing the buttons. Stinking sinners that don't follow my will and think I won't notice. Take that – and that!

Ten past three. I hunch the blankets over my right shoulder and pull my knees towards my chest. Impossible to sleep. Only the next minute my eyes open and instead of it being dark it's bright, or at least a grey through the bedroom curtain. The winds still whipping and slapping but more quietly now.

I was spreading marmalade on my fourth slice of toast, watching a dab of butter melt on my finger and wondering which part of Bernie I'd like to watch butter melt on, when footsteps sounded. Almighty Traynor, wheeling a ticking bike across the yard. Mrs Livingstone's. He propped it against the wall.

'Took her for a test spin – drop her off to Presumer's ma's on the way back. Providing I'm not killed.' He tugged at his Adam's apple. 'See if I'd been cycling two hours earlier past Knockbeg Park? Bike and me would have been crushed like an ant on an acorn.'

'An ant on a what?' Maeve said in a high voice.

'Acorn.'

'Will you take tea, Alphonsus?' Mammy said.

'Godalmighty surely, Mrs McGrath. Know something?' He leaned across the table, his neck stretched like a goose's. 'Take six carthorses to get it from across the middle of the road.'

I thought for a minute. 'There's a tree blown down?'

He nodded, pulled the neck in again. 'Nestlé's lorry driver said only he pulled on the handbrake, he'd have been pulverised. And the circus tent in the Show Grounds would have been blew down, only they got extra ropes tied on to the horses and then on to the tent, to hold it up. But there's branches every road.'

'Was any ones hurt?' Mammy asked, putting another plate of toast between us. Almighty took two slices and spread them thick with marmalade. Made a sandwich with them.

'A telephone pole landed on a house in Carrickmore – man in bed never even woke up. Daddy says they'll only be able to tell who he is by his teeth. The electricity had the rest of him made into jelly. And a policeman in Beragh was electrocuted. He was working with an electric drill in the garage and the wind blew it out of his hand and it went into his eye. Through his skull before they could stop it.'

'And him a policeman. God save us,' Mammy said. 'Eat up, Alphonsus, I'll get you two slices more.'

'Thanks, Mrs. But see Knockbeg Park – Godalmighty, you should see it. You should. Just. See it. Chimney-pots blown down all over the place. My daddy says if they light a fire, they'll choke to death, and if they don't they'll freeze. See if you give me a thousand pounds?'

I nodded. You had to nod at Almighty sometimes. Or kill him.

'Wouldn't live in Knockbeg Park. My daddy says they have it like a slum.'

'Your daddy's right there,' said Mammy. 'Most of them anyway.'

'And I suppose youse heard about the robbery?' Almighty gave his little lips-closed smile. He liked when people hadn't heard things. 'Mary O'Kane's brother, the boxer boy. Paddy. He's a projectionist in the Picture House. Well last night he goes to count the money and guess what? A load stolen out of it. Circus ones away with the whole pile.'

'Were they caught?' I asked. 'Was it the Great Collette?'

'I don't know – probably the whole lot of them.' Almighty took a swig of tea. 'Not that I give a dang what they do. Godalmighty, what would I care? The thing worrying me is *The Winning Maid*. That's what's worrying me.'

'The what?' Maeve asked.

'They play – *The Winning Maid* – in the New Hall. People that were going to come to the play might be afraid now, in case a tree would land on them and squash their guts.'

'Please God they'll cancel this céilí, then,' Mammy said.

'Please God they'll not bother,' Maeve muttered.

'What are you in the play?' I asked Almighty.

'A neighbouring farmer. I tell about the serving girl being seen weeping behind a tree on the small boreen that leads from the bog. "She was standing like a tree after rain, the tears chasing each other down her sweet face, and I didn't know whether to speak to her or hide." There's a big speech about her. At eight tonight. We have to rehearse at three. Brother Meehan says he thinks it'll be a powerful production.'

'A good play is better than a thousand of your TVs,' Mammy said. 'All the world's a stage, and the men and women a crowd of actors.'

'Well it so happens they have plays on TV too,' Maeve said. 'Sister Concepta told us, more people see a play on television than it would take four hundred years to get if you were doing it on a stage. We should have a TV.'

'We should have nothing of the sort,' Mammy said.

'Muck and dirt from start to finish. Is your play long, Alphonsus?'

'It has three acts, so two intervals. And guess who's appearing in both intervals? Go on, guess.'

'Grace Kelly,' I said. 'Jane Russell. Mary O'Kane.'

Almighty stopped brushing the crumbs from his trousers and stared at me, bottom lip hanging. 'Somebody told you. But I bet they never told you she'd signed a big contract with Larry Whatyoucallhim – the big London boy. Parnes. Mr Parnes says that the public's sick of all these glamorous women singers. It only makes other women jealous. The thing about Mary O'Kane is, she's not glamorous. That's the best thing about her, he says. "Little Smasher", they call the record she's doing. Cutting. You cut a record, that's what you do with it. Cut. My daddy says we're going to order over a hundred of them for the shop, because that's the least he could do and him her manager.'

'Cait says Bridie Gallagher is being sued by her manager,' Maeve said. 'For a million pounds.'

'I thought the Picture House boy was a singer too?' Mammy said.

Almighty nodded five times as he swallowed a mouthful of tea. 'Paddy – surely to Godalmighty. Or he was. Only then my daddy took over as Mary's manager and he knew first thing Mary would be better on her own. So he told Paddy he'd be better stop singing. It was too, the way Mary's cutting her own records and everything now. Wish Paddy had come back to the office earlier, though, and caught the circus ones stealing – he'd have pulverised them. He boxes, you know. Biff, bap, bam. Mr Parnes says Mary's going to be famous.' He wiped his mouth with the back of his hand.

'Godalmighty, that'd be great, wouldn't it? Mary O'Kane in the Top Twenty. Put Omagh on the map, my daddy says. Must fly. Thanks a million. Dress rehearsal at three o'clock, real thing tonight at half-seven. Might see youse there.'

'No might to it,' Mammy said but he was already gone, ringing the bell of Mrs Livingstone's bike as he rode out the lane.

There was a smell like a pub inside Livingstone's. Mrs Livingstone sat at the table with a mug of tea, her cheeks going hollow as she sucked a cigarette.

'Three o'clock?' Presumer asked me again. 'He definitely said three o'clock?'

'Definitely.'

Presumer put his foot on a chair and tied his laces. Seeing him prepare to go out, Sean wrapped himself round his brother's leg. 'Me too. Me too.'

'Ma! Lift this wee shite, would you?'

'C'mere, son.' Mrs Livingstone scooped Sean up under one arm and strolled to the dark doorway of the bedroom, a shaky trail of cigarette smoke in her wake.

We moved up Castle Street towards the town centre. The sky above the rooftops was the colour of the footpath.

'How do you think they got into the Picture House to rob it?' I said.

'Wrapped a hammer in a towel. Or made a key out of a bar of soap. How am I supposed to know?'

'Where would they get a key?'

'Or soap. Where would they get soap?' Presumer repeated his question a couple of times, laughing harder each time. 'Dirty buggers, circus ones. Except Collette,' he said. 'She's clean. A hoor but a clean hoor at least.'

'So what do you need to see Almighty for?'

'Because Almighty has something I want and I've got something he wants. He'll scratch my back and I'll kick his hole.'

As we approached the New Hall, Presumer nudged and pointed back up the street. Outside an open doorway, arms folded, two women stood talking. A thin figure in black – black trousers, black coat, black hat, all a bit too big – approached. Francie Ryan. When he got as far as the women he stopped, raised his hat, replaced it and stood talking. The sound of the women's laughter and excited cries drifted up the street to us.

'Ninth Station,' Presumer said. 'Francie meets the women of Omagh. They greet him as the arseless one and bust their bums laughing.'

When we opened the New Hall door the sound came crashing around us, like a wave at Bundoran. Mary O'Kane was standing beside a microphone in the middle of the stage. She was wearing a pink twinset and had her two hands at shoulder height, a bit like the priest at Mass, and was singing about a little smasher who one of these days was gonna make a dash for love, uh-oh, gonna make a dash for love. When she finished, Brother Meehan who had been conducting the orchestra beamed up at her and said that had been first-rate, but we'd still maybe do better sticking to Ruby Murray. Neil Traynor, wearing a grey suit, nodded and led Mary down the steps and away, his hand flat on her back below her shoulder blades.

'Can you believe it?' Presumer whispered, staring at the side door through which Mary and Neil had vanished. 'That oul' bastard checking if she'd a brassiere

on.' He sighed and, hand raised, approached Brother
Meehan. 'Brother, can we give Alphonsus Traynor a
message from Mr Baldwin of the bike shop? He said it
was urgent.'

'Go on, go on.' Brother Meehan struck a tuning fork
against his thigh, held it to his ear and said,
'Himmmmmm.'

We found Almighty in a corner of the green room,
crouched over his script. Presumer pulled up a chair so
that their kneecaps were nearly touching. 'I'm in a bad
way for something, Almighty. So tell us this. Where
would a fellow get a record player?'

Almighty looked up, mouth hanging. 'Record player?
What sort of record player?'

'One that works.' Presumer plucked at an invisible
violin. 'Birls records. What do ya wan', if ya don' wan'
money? Whish you wanted mah love – by-beee!'

'My daddy's shop has a whole pile of record players.'

'What's the cheapest?'

'Twelve pound, I think.'

Presumer shook his head, then leaned forward and
tapped Almighty's knee. Almighty pulled the knee away.
'Did I tell you our cat is expecting kittens? Sometime
between now and Christmas. Might be a spare one for
you. Black with yellow eyes. If, you know, you were able
to, er um, arrange a swap.'

'A swap for what?'

Presumer sucked his big scummy teeth, smiled. 'Oh, I
dunno. Anything you wanted. A record player, maybe.
Two kittens for one record player. A bargain, that.'

Almighty glanced to me then back to Presumer, not
sure whether to smile. He leaned forward, his voice a
hoarse whisper.

'Seven o'clock, at the back of the shop. My da'll be out at the golf club.' He pulled his head back in and pointed at me. 'You're a witness. Two kittens, and one has to be a she-kitten. He's a witness. Godalmighty, if my da comes back early, he'll scootrify me. You're a witness, remember.'

I nodded but Presumer was on his feet, staring at Almighty through narrowed eyes. 'You and your witness. No need for witnesses. My word is my bond. Get it?' He'd heard John Wayne say that in a picture one time – 'My word is my bond' – where big John had this argument with a Mexican bartender. 'Six o'clock, Almighty,' he mouthed as we left. 'My word is my bond.'

Almighty's da, Councillor Neil Traynor, was backing out of Joe Boyce's shop as we came along. He was laughing and shouting something back into the shop about the cost of cigarettes; so since Presumer was ahead of me, it was his toe got stepped on.

'Jesus – mind out!' Presumer yelled and crouched on the footpath, rubbing at the toe of his gutty.

'Hi now – less of that language, cub. And mind where you're walking!' Neil stood back, pointing his rolled-up newspaper. 'You're Livingstone – right? I knew to look at you you were.' He tapped Presumer's head with the *Irish Independent*. 'You're going to save me a bit of bother.'

Presumer sucked his breath between his teeth, stood up slowly.

'Tell your ma – listening? – to have a clean pinafore on her for the golf club tonight. Okey-doke? The Knights of Columbanus is having a do, so we want the staff to look right. Clean and that.'

Presumer said nothing.

'And I want her in an hour early as well. Make the place look super-duper for Halloween. Mind we'll pay her for it. Five bob for the extra hour, same as all other club staff. We're not misers, you know. How's Paddy!' he shouted, waving to a man twenty yards up the street. Grinned and gave him a thumbs up. Then looked back to Presumer, who had straightened up. 'Right so – what was I saying? Oh aye, cleaning. Right. You tell your mammy about the overalls. And an hour early. She was late twice in the last fortnight – there's to be no more of that. Okey-doke?' Presumer nodded and we started to move on. 'Oh aye – *and*,' Neil said, slapping his newspaper against his thigh, '*and* all employees must arrive in a fit state to work. That's club rules. Ah, mmh, yes. I think she knows that herself. Okey-doke?'

'Okey-doke,' Presumer said in a high, fragile voice as we made our way down the street. 'Okey-noke, nail your fat balls with a white-hot hammer.'

'Easy,' I said. 'Keep your voice down.'

'Humpy Knights of Columbanus, stuffing their faces. Humpy knighty bastards like Neil, licking their arse.'

We stopped outside Traynor's Electrical Shop on Market Street. Presumer stood with clenched fists, a slice of Brylcreemed hair falling between his dirty brown eyes. For a minute it looked as if he might attack Neil's shop window. Then he glanced behind him at the footpath and noticed the car. It had long mudguards and an RAC badge on its front. A quick check both ways: Presumer opened the car door.

'In quick – it's starting to rain.'

He was right. More rain, falling like bits of soldering.

Presumer vanished in a symphony of creaking leather, slammed the door behind him.

I clicked open the passenger door and got in. The dashboard was made of brown shiny wood.

'We'll be caught.'

Presumer sniffed the back of his seat, gripped the steering wheel. 'Caught my hole. Town councillors don't get caught. I'm a town councillor. *And* I own an electrical goods shop. *And* I manage wee girl singers. Vroom-vroom.' In the silence that followed I could hear the rain beating on the car roof. Even it sounded well-padded.

'This is stupid,' I said again. 'C'mon, let's get out.'

Presumer rubbed his palm along the leather, making it squeak. Cleaned off a circle of mist on the side window, making another, higher squeak. 'When I earn a packet I'm going to have one of these. Bring it from England and park it outside the house. Any wains want a spin, I'll drive at ninety, scare the shite out of them. You not fancy a car like this?'

'No.' It was a lie, though – I would. A nice big car. Driving it to the Astoria Ballroom in Bundoran. Getting a girl – maybe two or three girls – into the back seat, making the springs ping and the leather yelp. Crunching up to the Great Northern Hotel with a smiling wife and six children. Waiters bowing and scraping, and me wearing drainpipe trousers and a teddy-boy tie and giving them a fiver as a tip. That was the way to live. Not walking up and down the sideline of life, blessing yourself and reading a breviary.

'Hear that?' Presumer had swivelled round in his seat, his voice a whisper. We listened.

Rain. And through the rain, footsteps. Coming slowly

towards the car. We ducked out of sight on to the floor, our hands over our heads, waiting for the door to open. The footsteps drew level, paused, moved on. We peeped through the back window. Foxy. Hurrying down the street, his right shoulder higher than his left, boots leaving little traces of dung on the wet pavement. Had he looked in? Had he seen us?

'Who gives a fuck if he did or not.' Presumer produced a small penknife, opened it with his teeth, turned back and began to lunge at the side of his seat.

'You'll wreck the good leather!'

He ignored me, kept hammering. There was a popping sound and a hole appeared in the upholstery. I grabbed his arm but he pulled away, hooked the edge of the blade into the gap. You could see the white stuffing now, a little bit oozing out like gunk from a boil. 'He'll still be able to drive it. The wheels won't fall off because the seat's got a wee hole or two.' He gave another tug.

'C'mon, Presumer. Let's go!'

'Keep your drawers on.' A final couple of pops and he opened the door and got out, closed it gently behind him. 'Wouldn't want to damage her or anything.'

Hands deep in pockets we walked through the rain. Nobody about. At the Rat's Pad we stopped.

Presumer spat against the wall of McElroy's pub. 'Are you on for giving us a hand with this record player or not?'

I swallowed. 'If I can I will. Thing is, Maeve and Cait are going to the céilí, and I'm—'

'Good man. See you half-nine, Market Yard entry – OK?' Presumer raised his fist in the air and began to sing. 'I'll never forget the way that we kissed the night of the HAY RIDE.' The last two words and the noise of him laughing and singing was still in my ears as I passed Charlton's garage.

It was nearly five by the time I got home. In the yard, a hen going craaaawwk. Inside shadows and the ticking clock. And the sound of snipping from the bathroom. Mount the stairs quietly, peep round the half-open door. Maeve has brought a chair into the bathroom and is sitting in front of the big mirror, leaning forward, mouth twisted in concentration.

'Where's Mammy?'

She gasped, put the flat of the hand holding the scissors on her chest. 'You could have made me put my eye out!'

'Or your brains. When's Tea?'

'Do you like this fringe? It's supposed to complement my nose. Cait is going to comb hers like this too.'

Sometimes I felt like kissing Maeve's face, other times like hitting it with a hurley. This minute I wanted to do both. 'To complement *her* nose?'

Maeve didn't seem to hear that. 'Do you think would Presumer Livingstone take a picture of Cait and me dolled up for the céilí?'

'No.'

'He'd do it if you asked him.'

'But I'm not asking him because he's not going to the céilí. Where's Mammy?'

'In the orchard. She'll be back soon. If it was holy drawers St Bernie you'd soon ask.'

Five minutes later Mammy came along the back yard with a bucket of apples on one arm. 'Do you think is that Traynor child right in the head at all?' she said, putting down her basket. 'Him and his trees and his man from Carrickmore and his codology. I was talking to Foxy

Johnston – a pack of lies, the whole lot. A couple of biggish branches on the road and a cow killed in a field near Fintona, and not a word about lightning or men with false teeth melting.' She took off her old coat and hung it behind the back door. 'If the poor creature had of had a mother growing up, it'd have been a different matter you may be sure. But please God she's looking down from heaven this minute, praying for him, for he's in sore need.'

She took out the cooking bowl with the brown outside and the white inside. Sieved in flour, added buttermilk and butter, kneaded the dough. Bare arms, strong and white, coated halfway to the elbow. Had Our Father ever stroked those arms?

'Did Foxy say anything about a pony?'

Mammy's mouth tightened. 'Couldn't get him stopped. Stood at the orchard hedge, chatting and chatting till I wanted to hit him. Says he wants our pony – our pony! – to clean out that lavatory of his. The cheeky article. Comb your hair before we head off.'

Maeve appeared at the door, a ribbon in her hair. 'Head off where?'

Mammy turned the dough out of the bowl, leaned on it with her knuckles, squashing resistance. 'And wipe those hair clippings off your face as well.'

'Head where?'

'To the chapel. To pray for the poor holy souls.'

'But I'm already *doing* the nine first Fridays – the poor holy souls will get a plenary indulgence from me for that. That's all they need.' Maeve's eyes began to fill. 'What's the point in sending them to heaven twice? And making me late for the céilí.'

Mammy's knife harked and hissed around each apple

in turn, undressing it. The peeled apple was the colour of human flesh but smelt a lot nicer. When she tipped the apple pieces into the saucepan they hissed.

'A second round will never go to loss. Purgatory's packed with poor souls waiting to get into heaven.'

'How do you know? There could be none there at all for all you know!' Her eyes and nose were leaking at a good rate. 'Mammy, I don't have to go to the chapel, do I? *The céilí.*'

Mammy put the apple tart in the oven. 'Nobody's stopping you going to your céilí. All anybody's saying is, come into the chapel first like a decent Christian and say your prayers. That's all anybody's saying. If your brother's putting himself out taking you the length of this céilí and back, the least you can do is go and give thanks to the Almighty.'

'Did you tell Foxy he couldn't have the cart and pony?' I asked.

'I told him I'd mention it to Our Father. Danged oul' nuisance, that's all.' She pulled off her pinafore and hung it behind the door. 'Throw on your coat, you now – Our Father's coming in the lane and he'll not be pleased to be kept waiting.'

Omagh chapel porch was crammed. Mainly women but men too, caps in hand, pioneer pin in the lapel of the charcoal grey suit. Some had finished praying and were coming out, some were on their way in; but most were at the in-between stage of putting a foot outside the chapel so they could start a new visit. You had to do that to claim the plenary indulgence. The porch was full of people, hands groping into the font at the door, touching underwater.

Mammy led us in, looking neither right nor left, beeline straight for her usual seat three down from the pulpit. I slid into a row five from the back and Maeve knelt directly in front of me. The light from the altar made a halo round her hair.

Close eyes. Blobs of colour, black and red and green, drifting around inside my skull. Concentrate.

'Our Father, who art in heaven.' (Think of Our Father, fifty times his normal size, seated on a throne with his hair a good bit longer and wearing a beard.) 'Hallowed be thy name.' (A big shining sign saying 'God' with lots of people kissing the ground and waving their arms.) 'Thy kingdom come.' (Our Father multiplied by fifty, still sitting on his chair, coming down from a cloud and sending sinners scurrying for their lives.) 'Thy will be done.' (God/Our Father reaching down with a staff and eyebrows raised until they're nearly touching his hairline, me nodding, yes, yes, yes, I will, God.) 'On earth as it is in heaven.' (A giant hand touching the ground, then pointing up to the clouds.) 'Give us this day our daily bread.' (A giant hand coming out of a cloud holding fifty sliced pan loaves, then touching my cheek and making it smooth.) 'And forgive us our trespasses.' (Ghostly hand reaching down and patting me on the back, 'sall right, son.) 'As we forgive those who trespass against us.' (Me patting the back of Joe Nugent, who deliberately got people to gang up against me in Third Class.) 'And lead us not into temptation.' (God standing in front of a five-barred gate, hand up like a traffic policeman, waving trespassers away.) 'But deliver us from evil.' (God plucking us out of a dark hole and putting us on a dry safe ledge.) 'Amen.'

And God. I can see now from the amount of urges you've put in me, you want me to be a Catholic layman who's in the world and wears drainpipes and gets married. But at the same time I want to be sure that's what you want, so you won't start saying on the Last Day that you were really calling me the whole time and I turned a deaf ear to your Call. So give me a sign you don't expect me to go to Maynooth, just to be on the safe side. OK? Amen.

I was halfway up the aisle to start my third plenary indulgence which I was going to make for Mickey Harvey, when I looked back and saw Bernie. She was standing inside the main door, a green scarf wound round her neck, little wispy strands of hair hanging across her face. Her hand with a bead of holy water was raised to her face and as usual she was smiling.

A man with grey hair plastered straight back above his face entered behind her, doing that stuttering hand movement old people do when they're blessing themselves. When he spoke to Bernie his brown teeth showed. Bernie's smile widened.

Kneel down in the nearest seat, think of something else, don't think about knocking the man's rotten stumps out one by one with a small hammer. Think instead about Mickey Harvey, how small his coffin looked in the chapel when we were both in Third Class. How could somebody die from falling through a skylight? He had been really good at football, even if his nose had sometimes leaked a green dot of snot that vanished and appeared wobbling for a second, as he breathed in and out. Most days as we stood in line during milk break, he'd practise heading an imaginary ball. So when they put his coffin in front of the altar, I kept half-expecting him to head the lid open.

But Bernie kept coming back into my mind. Maybe I could offer one of my plenary indulgences for her? Then when she did die, she'd have the help there waiting for her, sending her zipping straight out of Purgatory again, a smile on her face . . . Although Bernie didn't need an indulgence. She probably had extra ones herself that *she* could afford to give out to *other* people. So I ended up giving it to Mickey Harvey's mother, who had been in a terrible state and died just a year after Mickey.

Ten minutes later, at the start of my fourth visit, we met at the chapel door. Nobody between us, just Bernie smiling at me and me smiling at Bernie. Why do people not just leave it at a smile and 'Hello' when they meet? Nerves, maybe. 'Hello!' they say, and then they start laughing. 'Haaaaaa-hhhaaaaa!'

So Bernie smiled and I laughed and then she said, 'Jim! How are you?'

'The best,' I heard myself saying. 'Powerful. How are you feeling yourself?' Feeling yourself, feeling yourself. The blood rushed up my neck and into my ears and face and my right cheek began to ache, the way it sometimes did on a warm day. Feeling yourself. Ohshiteshootmenow.

Tower of ivory, House of Gold, Morning Star, Virgin most pure.

CHAPTER 4

The tide of people was swirling out of the porch to stand inside the chapel gates, some of the men hunching their shoulders to light a half-cigarette, their noses gushing smoke. If they saw somebody they knew they'd nod without smiling or whisper a hoarse greeting. Was the grace of God working in them? Or were they just depressed thinking about dead people?

Bernie walked down the side of the chapel where there was less of a crowd. Beside us in the grotto, St Bernadette prayed and Our Lady looked down at her. Bernie leaned her head to one side and looked at me: 'I saw you earlier.'

'Did you? Funny, I didn't see you.' *Funny*. Why did I say that?

'You were kneeling with your eyes squeezed shut. And your hands like this.' She laced her fingers together and giggled. 'Like maybe you'd died.'

'Was I? Dead and praying for the holy souls – that'd be funny.' *Funny*. Stop fucking *saying* it. 'Ah. I was wondering if . . . How's your daddy?'

'He's – he's all right. Apart from his knee.'

What was she talking about? 'Does your daddy still play in that céilí band? You know, that does all the céilís?'

When she shook her head her hair swung like a bell. 'I told you – he hurt his knee. He was in the kitchen breaking this big stick for the fire and he was leaning on it really heavy, and then all of a sudden it broke and a bit of it went flying across the kitchen and he fell and hit his knee against the cooker. And now if he sits for more than twenty minutes he gets this pain in his knee, he has to get up and walk around. So he can't play in the céilí band any more, because they play for hours without getting up.' She giggled. 'Why?'

'Why what?'

'Why did you ask about Daddy?'

'Because . . .' I took a deep breath. 'I was just wondering about that céilí in the Foresters' Hall tonight. If you were, you know. Thinking of going to it.'

'The one for wee fifteen-year-olds?' When she laughed I could see inside her mouth. There was a little red thing hanging in there. 'Wouldn't be caught dead at it. Why?'

'Nothing, nothing, nothing.' Through the lining of my coat, I gripped some thigh until it hurt. 'No, what I was wondering was, if you might, you know, fancy the pictures. Tonight. Mind you, I don't mind if you don't, doesn't matter, I don't care.'

She stared at me. There were flecks of yellow in the brown part of her eye. 'I don't believe it,' she said. 'There's Mammy and Daddy coming.'

So it was. Her father walking out the chapel gates, yes, with a slight limp, his back straight like Roger Casement being led away after he was arrested. Behind him her mother, talking and pointing, occasionally pulling at his sleeve to emphasise something. Maybe telling how she'd seen me running down their path.

'I think I'll go myself anyway. To the pictures,' I said. A lie. No reason or motive can excuse a lie. 'To the Picture House, around half-seven. But as I say it doesn't matter. I mean you don't have to come, I don't care if—'

'All right. Half-seven, outside. Bye-bye.'

I watched her hair lift and fall as she trotted after her parents. Before she stepped through the gates she looked back, gave a mittened wave.

'I knew you were up to something,' a voice at my elbow said. Almighty Traynor, his lip hanging like a slack garter.

'What?'

'Daddy says you can tell a person is telling lies when they can't look you in the eye, and none of those circus ones could look anybody in the eye. They were definitely up to something, Daddy says.'

'You said you knew *I* was up to something.'

'Did not. They – *they* were up to something. That's what I said. The circus ones.'

A rush of relief. Then anger. Bloody big-mouth Almighty. 'OK. What. Are you talking. About?'

'A burglary. A burglary. Aaah, let go my arm. At the Picture House. Money stole.'

'Money?'

'I told you about it this morning. Cripes, that hurt, you know.' He rubbed his arm, scowling. 'Fifty pounds took, my daddy says. Paddy O'Kane, the boxer boy, does the projector as well, Mary O'Kane's brother, did you know that? My daddy manages her, you know, he's the one who made her really popular . . . Anyway, Paddy O'Kane – he nearly killed another boy in a boxing match one time, you know – my daddy said Paddy saw blood everywhere . . . all right, all right, he checked the drawer and the first time he checked it, nothing wrong. But then the second time he checked the drawer, God Almighty, there was fifty pounds missing. Fifty pounds! My daddy says they broke in the window. Noise of the storm, nobody heard them.'

'And how does he know it was the circus ones took the dosh?'

Almighty wiped his lip with the back of his hand and stared down the street. 'Blood where the window was broke. On the window sill. Police went to the Show Grounds this morning, checked the circus ones in their caravans. Got this man had a cut on his arm.'

'Could have been coincidence.'

'Godalmighty, how could it? He'd a cut arm.'

'Might have cut his arm with one of their machines. Or in a fight. Anything.' I looked at my watch. 'Anyway, I though you were supposed to be meeting Presumer about that record player.'

A muscle in the side of Almighty's head twitched. 'Seven o'clock. Plenty of time.'

'It was six you were to meet him. I remember Presumer saying you'd meet at six. Not seven.'

Almighty leant his head to one side, spoke in short, angry spurts. 'I'm the one is going to the bother, right? So I'm the one decides the time. And I say it's seven o'clock. Godalmighty, think I was a *slave*.' He paused, lifted his boot on his knee and looked at the sole of his foot. Cleaned his hand on his trousers. 'Anyway I was at confession this morning. Not much good in going to confession if next minute I'm stealing my daddy's property.'

Almighty developing scruples. That was a laugh. 'Not much good in confession if you tell nothing but lies either.'

'What lies? Who's telling lies?'

'Tree lies. Chimneypot lies. Men in Carrickmore getting their teeth melted by electric shock lies.'

'There was a man killed! Or could have been.' Almighty stared up at me, his face red and his eyes just a bit skelly. 'Lightning hit his barn and there was a pig in it killed. Stone dead too. And there were loads of branches on the road when I came out to your house. Maybe not big trees hundreds of years old or that sort of thing, who said there was, not me anyway, but plenty of wee-er trees or branches and a thing like that. Go you out and look, see for yourself. Godalmighty. Think I'd make something like that up.'

It didn't matter. None of that mattered. What mattered was, I would leave the céilí and go to the pictures with Bernie. And I wouldn't think about Presumer or the record player or Maynooth or any other complicated things for as long as I could avoid it.

Inside the chapel, kneel in a seat on my own. Concentrate.

Dear God. Thank you thank you thank you. You'll be glad you let me get off with Bernie. She's nice but I swear I won't do anything bad. I'll respect her body as a temple. And my own as well. That's the way a decent Catholic man who's not a priest acts and that's what I'm going to be. So thanksthanksthanks, God. Amen. Yippee.

'Did youse say one for me?' Our Father asked as we passed Foxy's shop. He rolled down the window and spat.

'Not allowed to,' Maeve said. 'You're only allowed to pray for the holy souls today – nobody else.'

'And isn't my soul holy?'

Mammy sighed and looked away, out the left-hand

window at the field where Councillor Traynor had promised they would one day build houses for the Rat's Pad people and Presumer had said some chance. 'Please God we all are looking after our souls and keeping them clean.'

At half-six, Maeve and I walked out the lane together. She had on a blue dress with a red sash and I wore my charcoal grey suit. As she walked, her hands swished against the dress material. Cait Cooley was standing outside her pebble-dash bungalow in Sedan Avenue, jigging from foot to foot, waiting for us. Up close you could see the shaved part of her neck, where she'd got her hair cut really short. Her pink frock had about six petticoats under it.

'*Nothing*'s wrong with me,' she told me in her thin voice.

'I thought maybe you, you know, needed to go somewhere.'

'For your information, moving from foot to foot does *not* mean you need to go anywhere. And they're my feet anyway, not yours.' She turned to Maeve. 'D'you bring "Livin' Doll" like you promised?'

'Sorry, Cait. I meant to, only—'

'My daddy says if anything happens to his Cliff Richards record, the person will answer to him. I'm just telling you what he said. "The person responsible will answer to me." He wanted me to tell him who got the lend of the record but I wouldn't.'

'It's Cliff Richard, not Richards,' I said. 'And how did he mean, answer?'

Cait laughed, a short angry sound like a half-cough. 'It means he'll beat them good-looking. That's what it means. He'll bust their snotter wide open for them.' She stared at me and then rubbed her right cheek. 'Anyway, that's what I said. Cliff Richards. Must be deaf too.'

The Courthouse clock was striking quarter past seven when we got to the Foresters' Hall. Four or five older men stood smoking at the door, watching the girls go in.

'Ten o'clock, then,' I said. 'Here.'

'I thought he was going to the céilí,' Cait said to Maeve. 'Is he not going to the céilí?'

'Me too. And you said Presumer Livingstone was going to take our picture.'

Two faces staring at me, tight little eyes resentful. 'No I didn't,' I told the faces. 'No Presumer, no camera, no picture, no me. OK? I'm going to the pictures. I'll be back for you at ten o'clock.'

'Who you going with?' Cait called after me. I put a finger to my lips and smiled. Cait said 'Huh!', narrowing her red-rimmed little eyes and following Maeve into the hall. One of the men nodded towards Cait and whispered to the man beside him. They both laughed.

It would take me about ten minutes to walk up the hill, past the Courthouse, as far as the Picture House. It wasn't until I was passing the Carlisle Restaurant that I remembered Presumer. I'd said I'd meet him at half-nine, at the Market Yard. Shitedamnhoor. The picture wouldn't be near over at that time. Buggerbuggerbugger. If I hadn't been so busy thinking about having said 'feeling yourself' to Bernie, I'd have remembered that. Anyway, why couldn't Bernie have been going to the céilí, the way I'd wanted her to? Now she'd have to miss a chunk of the picture and it was her own bloody fault. My cheek, from under my eye to near my neck, began to throb and get hot.

To the right of the Picture House was Bogues the Jeweller's window, glinting with engagement rings and bracelets made up of small animals. Maybe little ornament creatures like that were aware of us, the same as we were aware of them, except they never let on. Maybe they could see me standing here, gritting my teeth, trying to think things out. It'd be nice just to stop. Climb in through the glass, put my cheek on the dark blue velvet and talk to them, then fall asleep. Dream about life being over, nothing but heaven with its orchestra of a thousand harps and pleasure that tore your soul to bits.

Behind me, little high heels tick-tocking along the footpath. Wait until they're nearer. Think of ice on your face, cool, cooling. Hissss. Now turn, relaxed, in charge. Brown coat with a black velvet collar. Velvet like the jewellery window. Black high heels, smiling lips, yellow hair curling forward. Plump earlobes peeping through the curls. Um-tum.

'Hello.'

'Hello.' She stood with her little high heels neatly together, her hands laced in front of her. Looked up, waiting for me to speak.

'It should be a good picture,' I said. 'John Wayne.'

'I bet it'll be lovely. Is he the funny one?'

'No, he's the cowboy one. Except in this he's in an aeroplane . . . The thing is, it's half-seven now.'

'And we're both exactly on time. Tick-a-tick-a-tick-a-timing.' She smiled up at me again and her earlobes moved a tiny fraction.

'And the thing is, I have to leave at quarter to nine.'

Her smile shrank to a small pink O. 'Leave the Picture House? But the picture won't be over!'

'Well maybe not *all* of it, but you see I have to collect my sister—'

Her chin had begun to quiver and develop a lot of dimples. 'I wish you'd told me earlier. I thought we were going to the pictures.'

'But we are!' I took her elbow and moved towards the ticket box. 'It's just that I have to collect Maeve and her friend from the céilí, to make sure they get home safe. And nothing happens to them. *That's* all. You see I said I would. Mammy asked me to and I said I would.'

I waited, hoping that the mention of Mammy had impressed her. She pushed her fingers up the left sleeve of her brown coat and sighed, sniffed. Eventually produced a tiny handkerchief with lace edges and a B at the corner.

'If you wanted to, you could stay on. I mean, I wouldn't mind.' She bowed her head so I couldn't see her face. 'Is that all right? I mean I'm sorry. But I have to go at quarter to nine. I don't want to but I have to.'

She looked up at me, then away again, pulling the hanky across each eye in turn. For a moment I thought she was going to say something about never having heard of a céilí that ended at quarter to nine, but she didn't.

At last: 'That's grand. Thank you very much for inviting me. It's actually the nicest present I got for my birthday. I'm being ungrateful.'

'Oh, God that's right. Happy Birthday. And you're not ungrateful at all at all. I mean – would you like to stay? They won't make you leave just because I'm leaving. You could stay and find out what happens. If you want.'

She shook her head. Whispered: 'I'll leave with you.'

The woman with the white hair and the face powder peered through the glass. 'Ten dees?'

'No,' I said, trying to make my voice sound deep. 'One and sixpences. Two.'

The carpet in the foyer was so thick, your feet dragged when you walked. The usherette's torch led us to the first row of one and sixpences, just behind the ten dees. On the screen a lot of girls on water-skis were being pulled by boats. 'Even under pressure, the girls managed to keep a cool head!' the commentator said and everyone laughed.

Bernie took off her coat and folded it carefully over her knees. Her dress was chocolate brown with bits of red sprinkled through it.

The advertisement for Bogues the Jeweller's was being shown when three girls, pushing each other and letting little muffled laughs like farts, moved into the row in front of us. Ten seats along, a figure on his own. Francie, a bag of sweets on his lap, chewing. Without taking his eyes from the screen and silently, he unwrapped and ate.

The big picture was *Strategic Air Command*. It had John Wayne as a fighter pilot and all the women had red lipstick and white teeth. John Wayne's best friend got wounded, but he still managed to land his plane. John put a lighted cigarette between his lips as they carried him off on a stretcher.

'Your man's snuffed it,' one of the girls in front said. 'See the way his hand's gone all droopy.'

'Your diddy's droopy!' one of the others whispered and the three exploded. Fart fart fart. Francie gave a quick glance along the row towards them, then swivelled back to the screen.

I leaned forward to tell them to shut up and think

about other people, we'd paid to watch the picture; but Bernie put a finger to her lips, then reached and took my hand. Within moments our shoulders were pressed together and I could feel her hair tickle my ear. Everything in the Picture House – the darkness, the warmth, the giggles of the girls in front – seemed to fade. It was like winning a race or something. To think that a girl like Bernie would take my hand and put her head on my shoulder without my even *asking her to*. That felt good. So did thinking about her little earlobes hidden by hair. At the same time, although it was good to be with her and I was hoping some people I knew other than Francie might see us, I wasn't sure I really *liked* her that much. The way she was so neat and forgiving and nearly cried when I said about leaving early – I don't know why but it made me want to start shouting dirty words and hitting her. Except I didn't. I sat staring at the screen, trying not to breathe too heavily.

When the green clock to the side of the screen said half-eight I stopped the girl with the tray and bought Bernie an Orange Maid. Once she got the paper off she reached for my hand again. Then quarter of an hour later, just as John Wayne and a hundred American planes were taking off for Germany, I eased my hand clear of hers. It felt as if it had been cooked. Leaned towards her.

'Would you like to stay?'

She shook her head so that little strands of hair tickled my ugly right cheek. Then she unfolded her coat, stood up and followed me out. One of the girls twisted round to watch us leave, then ducked back to whisper to her friends, and the three did some more explosive laughing. When I looked back John Wayne was staring at the picture of the girl he had pasted up in his cockpit.

Out on the footpath, standing alone, a dark figure. Francie, knotting his black scarf, tucking the ends of it inside his black jacket, buttoning his black coat. Shadows under his cheeks, his face dwarfed by the black hat.

'Jim – the man himself!' His voice was deeper than I remembered. And jollier. 'A very violent film but exciting, wasn't it? The bit where—' He paused, pretended to see Bernie for the first time and lifted his hat. 'Good evening, miss.'

'This is Bernie. Didn't know you got home for Halloween, Francie.'

'Thought I mentioned it in the letter.' He glanced at Bernie quickly, then tightened his scarf inside his coat. 'Just the weekend.'

'You're away training to be a priest then, are you?' Bernie asked. Her mouth stayed open, as if Francie was just back from climbing Mount Everest. 'Must be *hard*.'

'Well.' Francie pulled the scarf around his throat so tight I thought he might choke. 'Not for me. For me it's just the ticket.'

'Bet it takes tons of will power, just the same. My will power is terrible. What time do you get up in the morning?'

'Six o'clock. But don't forget, the Pope gets up at four!' Francie looked delighted at the thought.

'Oh dear dear dear – my will power could never stick that!' The tip of Bernie's tongue stuck out between her teeth as she laughed.

Francie waggled his hands like Al Jolson. 'No, no, no, no! It's easy!' And we all laughed. Then Francie began to tell us about the football games and hurling games and the debates and singsongs they had at Maynooth. Bernie watched him, her mouth slightly open.

I took a quick glance up the street at the Courthouse clock: its faint, stupid face said five to nine. Was this person in black the same one who'd told me about the meaning of riding, that day we'd sheltered from the rain on the way home from primary school, just after the two big girls from the convent went past on their bicycles, the mud splashing the backs of their bare legs? Was the real Francie who'd laughed and made pointing movements with his fingers still somewhere inside that black suit? Or had he been taken out and a kind of negative of him left instead, black and white and faded?

'So you see it's strict but a grand laugh as well,' he said. Bernie shook her head and tugged a little silver cross that was round her neck, and when she did that, Francie patted his coat pockets as if trying to squash something. 'Well now! We'll have to have a proper chat before I go back, Jim. Catch up on this and that and the other. God bless!' With a final wave he ducked off into the night, bent forward, hands deep in his coat pockets.

A fine drizzle had begun to drift through the fog. All the way up the Courthouse hill and out the Derry Road it came down. Bernie stopped to put on a yellow head scarf, and when we began walking again she linked her hand into my arm. Squeezed my wrist and looked up at me, neat little features wrapped in a shiny scarf.

'Do you know who Francie reminds me of? Only he hasn't a – his face isn't the same as yours, it's . . . Sorry. Sorry.' She put the back of her hand to her forehead. 'I don't know what I'm saying. I think I've one of my headaches starting.'

'Hope it wasn't me gave you it. The headache, I'm talking about.' Had she been going to say that Francie . . .

'No, it's just—' she glanced away – 'I thought maybe you were sorry you'd ever asked me to the pictures.' We were at the bottom of her path. She turned and looked up at me.

'Sorry?' I said. 'No, no, no – I'm *delighted*. It was – it was the best hour and a half I've ever had. Honest.' *Fucking liar*.

She put her hand on my sleeve. 'Thank you very very much for bringing me to the pictures. You're a really really nice boy. Such a nice present. Take care.' Her lips came up and dabbed my cheek – the good one – then she went tick-tocking up the path to her door.

Quarter past nine. I hurried back towards the town, panting slightly. It'd take me ten minutes getting to the Market Yard, if I hurried. The wind pushed through the trees beside Andy Elliott's, making first a hissing and then a sucking sound.

Instead of waiting for me at the entrance to the Market Yard, the way he said he would, Presumer hid in the doorway of Armstrong the shoemaker's. Waited until I went past him, then tiptoed up from behind and clapped his mouth over my mouth. We stumbled against the shoemaker's windows and the shutters rattled.

'What the hell you do that for?'

'Didn't want you to give a startled cry,' Presumer whispered. 'And betray our presence to the enemy.'

'I wasn't going to betray anything, for God's sake . . . What about this record player?'

Presumer let go of me and straightened his jacket. 'There is no record player. Almightyshite didn't turn up. Jookey wee Almightyshite. I waited for hours and he never turned up.'

'For hours?'

'Hours.'

I thought of what Almighty had said about meeting Presumer at seven o'clock, not six o'clock, but said nothing. There was no point in annoying him even more. We walked past Brogan's pub, downhill towards Bridge Street.

'So where are we for?' I asked. 'I have to be back at the céilí by ten.'

'So you do. Maybe Cait Cooley will give you a wee ride for seeing her home. First, though, we have to get ourselves a metal mickey.'

'A what?'

'Almighty Shitehead didn't bring the mountain to Mohammed. Which means Mohammed will just have to tunnel into the mountain instead. Foller me, kid.'

He led the way over the bridge, past the Orange Hall, until we could see the lights of the Silver Birches Hotel up on the hill to the right. Twenty yards further on, up the road on our left, Stanley's house, with its neat blue slate roof, pale grey walls. Stanley was a retired dentist who lived on his own and went on holidays to Spain every year. The house was silent now, the windows reflecting the darkness around. When Presumer opened the gate I kept tight behind him.

'How do you know Stanley's not here?'

Presumer pointed to the gravel space in front of the house. 'No car. Stanley him no never walk. Therefore Stanley him no here. Elementary, Kemosabe.'

Humming, happy again, he walked quickly to the back of the house, where there was a wide yard and three outhouses in a row. The first had a padlocked door. So had the second. When we came to the third,

Presumer ignored the door and moved round the side of the building. A clump of bushes grew close to the back wall. He squeezed between the greenery and the building and I followed.

We were now beside a tall window that started at shoulder height. Presumer pointed silently to the ground, then my hands, then his dirty canvas shoes.

I crouched while he climbed: first his foot on my linked hands, then his knee on my shoulder. There was a rustling sound above me, followed by the chirp of breaking glass. Then a sound like drops of rain as the remaining bits of glass from the frame were pulled clear and dropped on the grass.

'Hold her steady.' A foot dug briefly into my left shoulder, then the weight was gone. I looked up to see his legs thrash the air, disappear inside.

Silence. 'All right?'

'Keep nix.' His voice was muffled, like the time I'd called at his house.

I pushed past the shrubbery again, peered round the outhouse corner. Nothing. In the distance a car engine, miles away and probably not even travelling this direction. The house itself stood lifeless. Somewhere in the distance, the click of a bicycle approaching.

Presumer was stealing. And he was stealing something here so he could do some more stealing from Almighty's shop. That much was obvious. He hadn't got the record player in a swap for the kittens, so now he was going to wait his chance and take it. And I was here helping him – I who'd been in the chapel only yesterday, talking to God about being a good Catholic layman! A bloody Samaritan, more like. Good Catholic laymen didn't go around stealing or being an accomplice while other people stole. All right, they didn't need to, but that wasn't the point.

Footsteps. The bicycle gone, now somebody walking along the road. Stanley himself maybe, big and square-jawed, out for a stroll. Or the cops. What should I do – stay and confront them, give Presumer time to escape, surrender myself? That didn't sound too good. Maybe this was God's way of sending me a sign – getting me to wise up. He was going to have me caught and sent to jail. Then even if I wanted to go to Maynooth like Francie, which I didn't, I wouldn't be able to, because if Maynooth didn't allow bastards, it was hardly going to allow thieves. So that'd leave me with no choice but to get married to a woman and go to bed with her every night for the rest of my life. The decision would be taken out of my hands. A life sentence of going to bed. Hard labour.

I slipped past the shrubbery to the back of the building again. There was a loud crash from inside, as if something had been dropped.

'Pre-zooomer!'

From the road, the footsteps were coming louder. Someone in boots, a man with strong, confident steps. Then the footsteps were out there on the road directly opposite us. I held my breath, tried not to think, squeezed my eyes shut. Step, step, step, step. And then after what seemed like years the steps started to get fainter and fainter, as their owner moved past Stanley's and on down the road.

Presumer's head and shoulders appeared slowly out the window, like his mother opening her half-door. 'Grab the end of this big thing. And mind your balls don't get poked off.'

There was the scraping of metal on concrete and a long crowbar began to emerge, its end jutting into the night sky. Slowly it dipped and I grabbed it. Lowered its cold weight to the ground beside me. A minute later Presumer jumped from the window to the grass, panting.

'What's this for?'

'You know yourself. To open things. Let's go.'

With Presumer carrying one end and me the other, we climbed the barbed-wire fence behind Stanley's, crossed three fields and a small stream. I called softly to Presumer that we were taking it too far, he'd have to carry it all the way back if he was going to break into Traynor's Electrical Shop.

'Not break into,' Presumer said. 'Effect an entry. That's what it'll be – effecting an entry. You hide metal mickey near fat-arse Neil's shop, somebody's bound to come on it. Hide it the other side of the town, nobody'll ever look there. See?'

It took nearly twenty minutes getting to the field at the back of Foxy's. There was a sheuch inside the fence and the mud tried to suck off your shoe when you stepped in it. Finally we got a dry patch under a tree near one corner. Presumer produced a small trowel from his jacket pocket. Using it and our hands, we dug out a long, narrow trench about six inches wide and ten feet long.

'Now.' Presumer straightened, cleaning his hands on the sides of his trousers. 'Metal Mickey is committed to the earth, ready for his resurrection. Which could be any night soon – even tomorrow night, for all anybody knows. OK? Darng-da-da-darng-da-da-da-da-darng-da-da-da-da-da-da.' He played a pretend guitar, pushing his front towards me the way Elvis did. In the darkness he seemed to glow with danger and promise.

My crowbar doth magnify the Lord, for he hath cast down the mighty and exalted the humble.

'What kept you?' Cait demanded. They were standing outside the hall, rubbing their arms against the cold. Her nose was the same colour as the rims around her eyes. 'Want me to get my death standing here?'

'Give me a wee minute till I think.' She didn't smile back when I said that. Didn't even speak until we reached her house. Then shouldered open her door and slammed it behind her with a muttered 'Bye' over her shoulder.

Maeve and I walked on out the Derry Road. As we came within range of a lamp post our hands and faces grew white, like a corpse. Then the light faded behind us and we were in shadow until the next one.

Halfway past the red-brick houses, I spoke. 'Cait wasn't in good form.'

'Well, I was dancing practically the whole night.'

'What about Cait?'

'Most of the time. Or some anyway.' She frowned and glanced across at me. 'Know who was there? That Almighty creature. Kept wanting to be my partner, and then when I told him to get lost he started sniffing after Cait. Dirty wee hallion. That was the only bad thing about the whole entire night.'

'You'd think Cait might have danced with him.'

'She's not that hard up.' There was another pause. We passed the last of the lamp posts. Darkness from here until home. 'Jim.' Another pause. 'You're not going away to be a priest, are you? Mammy said she thought you might be, but then this evening, you go off on a date—'

'Who said I was going anywhere? And who said I was on a date?'

She smiled. 'I said you weren't going away, didn't care what Mammy says; but Cait said she thought you might be too. And we were wondering—'

'You and Cait.'

'Yeah.'

'Wondering.'

'Yeah. I said going away would be pure cat. Swear to God – dressing up in black, Mass every day, no céilís or music or—' she gestured towards the night sky – 'anything. Cait said if somebody made her do that, she'd jump out a window and break her neck on purpose. So would I. Swear to God I would.'

But he will bear thee up, lest thou dash thy neck against a stone.

CHAPTER 5

By the time we arrived at seven o'clock on Sunday, the New Hall was nearly full. Rows of chairs all the way from inside the door, and as the rows got nearer the stage you could see the coats of the women getting better. Near the back navy blue or brown cloth coats, up at the front fox furs with little beady eyes peering over shoulders. Benches had been put out along the side, with people squeezed on to them, knees nudging against each other. Twin boys in matching grey shirts and short trousers stood on the bench beside their parents, staring at the curtain. One of them had his finger in his nose and the other kept pulling at the front of his trousers.

Our Father headed up the middle aisle, then stopped beside a row that was full. Mammy prodded him with her handbag.

'Would you go back down to somewhere where we can get in,' she whispered. 'Not have us standing here like gypsies.'

Maeve twisted her face as if she was swallowing medicine. '*Everybody's looking at us.*'

Our Father nodded slowly, staring round the hall to see how many people he knew. 'I suppose we be to move back.' At last we found a row near the middle and shuffled past people to our seats. Moments later the curtains twitched and Felix McGirn came through.

'Good evening, isn't it powerful, such a turn-out,

thanks be to God, and youse know we have a powerful evening ahead of us. All proceeds tonight and every other night for now and for ever, ha ha, for the school building fund and now the hall building fund as well, this brilliant hall that we have for concerts and plays and other functions and anything else we want to get up to. And speaking in my role as chairman of the Drumragh Players, I hope youse will enjoy our first play in this hall, *The Winning Maid*, that we'll be commencing in a short while, and you have my personal guarantee that it's quality laughs from start to finish. Now the special event and main honour for us all this evening will be, his Lordship the Bishop will be here to officially open the hall. The word from Newtownstewart is that the Bishop's or I should say the episcopal car for that's the right way of saying it, episcopal car, and it's well to get these things right, has just gone through, so we have still a wheen of minutes for the raffle of the bottle of whiskey so we would be as well to get weaving. Have we the hat with the tickets in it?'

Eventually the hat was brought on-stage and the twin boys were led up to select the winning ticket. They did it together, both of them gripping a single ticket which they took out of the hat. Everyone clapped as they clattered down the steps again, even though they pulled the ticket so hard it almost tore, and Felix had to twist their wrists to get it released.

He held the selected ticket above his head. 'One-four-seven, have we a one-four-seven, come up here till us quick or you'll get nothing.' There was a small cheer from the back and people stood up to look back and see who it was. Then after a good bit of laughing a girl with short black hair and wearing a red coat mounted the steps.

Felix put up his arm out and pretended to shield the bottle of whiskey from her. 'God, I don't know should a young cuttie your age be drinking!' he said into the microphone, and everyone laughed. But the girl in the red coat just gave a little smile, took the bottle from him and tucked it in the crook of her arm like a baby, then swung down the steps into the audience again, her opened coat swaying from side to side as she went.

The hall filled with the hum of talk again. People shifted in their seats, lit cigarettes, peered through the smoke to see who else had come to the play, come to hear Mary O'Kane sing.

Then suddenly Monsignor McLaughlin had gone out of the hall and was coming in again, walking up the aisle in front of the Bishop, who was all in black except for a purple waistcoat and a gold cross on a chain hanging on his little stomach. There was a murmur and a clattering of feet as everybody stood, and then a kind of cheer as the Bishop got nearer the front and more and more people saw him. A thunder of clapping and even some stamping of the floor. Then the Bishop was on the stage, Monsignor McLaughlin on one side and Felix McGirn on the other, and the three of them were smiling from ear to ear.

Eventually the cheering and clapping stopped and the Bishop made a movement with his little white hand for people to sit down again. The Monsignor and Felix sat on chairs behind him. The Bishop tapped the microphone and spoke in a soft voice.

As he travelled from place to place in the diocese, he met people in a whole range of halls and places. But coming to Omagh was always a special pleasure for him, and one he looked forward to, because he knew the Omagh people were a special people.

'In fact it is no exaggeration to say I am almost embarrassed by the strength of your reception and kindness. What sustains me is the knowledge that your welcome is not truly for me but for Our Lord Himself and His authority here on earth, the Church.'

At the side of the stage a head appeared through the curtains and vanished again. There was a giggle which subsided immediately.

'It is an especial pleasure to come here today for the official opening of your new parochial hall, dedicated to Blessed Martin de Porres. I know how hard everyone in the parish has worked for this hall, how much it means to you, and how determined you are to put your shoulders to the wheel with Monsignor McLaughlin here to reduce the debt which it must inevitably bring in its wake.

'When Monsignor McLaughlin came to me three years ago and asked me if he should proceed with plans to construct this hall, we spoke for a considerable time. Then when we had finished speaking the two of us went down on our knees in my office and prayed to Almighty God. And after the Monsignor and I had prayed for guidance I gave him my answer. "Monsignor McLaughlin," I said. "In God's name take off your coat and go ahead with this work." That was three years ago. Today you see this marvellous, marvellous modern hall with all its amenities – the fruit of his and your efforts.

'But let there be no mistake. This hall, soon to be under the protection of Blessed Martin de Porres, and of Our Lady and all the saints – this hall is very necessary.

For in some halls today – in a lot of halls – it is impossible for Catholics to participate fully in the enjoyment offered without violation of their consciences.'

There was a silence. Men looked at their shoes or the ceiling, women pulled their handbags in tighter to their stomachs.

'It pains me as your bishop to say that, but it is sadly the case. It is also my conviction that a lot of older people are not fully aware of what is going on in some of these halls. For if they were, they would be as concerned as I am.

'This hall, though, will provide a refuge from such things. As Mary is the refuge of sinners, so this hall will be the refuge of those who seek to preserve their faith, in the face of those who seek to be modern and godless. For this will be our Church hall, dedicated to those things that are good and worthwhile in our Irish Catholic tradition. This will be a hall to be proud of, the equal of any of its type to be found in County Tyrone, or indeed any county in Ireland. This will be a place where wholesome entertainment and innocent enjoyment will be available to those who come. I know that Monsignor McLaughlin is proud to see this day, for I know that I am proud to see this day and to share in your rejoicing.

'So with gratitude in our hearts to Almighty God and to all those who have worked for this day, particularly Monsignor McLaughlin, let us stand and bow our heads for the blessing of the hall, and the protection of the Holy Ghost on all that happens within its four walls in the years to come.'

After the Bishop had prayed in Latin and moved round the hall shaking holy water over people, he took a seat near the front. Then Mary O'Kane came on, and she got nearly as big a clap as the Bishop. She was wearing a white dress and a pink sash, a bit like Cait's only the dress was ten times nicer and she was a hundred times nicer. From where we were sitting you could see the top half of Neil Traynor standing in the wings, his face red and shiny, his two big hands clapping.

Brother Meehan sat down at the piano on the left-hand side of the stage and Mary stood behind the microphone in the middle, her hands joined in front of her. Felix McGirn hurried over and adjusted the microphone so it was low enough for her. Brother Meehan played a few bars to warm himself up, rounding them off with a brisk zip of his thumb up the length of the keys; Mary turned away from the microphone and gave a little cough into her hand.

Then Brother Meehan hit a single note two or three times, very clear and loud, and peeked at Mary over the top of the piano. Note note note note note. 'Nah, nah, nah, nahhhh,' Mary sang in a whisper. Her head tilted back, the spotlight made her eyes glint and she leaned towards the audience, her mouth open in a dark little cave.

'Softly, softly, come to me. Touch my lips/ so tenderly.'

Apart from Mary's singing and the notes of Brother Meehan's piano, there wasn't a sound in the hall. Not a cough or a foot moving. All of the audience, even the women, were absolutely still, staring up at Mary, wondering what it would be like to touch those lips. They looked soft and puffy, the kind of lips that would maybe stick to your neck for a second after they'd kissed you. I imagined all the people who wanted to touch her lips forming a queue, the way people lined up to kiss the cross on Good Friday.

Halfway through the song Presumer tiptoed up the middle aisle with his camera. Smiling he crouched on one knee, bent over the top of the camera until he had Mary in his sights. Click-click, the camera went. Presumer moved back a little to the right, aimed again, clicked again. And again. Then with a wink to someone he knew, he scurried half-bent back down the hall. Some of the older people looked at each other and shook their heads as he passed.

'– and open up. Myyyy. Heeeeeeart,' Mary sang, and you could hear the notes go zinging down the hall, through the smoke, before sliding soft and warm into all the ears. People were as still as statues in their seats, eyes shining, listening to Mary asking to have her heart opened up. You could tell the men especially liked the thought of that.

When Mary got to the end Brother Meehan played two more notes, very soft and slow. There was silence for a quarter-second; then an avalanche of noise. People standing up clapping, their hands in front of their faces, women laughing and looking at each other, some people at the back stamping their feet. Every time Felix tried to calm people down so he could be heard, they clapped and cheered some more. All this time Mary stood to the side of the microphone with her hands behind her back, a shy little smile on her face.

The play was a right laugh, all about a will this old bachelor farmer made, and a contest they had to see who was the maid he said he was leaving all his money to, and in the end the spiteful maid that pretended to be very nice was caught out and the quiet one who never stuck up for herself was found to be the winner and she was able to get married to the farmer's boy she'd always loved. I kept hoping Almighty would forget his lines but he remembered every single one, said them off like bullets from a machine gun. At the end the actors all lined up with their hands joined and did a bow for the audience and got a great clap. During the clapping they waved, especially Almighty, who looked like one of those people standing beside a plane.

'For flip's sake,' Maeve said, not moving her lips. 'Look at that Almighty eejit. Waving. *Waving straight at me*. Oh Mammydaddy – do you think does anybody see him?'

'See what?' I asked.

'Oh God I don't know where to look.' She ducked behind the seat in front, moaning. 'If I had a hammer and a spike, I'd nail his hand to his head, swear to God. Oh blessed Christopher.' She stayed bent forward in her seat where she couldn't see Almighty.

They were still clapping as I slipped to the back of the hall and downstairs to the toilets. Even they were nice and new, with five cubicles and ten white shiny pee-places along the wall. When I came upstairs again, Felix was announcing that there would be one last final encore, definite last, no more, mind; and Mary came back on-stage and Felix and the Monsignor clapped and smiled at her as she positioned herself behind the microphone again. Then the quiet settled on the hall again, just like before, so I didn't go back to my seat but stayed near the back in a side aisle, roughly six feet behind where the girl with the red coat was seated. Leaning against the wall, I could see the way her teeth stuck out a tiny bit over her nice bow-shaped lower lip, as if she was ready to bite into Life.

This time Mary sang 'Good Night, Irene'. She didn't sing in her nose the way Ruby Murray did – her voice was clean, like a piece of polished silver or the moon on a frosty night. And this time instead of staying quiet throughout the song, when it got to the chorus everyone joined in. They sat back in their chairs swaying from side to side, smiling, singing, glancing at each other. 'Goooood niiiiiight, Irene, good night. Goooooodniiiiiight, Irene.' I even joined in myself, a kind of ache in my chest as I sang. This was a feeling I wanted to keep going: all of us warm in here, singing, the darkness outside, everybody smiling and healthy and singing about Irene. This was how it would be, I thought, if I behaved myself as a Catholic layman and died and went to heaven. I'd wake up to the sound of a hundred Marys singing in a celestial chorus, while all the people around swayed from side to side and joined in.

Or nearly all. Because the girl in the red coat wasn't singing. She was sitting with her two hands gripping the bottle of whiskey, looking from side to side. Then suddenly she'd swung round and two brown eyes, glistening like chestnuts just out of their spikey shell, were fixed on me. It was too late to look away. Her hand went up and pushed a strand of crisp black hair from her face. Then she rubbed one cheek, crossed her eyes and made her teeth show like a buck rabbit. What the hell was she doing it for? I tried to stare back, hoping I wasn't blushing and that she'd take the hint and stop. But she didn't – just kept looking straight at me with her skelly eyes and buck teeth, never smiling or anything. In the end I had to look away.

On the stage Mary finished her song and Neil Traynor in his brown suit came on and stood with his arm around her shoulders. The audience kept clapping, clapping and whistling because she looked so small standing there and her smile was so nice. 'Have you bought my record yet – "Little Smasher"?' she asked the audience. About three people put up their hands. 'When you get a chance, how many of you will buy it?' And practically all the hands in the hall shot up, some people even put two hands up, and everybody cheered and Mary waved her hands like Al Jolson and did a little dance, right there on the stage. Then Neil was behind her, his hand a spread of fat fingers in the middle of her back as he eased her off the stage.

When I looked back to see how the girl in the red coat was reacting, her seat was empty. She must have stood up and walked right past without me noticing.

I will sing a new song to the Lord.

CHAPTER 6

It was 16 November – only forty-six days of the 1950s left. Time tick-tick-ticking away, as Mícheá Ó Hehir always said towards the end of every All-Ireland Football Final. Branches black and dripping with rain. Classroom windows misting over. Teachers with knotted scarves and tweed coats, hurrying up the schoolyard, faces grim.

Brother Dickey came into our Maths class. He taught English and music, and at Christmas was in charge of the school production. And, later in the year, of Vocations. But that was later, no call to think about that, and anyway I was going to be a Catholic layman. Now, with his eyes glittering behind his horn-rim glasses and his chest and backside stuck out farther than usual, Dickey was asking Mr Carragher to excuse him and announcing that auditions for the Christmas musical would be after school.

'Boys who were in last year's operetta,' he said, scratching under his arm, 'should attend. Any boys wishing to offer their services afresh, on stage or as stagehand, should also be there. Three-thirty sharp in the gymnasium. Fail not our feast. Thank you, Mr Carragher.' And he went out, his black shiny boots shaking the temporary hut that had been built twenty years ago, his backside bulging through the back of his soutane.

That afternoon the sky was the colour of dishwater
and the cindery ground around the classroom huts
glistened with rain. Inside the gym around seventy – no,
maybe a hundred – boys were talking in groups or
leaning against radiators. As Dickey entered and strode
on-stage, the talk collapsed, flattened into silence. The
other music teacher – Fly Dolan, a little dark-haired man
with a Southern accent – stood at the side of the stage,
buttoning and unbuttoning his tweed jacket.

'Attention, gentlemen . . . Now. This is our first
operetta meeting and I want to make a few things clear.'
The back door of the gym rattled and opened. Presumer
stood in the doorway, out of breath. 'Completely,'
Dickey repeated slowly, 'clear.' Presumer grinned and
slouched towards the nearest wall.

'You're here for one of two reasons,' Dickey
continued. 'Either you want to sing and act in the
operetta – which will be *The Pirates of Penzance* this
year, by the by. Or you want to assist as a stagehand.
They also serve, etcetera, etcetera. There may even be a
few here who see themselves as future Mary O'Kanes.
Little smashers, so to say, swathed in trousers, not
skirts.' Everybody laughed. 'Whatever your motivation,
we have less than six weeks to prepare. In five weeks'
time, an audience will fill this gymnasium, the curtains
behind me will draw back, and ready or not, our
operetta will begin. So. There's not time for tomfoolery,
and there's no time for time-wasting. If you have
tomfoolery or time-wasting in mind' – his arm shot out
at shoulder-level, pointing down the gym – 'there's the
door now.' There was silence as we waited to see if a
tomfool or a timewaster would move. No one did.
'Good,' said Dickey, lowering his arm slowly and

staring at each of us in turn. 'Because when I put my hand to an operetta, I take pride in it. I like to think it's going to be the very best that human effort can produce. And that those working alongside me will also have the character to put their shoulder to the wheel. Let's make something we can be proud of, men, something that thirty, forty, fifty years from now, people will look back on. "D'you remember *The Pirates of Penzance* in 1959? The last operetta of the Fifties? Was not that outstanding work?"' He paused, eyes like brandy balls behind his glasses. 'Right. Stagehands first. Approach briskly please, gentlemen.'

Eleven of the senior boys scrambled on-stage and gathered around Dickey. Some of them were taller than him but none of them looked as solid, as sure of themselves. 'And do we have a twelfth?' Dickey asked. 'A twelfth apostle, to join these eleven?' Bill String, who was nearly six foot, bounded up beside the others. 'At last,' Dickey said. 'Gentlemen, Mr Dolan will take your names – off-stage, please. I would like to continue with auditions.' Fly buttoned his jacket a final time and shooed the stagehands into the backstage darkness.

'Now,' Dickey said, producing a hard-backed exercise book and a fountain pen. He put them on a table in front of him and scratched his bum briefly. 'How many of you were in last year's cast? Very well, hands down. Sit at the back, last year people. The rest, over here.'

Dickey took his place at the piano and then each person had to sing the scale, followed by the first verse of a song they knew. Presumer sang 'Davy Crockett'. Dickey stared at him over his glasses.

'Front of house, I think. For the dispersal of pro-grammes and the location of seats. McGrath?'

I sang 'Kevin Barry'. Mammy used to sing it, when she was making the dinner or cleaning the house and I was trotting behind holding her skirt. When I got to the third line, 'Just a lad of eighteen summers', Dickey put his finger to his lips. 'Enough, oh God enough. Programmes and seats, programmes and seats.'

It had stopped raining by the time Presumer and I made our way down the schoolyard. Over the wall with the broken glass set in it the wind came whipping, slapped at our faces. 'Did you see Fat-arse scratching his hole? Even thinking about these operettas gets him excited, you know.'

'I sort of like them too.'

'There's excited and excited.' Presumer strummed an invisible guitar hanging in front of his fly. 'Oh the Rock Island Line is a mighty good road/And Brother Dickey-arse is the boy to ride.'

'What about that picture of Mary O'Kane – are you entering it for the competition?'

'Haven't finished the film yet. It'll be a beaut, though. Got her hands in as well – the way she wiggles them around in front of her. I'd've preferred Collette's legs, mind you. "Oh the Rock Island Line is the road to ride"—' He went down on one knee to tie his lace, looked up at me from under a wrinkled forehead. 'I was thinking of New Year's Eve.'

'For what?'

He stood up, pushed a Brylcreemed strand of hair from his face. 'If it's cloudy, definitely. And if it's pissing rain, even better. What you want is nobody about. Or at least out in the street. Right?'

'Isn't what right?' I knew what he meant but I wasn't saying.

'I even know where they're kept – saw Fat-arse Neil stacking them inside the back door one time I was in getting a plug. Some of them can stack three records at a time and drop them down one after the other. Dead cinch once you get the back door opened. Do you think you, you . . . ah . . . you might want to assist in some musical liberation, McGrath?'

'Some what?' I needed time to think.

'We'll only take one. To hear wee Elvis P and sweet Jerry Lee. Know what Francie claimed one time? That Elvis was in jail six times for sex crimes.'

'What's a sex crime?'

Presumer leaned his mouth into my ear. I could feel his hot breath. 'Pulling out your thing and waving it at women. Or using it to stop a bus instead of your hand. "Hi, driver. I'm Elvis Presley and I'm looking to go to Drumquin and my thing is half-foundered."' He straightened up and sighed. 'Did you know the Duke of Edinburgh's is the size of Errol Flynn's?' I shook my head. 'So anyway. Are you coming?'

'I might. I would if—'

'Great stuff – if you're not in you can't win, as the actress said to the bishop.' Presumer grinned and put a finger to his lips. 'Shhh-hh!' Then he turned in at the Back Lane.

I walked on for about a minute, then retraced my steps up Castle Street to the chapel. It was cold and dark, but the red light in front of the tabernacle was soft. No sound, only the whisper and rosary bead rattle of a woman doing the Stations of the Cross.

Did they have an actual red light in places like Soho? Did people like Elvis and Errol Flynn know they were committing sin, headed for hell? Or was Uncle Father

John right and people like that believed in nothing, because they hadn't enough imagination to believe in a God?

I stared at the tabernacle door. God the Father, the judge of all creation, was in there. The gold door suggested wisdom and goodness but also toughness. The red light, in contrast, was all soft depths. God the Brother's place. Not the Son, the Brother. Maybe not even brother, but pal. Somebody who wouldn't mind checking rabbit snares or lying on his belly with a fishing rod. Somebody who might even go to a dance, chat to a girl. Not coorting – it'd be blasphemous to even think of God the Brother coorting. Or assisting with the stealing of a record player. But at the same time, somebody who could enjoy life. If he was here, he'd be one of the first to volunteer as a stagehand. With the twelve apostles. And he'd let people do whatever they felt happiest doing.

I left the chapel slowly, watching my scuffed toecaps appear in turn. Foot, foot, foot, foot. They were taking me home. And, at the same, to my grave. It'd be no small help to have a pal like God waiting for you when you'd been dumped into the trench in the ground and clay piled on you. Great getting excited about girls and food and helping out at operettas and stealing record players and going to bed every night with your wife, but then the journey had to end. And you'd need to be sure as you could that there was somebody waiting for you with a warm welcome. Not hot, warm.

That night I dreamt about sheep. They kept pushing against the side of my leg, rocking me like waves on a lake. Then they began to rush away down a field, right and left, some leaping a fence that had appeared. A space opened up in front, and at the end of it stood a giant ram, pawing the ground like a bull in a comic. Then it came charging towards me, across the snow that had suddenly appeared on the ground. I barely had time to get out the knife that was in my pocket and hold it up in front of me so that the ram, nostrils blowing smoke, rushed chest-first on to it. It gave an awful groan and the snow around our feet began to fill with blood, spreading out on either side to form a shape like the map of Ireland. I bent down and touched the map with my fingertips. It felt warm and sticky.

Then I was awake. Had I given in to the rush of passion? Because if I had, that was a mortal sin. But hold on: you can't be guilty of sin in your sleep. The religious adviser had said that in Third Year, when he had called us up one by one and told us the facts of life, half turned away and reading from a little book with a black cover and talking about pens dipping into bottles of ink. So although my pyjamas were damp at the front, God wouldn't hold them against me. I still felt rotten, though.

Eyes closed, knees drawn up to my chest. Maybe this was a sign – God showing me that I definitely had the right number of hormones for a Catholic layman but too many for a priest. Sending dreams into my head that someone made of priest material couldn't possibly dream. Francie wouldn't be dreaming about rams, you could be sure of that. '*Domine non sum dignus*,' I said. 'Lord, I accept that I'm not good enough.'

Debbie Reynolds stroked my face and nuzzled her lips under my chin. 'I thrilled to your touch, you big ram you,' she said.

We didn't have to attend the first three weeks of

rehearsals – all that was needed was the actors, Dickey said. Then from the ninth of December on we had to go with the chorus and actors to the school gym immediately after school and stay there helping behind the scenes until nine o'clock. The actors and chorus brought an extra lunch with them to eat at six o'clock; after they'd finished Dickey would pass round a tin of biscuits, really nice ones like custard creams and fig rolls, and some nights two bags of sweets: one dolly mixtures and the other bull's eyes. For the twelve stagehands and Presumer and me, he sent out for bags of chips every night. Maybe it was because we had to do a lot of heavy work – lifting flats and pulling on ropes to get lights up, sweeping the backstage – that he brought us chips. During our break we would sit on the radiators shaking the little purple twist of salt over our chips, chewing and listening as the policemen's chorus did 'Ta-rant-arah' and the maidens did 'Go to Glory' another time. When they didn't keep time with each other, Dickey would roar at them to in the name of God *listen* to themselves, could they not *listen* for *once*, which was a laugh, and his eyes would bulge behind his thick glasses. But when he looked in our direction we kept our faces straight.

There was a sort of rule that during rehearsal time you were allowed to smoke in the green room provided you didn't do it too obviously. Tommy Harvey, the third year who was playing the main part of Mabel, jooked in any time he wasn't on stage, which wasn't often.

'Fucking gasping for a drag,' he said, tugging at the neck of his yellow dress. 'Anyone give us one?'

Presumer passed him a freshly lit cigarette. 'One pull.' Tommy dragged hard, a vein in his neck standing out with the effort. 'Know what beats me, though – how you remember all your lines.'

'I don't,' Tommy said, grinning from behind the smoke. 'Forget half them. Listen.' He put his hand behind his ear. 'Bong, bong, bong! That's Dickey's balls clanging. "You slimy little boy, bong-bong-bong!"'

'He has three balls, then,' Presumer said.

'There's only one way to learn songs,' Skelly Murphy said, passing Tommy a handbag. 'And that's backways.'

'Not much good backways when I have to say them frontways.' Tommy winked at the rest of us and hurried back on-stage.

But then the first night came with the hall nearly full and Tommy only needed one prompt, where he meets his father the Major General for the first time. And then the second night, he didn't miss at all.

The third and last night of the operetta was a Wednesday, three days before Christmas. The first cars began to arrive from quarter past seven, droning up the central driveway of the school, even though the curtain didn't go up until eight o'clock and the doors were locked. When people found they couldn't get into the gym they got back into their car and sat there, smoking and waiting, the driver sometimes spitting out the open window.

I saw them because I was on my way round to the back door. Since this was the last night, Dickey decided to get Fly Dolan and another teacher to stand inside the main door and give out the programmes so they could be introduced to the Bishop when he arrived. Presumer and me were told to go backstage and help anybody that needed anything done.

Up close the police uniforms looked great – like real

policemen, shiny peaks on the caps and everything. And the juniors dressed as chorus maidens were better-looking than a lot of girls you'd see. Dickey was striding around smiling and clapping his hands. 'Once more unto the breach, dear friends,' he kept saying. 'One last push and we're there.' He stopped and pointed a nicotined finger. 'Harvey: mind on job. Practised your scales? Good man.'

Tommy was half into and half out of a black and yellow dress, making faces and swearing quietly. Dickey started to help him, tugging at the back part, but then Fly came and said one of the flats had fallen down. 'Livingstone,' Dickey called. 'Help Harvey into this.'

'How many lines do you have to know again?' Presumer whispered, pulling an eye and a hook together.

'Aaagh!' Tommy glared over his shoulder. 'Go easy, you fucker.'

'Don't know how you do it,' Presumer said. 'The bit where you meet your father and the bit where you do the lament – practically the same, aren't they? In the father one, it's about a maid who longs to greet her father, and in the other one it's a heart that longs to meet its mate. Or is it the other way round? And then there's that song about being late, it's like those two as well. Father, mate, late – makes me dizzy just thinking.'

'Hurry up and finish that bucking thing,' Tommy told him. 'I need to look through the script.'

After half-seven we could hear the murmur of voices on the other side of the curtain getting louder and louder. It was like a huge wasp, filling the space, getting bigger and more excited as eight o'clock approached. Dickey had warned us not to let ourselves be seen once it passed half-seven. But he was nowhere around so I opened the door at the side of the stage just a fraction.

The first two rows were empty. Behind that girls from the convent were seated. Line after line of brown uniform, with above the uniform dark eyes, blue eyes, fair hair, red hair, fat noses, tiny noses, buck teeth, pearl teeth. Maeve and Cait among them somewhere. Bernie too. Maybe even the girl in the red coat.

The buzz of talk rose briefly and then evened into a hush. People twisted round in their seats and gawped towards the back. The Bishop had arrived. He was standing just inside the main door, his purple waistcoat and gold crucifix shining and the college President smiling at him. Fly Dolan kissed his ring and gestured to some seats, the Bishop gave a nod and moved with little bobbing steps to the front row. The President walked behind him, and behind that came Mary O'Kane, with her mother and father on either side of her and Neil Traynor just behind. No sign of Paddy – he was probably working the projector in the Picture House.

Then the orchestra began to tune up in a loud, final kind of way and the talking faded. Dickey appeared backstage and began hissing at people to get to their positions. If a Senior was slow he got a push between the shoulder blades. Juniors he grabbed by the collar and propelled, with a knee in the arse.

Finally the orchestra started playing the overture and the curtains swished back like a dressing gown falling open, and the chorus trotted on-stage from both sides, meeting in the middle and singing about how hot a day it was. No hiding now from the rows of faces, mouths open, eyes hungry, waiting to be fed entertainment.

At the end of the first act we couldn't believe how well things had gone – it was the best night yet. The audience

said 'Aaaah' and laughed when the maidens came
running out, and they clapped for a long time after the
first chorus. They laughed, one or two uncontrollably,
at the bit where the Major General pretended to fall over
his sword. And they went 'Ooooh' when Tommy
appeared at the back in the spotlight, swooping up to the
high notes on his own while the other maidens stood
back.

Backstage, people acted a bit mad – eyes bulging,
grabbing at each other for no real reason. Dickey came
round the groups, occasionally tapping a Senior's back
with his fist or jabbing a Junior's back with his finger.
But he was pleased, you could tell. Even smiled,
although he turned away to stop us noticing. It was near
time for Act Two. Shhhhh.

And Act Two went grand as well. It wasn't until Act
Three that the problem started. Near the end of the Act
Tommy had to appear at the back of the stage, interrupt
the Major General and sing his song about the very
sweet buttercups doting on sweet Mabel. It was a love
song and full of high notes, so high that the orchestra
would wait while Tommy went up another flight, then
they'd follow him. Then another. And another. Until the
last flight which Tommy had to take alone, climbing up
and up like a mountain goat. Breaths would be held, fists
clenched. And when he at last landed safe on that top
note and held it, steady and triumphant, you could hear
the audience sigh with relief as the orchestra poured in
behind him: ''Tis Maaaaaay-bell!'

Things were all right until the last two lines of the
song that would take him to the very top. Without
warning, Tommy paused. Then instead of going on and
up, he repeated the lines he had just sung. The orchestra,

whispering and page-turning, scrambled to adjust. The audience drew in its breath a little, there was a shuffling among the seats. Then the orchestra wound up again for the big final explosion of notes . . . Again, Tommy backed down and repeated the last few.

By now you could practically smell the anxiety. Dickey was standing at the side of the stage signalling, going 'For ever love sweet Nature's waaaaaayssss', only about four octaves lower, trying to sing in a voice loud enough so Tommy would hear but nobody else would. On stage, several of the maidens had started to giggle. Mickey McElhone, the maiden nearest Tommy, was giving little nudges and mouthing something. Beside the Bishop, the President was gripping his gold cross in a white little fist.

The orchestra struck up the lead-in for the third time. Da-da-da-da-DUM, da-da-da-da-DUM, da-da-da-da-DUUUUM . . . Everybody – audience, chorus, speaking parts, Dickey – waited. Tommy's face was calm, he opened his mouth, took a breath, aaaaannnd . . . No sound came out.

People had started to look down at the floor. Some were turned with embarrassed smiles to the person beside them; two people in different parts of the hall began to cough. Mary O'Kane had her hand up to her mouth, as if to stop herself singing the words for him. In the wings Dickey stood perfectly still, his face in his hands. For a moment the orchestra sounded lost, then it regrouped and struck up the next chorus, where the maidens do a dance and Mabel looks on. The maidens weren't expecting this and a couple of them bumped into each other at the start of the merry traces bit. But they recovered, and halfway through the dance, when they began to wave the coloured ribbons, Tommy was able to slip off-stage. And when the Pirate King made his entrance and started waving his Jolly Roger about, the audience cheered up and seemed to have put the whole thing behind them.

Only then, ten minutes later, it was time for Tommy to recognise the Major General as his long-lost father. Appearing at the back of the stage, Tommy had to spread his arms and say, 'O Papa! My heart has hungered for this day. The time has come for grief to melt away. Behold your fondest daughter Maaaa-bel.'

Only he didn't say it. When the Major General sang, 'Speak, pretty maid, and say to me your name!' Tommy stood looking at him. Willie Melaugh, the boy doing the Major General, stared for a couple of seconds and then began to shrink, or at least that's what it looked like. His hand came up and patted his hair, which was a wig with powder in it. Each time he patted, a puff of powder went up. And with each puff he seemed to get smaller and more afraid.

'O Papa! My heart has hungered! In the name of God!' Dickey's voice, strained with anger, could be heard from where I was standing, at the opposite side of the stage, but it didn't seem to make any difference. If he'd walked on to the stage and pulled Tommy's jaw open and shut with his hand, maybe that would have worked.

Somebody at the back of the hall let a yelp of a laugh and a giggle picked up on it and went skimming through the audience. Tommy glanced right and left, as if thinking of making a run for it. From the wings Dickey could be heard snorting through his nose.

In the end the Major General saved the day. 'Oh

daughter!' he sang, about three octaves lower than Tommy. 'Can your heart have hungered for this day? Do I behold my loving daughter Mabel?'

It didn't make sense but at least it let the figures on the stage break out of their frozen positions. The audience applauded and the Bishop sat back, his face red and what might have been a smile on his face. Now it was nearly time for the last scene, where everybody made up with everybody else, and a big swaying farewell chorus was sung that filled every inch of the hall.

You'd have thought that would be the end of it. That when the last chorus had been sung and the audience had clapped to the music as the cast came out in order of importance and bowed, and Tommy got one of the biggest cheers of all, and the President had gone up on the stage to thank His Lordship the Bishops for gracing our school with his presence, that by then things would have simmered down.

When the curtains had come across for the last time the Bishop moved slowly down the main aisle, nodding at something the President was saying to him, sometimes raising his eyes and glancing at the audience and nodding, as if they'd said something he agreed with as well. It took nearly fifteen minutes for all of the audience to troop out after him. I stood with the stage door a little bit open, watching the hall empty, the back first, then the middle, and finally the rows of convent girls near the front. And there she was. The girl in the red coat, at the end of the second last row, only she wasn't wearing a red coat now, she was wearing a brown uniform like all the other convent girls, and she was already in the aisle and moving towards the exit. Her legs were sort of plump and her black hair was just ordinary, not long and fluffy like Bernie's, but . . . I can't explain it. My bad cheek had begun to throb even before she glanced over her shoulder and sent a quick smile back up at me.

It was like Foxy said – things so easily mightn't happen when they do. I could have been somewhere else when she glanced back. I could have been at the toilet, or blinking, or blowing my nose. I could have seen her and thought she was smiling at somebody else . . . No, that wasn't likely. The smile was definitely for me. But there were still loads of ways in which I could have missed her smile, not even seen her that last night of the operetta. Only I did see it, and I knew she knew I saw it, even though I only had the door at the side of the stage open about six inches and she was at least thirty feet away from me.

And in the moment that she turned and sent the smile up to me, an amazing thing happened: I saw a beauty spot on her neck. Don't ask me how I did it – it should have been impossible to see something that tiny from that distance, but I did. It was as if my eyes were telescopes. A nut-brown beauty spot, just above one of those two little bones that come across below your neck and meet in the middle. And down lower, only of course I couldn't see them except I happened to be in her bathroom when she was getting ready to have a bath, which wasn't going to happen, she would have nut-brown nipples matching her eyes. Two of them.

There wasn't time to think about that any more, and just as well too. Because now the main door had slammed behind the final girl and Dickey was striding up the hall, mounting the steps, creaking at speed across the stage. Everybody stopped what they were doing and watched. Tommy stopped unhooking his dress and stood, holding his breath. Dickey approached him, creak creak creak creak. Stopped. Spoke to him in a low voice. Ppsssswsssst.

For the next few minutes it was practically all Dickey doing the talking. Tommy just stood there, his head hanging, occasionally saying a word or two back. Then at last Dickey gave a tight half-smile and wheeled away, and we all sighed and looked at each other. It was over, it was all right. It was finished.

Except it wasn't. Because Dickey went straight from Tommy to the other side of the stage where Presumer was folding the pirate flag. The stage scenery creaked and shivered again. Dickey planted his thick black boots apart and made a noise in his nose like a bull. 'So you think you can get up to any trick comes into your head, do you, Livingstone?'

Presumer stared at him. 'Trick, Brother?'

'It's not an African explorer they should have nicknamed you after, it's an African savage. A half-washed heathen who thinks he can sabotage what others have worked night and day to construct.'

Presumer scratched his head. 'Sabotage, Brother? How do you mean, sabotage?'

'Well, let me think. I suppose I mean this,' Dickey said. And he hit him. It was a short swing, not more than six inches, but it had plenty of beef behind it. Presumer caught it high up on the cheek, below his right eye, and staggered back. The pirate flag clattered on to the stage.

Dickey took two quick steps after him. Again there was a thwack like a ball against a handball alley, flat of hand along the side of head. 'Ooooohhmmmm,' said the cast and the stagehands, watching. I felt sorry for Presumer but at the same time it was exciting.

Dickey told Presumer to put his hands down from his face: and when he did, he hit him again. 'Confuse deliberately!' Dickey shouted, sending little sparks of spit into the air. 'My main soloist! To amuse yourself! After all my time! And effort! My time! Everyone's time!' Each time he said something, he hit Presumer. Some blood from Presumer's nose flicked into the air like holy water and a couple of drops landed in Dickey's hair. He pretended not to notice. When Presumer leaned forward, shielding his face with his hands and elbows, Dickey drew back for a final swing and whacked him on the back of the head.

Presumer went down on one knee, then keeled over on top of the pirate flag. His hands fell away from his face and you could see the space between his front teeth fill with blood. His lips looked puffy.

'Now escort him from my hall!' Dickey's voice was hoarse. 'And mind no blood gets on my floor.' Four boys rushed forward to help Presumer up. I thought I saw Dickey take a quick look at Presumer as two of them wedged themselves under his oxters. But when I blinked and looked again he had turned away, was folding costumes and lifting props into a tea chest.

At first Presumer groaned when we took him outside to the cold air. Then he whispered that he felt sick, so we brought him to the back of one of the teaching huts. ''S all right,' he said. Almost immediately he started vomiting, and that must have continued, off and on, for about two minutes. I thought of the caretaker coming round in the morning and finding these pools of light brown puke outside one of the classrooms. I almost felt sick myself thinking about it.

Eventually Presumer stopped. He turned towards us,

wiping his mouth with the back of his hand. His eyelids looked pale blue and there was a terrible smell from his breath.

'Beat me, Brother, for I have sinned,' he said, and drew a comb through his dishevelled hair.

He will be the most outcast of men/And in his countenance will be found no comeliness.

CHAPTER 7

The Christmas decorations reflected as sliced red and green in the chrome bar of the Aga. The table had been scrubbed clean of the turkey blood that had soaked through the newspaper spread on it the previous night. Against the wall beneath the window my father's boots, my mother's shoes, Maeve's shoes, my shoes – all winking with a polish level higher even than on a Sunday.

'As long as the car starts now,' Our Father said, spitting on a hairbrush. He pulled it through the stubborn grey mass of hair with little effect. A quick swipe at each wild black eyebrow, equally useless. 'Now.'

'We'll say a prayer for it while you're out trying,' my mother said, picking the hairbrush from the chair where he'd tossed it and replacing it on the ledge beside the mirror. Had they ever fought? Thrown plates at each other, like Marlon Brando in that picture? Then maybe afterwards grabbed each other and planted kisses, sweat running down their faces? I took a deep breath. Christmas Day. The second most important feast of the Church year, and I was standing in the kitchen thinking about my parents' sweat. Better watch out or I wouldn't be able to go to communion.

Our Father gestured for me to follow him outside, where the starting handle jutted from the front of the car. Upholstery squeaked and springs creaked as he manoeuvred himself into the driver's seat. Then: 'Turn her now!' I gripped the starting handle with one hand, braced my other against the pleated metal front of the engine and pulled. Almost immediately the handle whipped back into place; the engine sat silent.

'Pull harder than that, man!' He was waving with one hand and tugging on the starter knob with the other. Stirling Moss roaring at his mechanic. I flexed my chest muscles so my heart wouldn't slither out through the bars of my ribcage. Crouched, gripped the handle with both hands, pulled upwards. Above my groan, the car roared into life.

It was odd, driving in the morning darkness. All the way to the chapel, hedges and tree trunks lit up for a moment, then slipped past on either side, like a beast or maybe God watching us, thinking about us after we'd gone. Nearer town, people began to appear, walking singly or in straggling groups, the headlights catching women with hats and handbags, the men with gaberdine coats and flapping trousers. It was like the feeling you got when it's getting near to the end of a picture – the music changes and people start saying things slowly and you see the sun going down behind the man and the girl. This was God's birthday, a time for presents and maybe signs. Although strictly speaking I should be giving presents to God, not the other way round. That was a bit worrying. But I still had a feeling that today would end with something definite, make my life click into focus.

Inside the church the altar was muffled with flowers – huge bunches on either side of the tabernacle, half-hiding the marble angels. And there were at least twenty fat yellow candles on the altar. Dessie Duffy the sacristan was lighting them with a taper the same colour as the communion wafer, stopping to bow towards the tabernacle each time he passed it.

We took our usual seats, five rows from the front. Three rows ahead of us was filled by Christian Brothers: a line of black backs, shoulder to shoulder, not a single arse resting on the seat behind.

Father Breen emerged from the sacristy, led by twelve altar boys. His parting was as straight as Dessie Duffy's taper and his hair greased flat on either side. Sometimes the oil ran down his forehead and he had to take out a hanky and wipe the gleam dry. He was a great man, Father Breen, everybody said, and the Monsignor would be lost without him. The work he did was powerful, especially keeping the Boys' Club going. When they weren't at the Boys' Club the town boys hung around outside the Rex Café spitting on the footpath, or in the Market Yard playing pitch-and-toss and threatening to thump each other. None of them would have dreamed of being an altar boy. And if they had Dessie Duffy wouldn't have let them join.

There was a cough and a clattering noise from the balcony as Mickey Muldoon stood up to do the first verse of 'Silent Night'. Some people said Mickey could have been another Mario Lanza – he even looked a bit Italian with his belted raincoat and his brown eyes. Mrs Moore would do the women's solo later on. She took the 'r's off her words, the way English people did, and she always sounded louder than Mickey on the top notes. When children heard Mrs Moore singing for the first time they looked at each other and giggled.

Father Breen had to give out Communion because the Monsignor wasn't fit to get up for six o'clock Mass any more, not even on Christmas morning. Father Breen went along the line of tongues like a bee, buzzing his words and moving the host in a tight little spasm before setting it on the waiting tongue. Pointy tongues, fat tongues, smooth tongues, tongues with a coating of grey or white or even green. It was a bit like seeing their bums except it went into their mouths. Wet.

I closed my eyes after Communion and prayed that the peace of Christmas would come down on my mind and leave me happy with the decision I had made about my life. In ten years' time I could be married to the girl in the red coat, have three children and every evening be thinking of going to bed with her as I had a fry and home-made bread and jam for my tea. Or maybe I'd go off the rails in London and wander round the strip shows . . . Or who knows – I could surprise God. Catch him off-guard and become a priest like Father Breen, only not as fat and a lot more cheerful. But no, God wouldn't be surprised, because he was always a step ahead of you. Besides, it was obvious now that I wasn't worthy to be a priest. Which suited me.

Five minutes of head down, thinking hard about God melting inside me, becoming part of every bit of me, little bits of him floating up my veins and spinning around inside my chest. Then I opened my eyes and found myself staring at the seam up the middle of a brown coat with black teddy-boy collar. Bernie Dunne, sitting directly in front of me. On purpose? Below the coat edge, her calves came out in a swell that made me think of the arms on our sofa. And unlike the Christian Brothers, she had her bum leant against the seat.

Squeeze eyes shut quick. Had she seen me when she was coming down from Communion? Maybe she hadn't

– I hadn't seen her until now. But if she had seen me she would be waiting outside after Mass. Smiling. Wanting to talk. Expecting me to bring her to the pictures again. Blinking back tears if I didn't say what she wanted to hear. Ohshiteshootmenow.

'Holy Mary, Mother of God,' I whispered. But that was worse, because now the girl in the red coat was facing me, her convent blouse open at the neck down to the third button, and she had started to open the fourth and fifth button as well. 'Bernie Dunne's aren't *half* the size of these – Heavens above, *everybody* knows that,' she was saying.

All it took was one second. One split second of indulging, enjoying the thought, and Christmas Day would be plunged in mortal sin . . . Was that one? Did I waver there? No, no, no, sing a song or hymn or something, da, da, da dahahhhhhh . . . Had I driven the thought out before it got time to settle? 'Holy Jesus,' I whispered, my face in my hands. When I looked up my mother was looking along the row towards me.

At the end of the third Mass – there were always three on Christmas Day – Father Breen came down off the altar and mounted the steps to the pulpit. His face was shiny red, as though he'd shaved a second time to be extra smooth this Christmas Day. His stomach, big and manly, pushed against the red velvet edging of the pulpit, and his eyes behind his wire glasses softened to something nearing friendliness. 'Rejoice with me,' he said, staring round the chapel and stopping when he came to a group of men huddled at the back, 'for a saviour is born in Bethlehem. The word is made flesh and our joy is unconfined. Those men at the back, there's room for you up here. Come on, come on – I'll hardly eat you on Christmas morning.' The men shuffled and stayed where they were.

The minute Father Breen had finished the *De Profundis*, I squeezed past a radiator and was out the side door while the rest of the congregation were still dusting off their knees. Neil Traynor was in the porch, lifting a St Vincent de Paul collection box into place. His mouth opened as if to say something, but I stretched my face into a half-smile and hurried past him. By the time Mammy and Daddy and Maeve and the rest of the people emerged from the main door I was in the back seat of our car, shivering. Had Neil really been going to say something to me, or was it just his big lower lip hanging a bit more than usual? Or maybe his nose was blocked and he had to open his mouth to breathe. There was no sign of Bernie Dunne. *Gloria in excelsis.*

My job first thing when we got back from Mass was to light the two fires – the stove in the kitchen and the fireplace in the dining room. Mammy had arranged the sticks and coal and paper in both last night. The flame went up nearly white from the newspaper to the sticks, sent bits of twig crackling and bending, licked round the coals.

Maeve had got Mammy a green plastic bracelet, which she was never going to wear and would eventually give back to her. For Our Father she had got a tiepin which was pointless too, since he tucked his tie inside his waistcoat. And for me a book – *Martin Chuzzlewit* in two volumes, with 'Loreto Convent' stamped on the second last page. 'They had a sale,' she said, looking over my shoulder. Mammy and Our Father gave me a ten shilling note and Maeve two half-crowns since she was younger, which she didn't like and rolled her eyes and didn't speak for a while. I had got Maeve a bottle of scent and them a box of Quality Street, which I hoped we'd all get some of later on.

In the kitchen Mammy's face was getting redder and shinier as she moved from kitchen to scullery and back again. She'd greased the turkey's back last night, making it look like a cross-Channel swimmer. Now all that was needed was to slide the tray on which it lay inside the oven. After that she had to check the trifle with bits of sponge and fruit held in a wobbly grip, and the whiff of the sherry she had put into it, and the smell of porter from the plum pudding.

But they didn't like me being in the kitchen. Especially Maeve. She said a kitchen was no place for a male, so I took that as a compliment and went into the dining room where Our Father was sitting back in the armchair with yesterday's newspaper. The fire was going nicely.

He looked round the side of the paper. 'Any talk of the dinner yet?'

'Half-two.'

His mouth opened as if to say something. Then he ducked back behind and cleared his throat for a couple of minutes.

Should I speak? This was Christmas Day, after all. 'Talk to him,' Mammy always said. 'Our Father is just dying to know what you're up to.' Do you feel guilty even when you're married, enjoying all that sexual pleasure after your tea? Have you ever thought what it'll feel like, dying? He didn't look as if he wanted me to ask questions like that and I certainly didn't feel like asking them. Maybe he was happy just sitting behind the newspaper picking his nose.

I went upstairs to my bedroom, took out my English exercise book. Dickey had given us an essay on the Keats poem to be finished by the end of the first week back at school. 'Thou still unravish'd bride of quietness.' When he was dictating the notes, Dickey had said 'unravish'd' meant unmarried. But in the dictionary, it said unsullied, inviolate, pertaining to a virgin. When you thought about it, a vase *was* like a virgin. Except you didn't put flowers in a virgin.

I'd got two pages written when a car came in the lane, crunched to a stop under the window. Blotting paper on the last sentence. Now peep out. Uncle Father John opening the car door, a smile on his big face, his hat tilted back. Five minutes later Maeve peered round the door.

'You're to come down this minute, Mammy says. You shouldn't be up here at all on Christmas Day – it's not right or normal, Mammy says.'

He was waiting in front of the dining-room fire, hat and overcoat hung up, a Waterford glass of whiskey in his hand. Big dark eyes bulging from his big broad face.

'What sort of trade are the cattle doing these days?' Smile and sip.

'If I was doing half as well as Isaac Norby I'd be rightly,' Our Father said. 'Fifty head of cattle shipping over to Glasgow before the New Year, wants them held in our boiler house till he gets transport.'

'Would that boiler house of yours hold fifty cattle?'

'I was saying the same thing, Father,' Mammy said, touching her bun of hair and pressing both combs deeper into the brown and grey mass. 'Nor nowhere near room.'

'A big Protestant dealer like Norby, you'd be stupid not helping him out,' Our Father said, clearing his throat and spitting in the fire. 'Never know when you'd be glad you did. And two pound a head for housing them forbye.'

'Decent enough money,' Uncle Father John said.

'I don't know what way the whole of them'll be got in, well,' Mammy said.

'Tons of room, hold your tongue, woman, what are you talking about,' Our Father said.

'Where there's a will there's a way.' Uncle Father John wiped his mouth with the back of his hand, set his glass on the mantelpiece. 'Stopped off beyond Norby's this morning, further up the mountain at Paddy Murphy's. Not as much swank there. Whole household lamenting this pet lamb – that was their whole bother and it was Christmas Day. You could have took it for a house holding a wake.'

'Pet lamb?' Maeve asked. 'Who has a pet lamb?'

'*Had* a pet lamb. Died on them yesterday morning – Christmas Eve. Thought for a while they'd maybe ask me to officiate at the funeral.' Our Father gave a bark of a laugh. Uncle Father John swirled his glass, peered into it as if it might contain some sort of message. 'And what way were the report cards this time, I wonder?'

In the end, Uncle Father John always got round to asking about report cards. I took a deep breath. 'Sixty-one in English, fifty-eight in French, fifty in History.'

Uncle Father John put his thumb inside his round collar, tugged it clear of his Adam's apple. Rocked back and forward on his heels without looking at me. 'The English mark has a nicer kind of lilt than the History.' Tight bastard. Could you not say 'Well done!' for once?

We looked up as Maeve came through from the kitchen carrying a tray. On it was the jug the shape of a boat that Mammy always kept special, never filled with apple sauce except for Christmas Day, and beside it a cut-glass bowl filled with cranberry sauce.

Uncle Father John beamed up from the armchair. 'That's what I like to see – a girl that can jump up and help her mammy. And a cook as well! The boyfriends will be lining for miles when they hear about this. Ah, Maeve?' And he reached out and pinched her bare upper arm, just below the sleeve, as she passed.

Maeve mustn't have been expecting that, because she gave a loud squeak and jerked her arm forward. The jug and bowl shot into the air, and even though she made a wild effort to catch them, they smashed to the floor, splashing the tiles with red and yellow. Maeve set her tray on the table, bent her knees, put her hands in her face and began to howl. If it had been her own blood spilled on the floor, there couldn't have been more fuss.

'She'd be quiet if you stuck a knife in her chest,' Debbie Reynolds whispered.

'Hold your tongue – are you doing your damnedest to ruin Christmas Day on us?' Our Father shouted, jumping out of his chair and standing on something that crunched. He towered over Maeve, hand raised as if about to thump her. Mammy appeared from the dining room, tugged at his arm, whispered for him to come down from high doh and go back to his chair.

'No harm,' Uncle Father John said, staring at a splash of cranberry sauce on his trouser leg. 'A dab of food never killed anyone.'

'She has your good trousers ruined on you, Father,' Mammy said, darting at them with a damp cloth.

'Not at all, not at all.' Uncle Father John rubbed at his leg and Maeve howled even louder. 'Did I tell you about poor Charlie Monaghan? Parishioner of mine, fifteen stone last Christmas and what is he this Christmas? Seven and a bit.' He sat and picked up his whiskey glass again. 'Seven and a bit. You'll not hear much lament from him about broken plates, I may tell you. Cancer, God protect us.'

When Mammy had swept up, Uncle Father John said he hoped it hadn't been her wedding china, that would be a tragedy.

'Sure what harm,' Mammy said. And she got the whiskey bottle and we all trooped into the dining room after her, Uncle Father John saying no, no, not at all, he wouldn't have another whiskey, but a splash of wine might be another matter. So Mammy poured him a big glass of dark red wine and a half glass of whiskey. Then he said Grace and we got stuck in.

Heads bent as loaded forks came up, bits of turkey, a fluff of mash, a glob of HP Sauce or maybe gravy dripping back down. Chew, chew, chew. Maeve didn't say much because she was still puffy-faced and weepy. Mammy was too busy serving things to say much except ask Uncle Father John if he had everything. Then Our Father would sigh and make a glugging noise drinking his orange juice and Uncle Father John would half-lift his wine glass and bend his head to meet it and say, 'The best hotel wouldn't do this, nor quarter this either I may tell you.' Then he'd wipe his mouth with his napkin, leaving a purple stain on the white cloth.

Our Father kept the talk moving by asking questions. What had become of so-and-so's business, was old Father Thingummy still saying Mass, hadn't there been a powerful crowd at that funeral of old McLaughlin the auctioneer, what age was he, ninety-eight, my God such an age. If the rest of us did as well, Our Father said, and Uncle Father John nodded and said fit as a flea up until the last month or so. He swallowed, looked round the table and then sang in a soft, quavery voice: 'Who fears to speak of ninety-eight/ Who trembles at the name?' Maeve started to giggle and then went back to sniffling. 'Mind you, I could do the whole song, only the dinner would be cold. Wouldn't it, Maeve? And for a banquet like this that'd be a sacrilege.' Then Maeve giggled again and everyone smiled and it felt good. Death might be out there but it couldn't come in here, or if it did it would have to be on our terms.

By the time the plum pudding and the trifle had been brought to the table and eaten, my belt creaked and I had to breathe through my mouth. The table was covered in plates of half-eaten food, the bowl of whipped cream and the jug of custard with the thick dribble down its front. Then that was gone and I had left the table and was on a diving board, trim and broad-shouldered, looking down twenty feet into a blue, blue pool where three girls in bathing suits were looking up at me and waving. When I hit the water it gave me goose bumps all over my chest, and then I was coming up, gasping for breath.

Except that I wasn't. The meal was over and the table had been cleared and I was sitting upright in a chair to the side of the fire, while Uncle Father John whispered his Office in Latin in the big armchair and Our Father snored in the smaller one.

Uncle Father John ended his prayers in a soft singsong voice, closed his gold-edged breviary and sighed. 'Well now, Jim. You'll be well on the road to whatever you're up to next year by now.'

'Hmm-hmm,' I said, trying to smile. I could feel the sinews in my neck tightening like a football lace.

'We all need to be praying to God all the time for guidance, that He'll put our foot on the right path and keep it there.' Uncle Father John stood in front of the fire and lifted the back of his jacket. 'There are that many voices calling nowadays, it can be hard for a man to know which voice he should heed.'

It was good to be called a man. Like Dickey calling us 'Men'. 'That's right.'

'Last year our diocese had a vintage year – did you know that? Only word for it. Fourteen – fourteen! – recruits went to Maynooth, and I think it was another six or eight went to study for the foreign missions.'

'Wheeoh,' I said.

'Or else twenty. One of the two.' He paused and jangled his change. 'So what about yourself? Mmm? Along those lines, I mean.'

'Lines?'

'The lines of a vocation, maybe.'

'To the, to . . .'

'To the priesthood.'

'To the priesthood.' I knew I was just repeating what Uncle Father John was saying, but I didn't seem to be in control of my own voice.

'Sometimes we try to blot out God's voice, you know. We're frightened of it, don't want to hear it because it might mean too many sacrifices.' He turned from the window, shadows beneath his eyes and nose. In the gloom Our Father's snoring could be heard. 'I did that for a time myself. Not a thing I tell everybody, mind you. But that's what happened. For a time.'

'A time?'

'Tried to blot out the call for a time. When I was your age. For a full year.'

'A year?' If I didn't stop repeating words he was going to murder me.

'Oh yes yes yes.' He put his head back and looked at the ceiling. 'Went down to Dublin and got myself a civil service job. Junior executive, they called it. Earned money, lived in lodgings, got myself a new overcoat and hat. For a full year. Trying to shut out the voice.' As he spoke, he put his hands over both ears. Then glanced at Our Father's sleeping form, leaned closer to me and shook his head. 'Useless.'

'Useless?'

'Use-eh-less. Do you know that poem "The Hound of Heaven"? "I fled Him, down the nights and down the days." About a man that tries to escape from God but God – the hound of heaven – hunts him down in the end.'

'God the hound.'

'No point in codding ourselves if we hear the call.'

'Right.'

'I know one thing, nothing would please your Mammy more than—'

'Aw,' said Our Father. 'Aw Christ Almighty.' He sat up in his chair and burped, rubbed his face with his hand. 'Aw Criminey. I hate wakening up like that.'

Half an hour later, after tea and mince pies, Uncle Father John pulled on his overcoat and gloves, adjusted his hat. He had other brothers and sisters who must be visited before the end of this Christmas Day. 'Maybe Jim would shine the flash-lamp as far as the car?'

Outside the stars were stabbing holes in the sky and frost squinted from the hedges.

'Mind you, when I think of it!' Uncle Father John laughed and the sound bounced off the boiler-house wall. 'Wasting my time.' He sat in his car and started the engine. Rolled down the window and thrust a ten shilling note into my hand. 'Don't tell another mortal soul, whatever you do.' I smiled and nodded. Stood smiling and nodding even after he'd passed the turn in the lane.

Maeve was in the back room, listening to Cliff Richard over and over again on the record pick-up attached to the wireless. Mammy was washing plates in the kitchen and Our Father was reading yesterday's newspaper again. I started to read *Martin Chuzzlewit*, but there was nothing in it half as exciting as where Robert Jordan and Maria got into a sleeping bag in *For Whom The Bell Tolls*. Eventually, at half-nine, with Our Father asleep again in the big chair and Mammy and Maeve in the scullery washing dishes, I went upstairs to bed.

Once under the cold sheets I closed my eyes. Presumer was lying on the couch with the cats, a bottle of stout in one hand and a magazine about Marilyn Monroe in the other. When I flew over Francie he was kneeling, eyes turned to the Infant of Prague on a table by his bed, lips moving – pssssss-wsssss. At Bernie's house her da was eating cornflakes straight from the packet, her ma dodging round him to get at the mirror to give it a rub. Bernie was upstairs, punching the pillow into fluffiness, leaning back with her hands laced behind her, the bed clothes a tent over her knees which were tight together, her mouth a little smiling rosebud.

And the red-coat girl? I toed the hot-water bottle up from my feet, between my knees and then my thighs.

Cosy. Like having your arms around someone warm, except this was my legs . . .

'You've got a torso on you like Gary Cooper's,' Debbie Reynolds whispered. 'Honest to God.' Her breath was like thunder in my ear. She was wearing a pink baby-doll nightdress, with a sprig of holly on the front which didn't prick even when she squeezed tight against me. I closed *For Whom The Bell Tolls*, moved the bottle up higher and felt sweat on my forehead.

'Do you know the thing I'd love this minute, is a bath,' Debbie sighed, her mouth open and her little tongue pointed and wet. So I closed my eyes and took her into the bathroom where I helped her get out of the pink nightdress while the bath was filling. There was a smell of daffodils from her. 'Can you give me a lift in?' she said, her breath tickling my neck. I said I could surely, it was no bother at all. In fact she wasn't much heavier than a bucket of twigs. A couple of little bubbles gurgled as she sat back, and I felt another layer of sweat form on top of the one that was already there. Inside my thigh and above it had begun to feel scorched, but that didn't mean I was going to move the bottle. It was right that I should suffer. 'Thanks, love,' Debbie lisped, her hair spreading and floating behind her. Slowly, looking very brown and shiny, her nipples broke the surface and pointed in different directions. I felt a nudge and there was Uncle Father John beside me, pointing towards Debbie with his thumb. 'Cleanliness is next to godliness, according to my breviary. Good man yourself.'

It was as if the rest of the day – the heat of the fire, Our Father's snorts, Uncle Father John's talking about walking the streets of Dublin – had dropped away and been replaced by something fresh and vigorous. I squeezed the bottle harder against my balls, closed my thighs on it. Suddenly, Debbie Reynolds had pulled me into the bath with her and was biting my neck and licking my burnt cheek with all its bumps and furrows, and the girl in the red coat had somehow got in with us as well and was twisting her plump leg around mine and widening her brown eyes and telling Debbie to give her a bit, not be so greedy. Then as I struggled to get my breath because the two of them were pulling me underwater, I felt the hiccuping begin. Down where the bottle was. Hiccup, hiccup, hiccup, before I could stop it, like a pup leaping between my legs. Golden honey, out of control.

Except when I pulled back the sheets so they wouldn't be wet, it wasn't golden, it was green. Felt like honey but looked like snotters – as if somebody had blown their nose over my stomach. He could have made it any colour in the rainbow, and he had made it the colour of snotters.

Which meant that now I was in mortal sin. Squeeze the eyes tight shut. Dear God, I am heartily sorry and don't let me die before confession. Yes, I know there's forgiveness by desire but it'd be better all round if I could get confession. Maybe I should knock up the Monsignor? Or Father Breen? Only it'd take at least half an hour explaining what was wrong. Better wait until Saturday. Just two days, and I'll keep my repentance fresh until then. Not too hard, with Hell so near I can smell the brimstone.

I wiped myself with an old hanky and turned out the light and tried to think good thoughts. It hadn't even been pleasure, more like a tap that had suddenly turned itself on, then off. That's what happened when you lived in the layman's world. Temptation and sin jumped on you when you were least expecting them. If you were to live a life tied tight to spiritual things, you'd be free from snot and sin.

Close eyes. Listen to my panting, getting slower, quieter. Peep between lashes. From the dark corner of the room Debbie Reynolds glances at me, then away. Wraps a long gaberdine coat around her treacherous body and slinks off up the chimney, out into the Christmas night.

Caught like a rabbit in God's headlights, falling into darkness as my hair crackles and singes, flames thundering all around. 'O God I love you, please don't hurt me, I'll never do it again!' But the scream just goes echoechoecho and I keep falling.

CHAPTER 8

On Saturday morning, as soon as I'd finished a third round of toast with plenty of butter and a wobble of Chivers marmalade, I went out to the shed where the bikes were kept. The door scraped against the cement floor as I opened it. Inside Maeve's bike was lying on the floor, on top of mine, a girl's bike on top of a boy's bike, hmm-mmh. I wheeled it out first and propped it against the side of the shed. Then I lifted my own from the ground.

Our Father had got it second-hand, from a man whose son had outgrown it. Even though he knew it was miles too big, he gave it to me on my tenth birthday. 'You'll grow into it,' he said, scratching the tiny space between hairline and crow's-nest eyebrows. For years I could ride it only with one leg under the bar, bent at an angle. Occasionally, when I wanted people to see me as more grown-up, I'd swing a leg over the crossbar, stretching to tiptoe on either side, the metal grinding into my balls and making me gasp.

Now I skipped alongside, left foot on the pedal, right swinging in a slow, manly arc, settle down in the saddle. Ball-grinding days long gone. Crackle of frozen puddles in the potholes under my wheels. From the boiler house the sound of cattle shifting and bawling. Four of Mr Norby's men had arrived with them in two lorries the previous evening, shouting and whacking for a full half-hour as they squeezed the last few in and shut the door behind them. The cattle's halfwitted roars followed me out the lane.

Right, concentrate. Confess the ordinary things first. I told lies ten . . . fifteen times. I was disobedient . . . three times. I let my mind wander at prayer . . . fifty? Seventy? Split the difference: sixty. I lost my temper five times, was lacking in charity, oh, eight, say eight times. I had bad thoughts . . . seventeen. Eighteen, counting the girl in the red coat's nipples being nut-brown. Or should that be nineteen, one for each nipple? Make it twenty to be on the safe side. That left just the bottle. Couldn't say, 'I pushed a bottle up against my thing and made stuff come out.' I pleasured – no, abused – no, it wasn't that. I held a hot-water bottle in a position that resulted in my climaxing. Right that was it. Bottle, position, climaxing. Close my eyes and say it.

I parked my bike inside the chapel grounds, against the railings. Our Lady in the grotto stood silently listening to St Bernadette, ignoring me and my bike and the farmers' wives moving in and out of the porch with their loaded bags, flicking holy water in all directions.

A queue outside both sides of Father Breen's confession box, none outside the Monsignor's. No wonder. The Monsignor gave lectures, leant his face close to the lattice screen and talked loud and slow, as if he'd cement in his mouth. When you came out your face would be on fire. Outside Father Breen's there were six people, five on the women's side, two on the men's. I knelt behind the second man, covered my face in my hands. Forgiveness – the word had a soft, sighing sound, like air being let out of a tyre. Father Breen wasn't the one would forgive me, it was the presence of God, hovering a few feet above him. God was a beam of light, and he would fill all of us with his love. Even if I was a dirty rat who did things with hot-water bottles.

From the women's side of the confession box a whisper. It sounded like an argument, except there was only one voice. 'It was dark . . . he said . . . my hand.' And then the sounds of what could have been coughing or maybe crying. Several of the women in the line exchanged looks before going back to their rosary beads.

The ear of the man in front of me had hairs coming from it. He kept trying to shove a finger into it with no luck, because the hole was small and his finger the size of a sausage. From the women's side of the confession box came the slam of a shutter. A middle-aged woman came out, mouth bunched as if she was sucking a sweet, eyes hard and dark.

Then the man with the hairy ear had ducked in, and he must have been a saint for he was out again inside two minutes. My turn now. Pull aside the curtain, step into the box, kneel down. No sound except the whispers from the other side. Did they test these boxes out before they put them in churches? Maybe there was a man in the confession box factory whose job was to sit in there and see they met standards. Maybe he sang or recited poetry, while a workmate sat outside and strained to hear. Thou still unravish'd bride of quietness . . . What'd you say, Willie?

Right. That was . . . disobedient, distraction at prayers, temper, lack of charity, bad thoughts. Right. 'And I placed a hot-water bottle in such a position it resulted in my climaxing.' Fix my eyes on the pale yellow image of Christ on the cross, he would take my sins away and Father Breen would be the tube up which my sins would flow to him.

Rustling and door-banging on the women's side, someone sneezed, and the hatch in front of me opened. In the thin light under which he sat behind the lattice, I could make out the form of . . . the Monsignor! He'd switched with Father Breen. Ohshiteshootmenow!

Too late to back out. 'Bless me, Father, I mean Monsignor, for I have sinned; it is two weeks since my last confession.' Well, more like two and a half, but no need to be over-scrupulous. 'I was disobedient . . .'

My sins oozed out like HP Sauce from a bottle. As they did I darted mentally ahead, trying to get the words right.

'Mm-hm,' said the Monsignor. Maybe he had changed with Father Breen to catch people out. Maybe the confessional seal was all a cod and they had a good laugh every Saturday night over dinner in the parochial house. *So this young one – nice-looking bit of fluff too – said to me – pass the HP Sauce, Father – good man – she says* . . . Concentrate, concentrate.

'. . . and pleasured my body to climaxing.'

There was a pause from the other side. The face leaned closer. 'What did you say there?' Slow thick cement.

'I pleasured my body to climaxing, Father. Monsignor. Once.'

'Was this alone or with another?'

The blood had started pumping into my cheek. 'Monsignor, alone.'

A sigh. Pleased or angry? 'And did you touch yourself, my child?'

'Mmss.'

'Speak up, would you.'

'Monsignor, I did.'

A pause: 'Where?'

'On my – my – my thing.' I couldn't remember the name of it. Go on, go on quick. 'But not with my hand.'

Heavy breathing from the other side. 'You touched your private parts but not with your hand. How did you do that?'

'With a bottle.'

'A *bottle*?'

'I had a bottle in the bed, and then I moved it up and it – it touched my – my private parts.' This was awful. I felt like crying.

'What sort of bottle?'

'Hot-water bottle.'

'Hot-water bottle.' Pause. 'And you were alone at the time?'

I'd already told him – what did he want to know again for? Of course I was alone, I was in my bed. *Alonealonealone*. But then the longing to tell all, to lift the ache from my heart overcame me. So I told him how Debbie Reynolds got into bed with me sometimes, and I wasn't totally sure if she was there that night or not, although I had taken her to the bathroom.

There was a release of breath from the other side. 'You sometimes have a woman in the room with you? In the bed?'

'Not a woman – Debbie Reynolds. She's in the pictures – a film star. She wasn't really there, it's just that it seems as if she might be sometimes.'

The Monsignor made a snorting noise. 'You realise that this is grievous sin. Are you a schoolboy?'

'Yes, Father. Monsignor.'

'Age?'

'Nearly eighteen.'

'Leaving school this year, then.'

'Yes, Father. Monsignor.'

A pause, then a sigh. 'What are you for doing – what line of work?'

For a moment I said nothing. Then half-wanting to pull it back even as I said it: 'A priest maybe.'

He may not have said 'Jesus'. He could have been clearing his throat, or the confession seat could have creaked. 'Eee-susss'. But I did hear him making a panting sound immediately afterwards, like one of the cattle in the field along the lane.

His face pushed against the grill. Eyes glinting. 'If God is calling you' – he cleared his throat – 'If it's God's holy will that you follow a vocation, then this kind of activity could be . . . the devil tempting you.' His voice was hard and quiet at the same time. Hard cement.

'Yes, Monsignor.' My whisper was even quieter than his.

'Putting your immortal soul on the brink of hell.' He sighed, tugged the purple stole that hung round his neck. 'Eternal torment for a moment of sinful pleasure. Not a great bargain.'

'No, Monsignor.'

A long period of throat-clearing. I waited quietly. 'Will you promise me something?'

Walk a million miles, eat glass . . . 'Yes, Monsignor.'

'Pray to Our Lady.' He was so close I could smell his breath through the lattice. Oranges. Had he a bag of Outspan in there with him? 'Her heel crushed the devil before and she'll do it again for you. And pray to St Joseph, who knew more than his share about chastity.

Pray to the angels and saints, for support against temptation. For we know not the day nor the hour.' There was a pause. 'Anything else?'

For God's sake – anything else! 'No, Monsignor.'

'For penance say the five Sorrowful Mysteries of the rosary and avoid all occasions of sin. Mind now.'

As the Monsignor said the absolution and sent his arm up and down and sideways in the dark, the expression on the face of the little crucified Jesus seemed sadder than ever. He knew what I'd been through, how these things happen when you don't intend them to, although it'd be impossible to try explaining that to the Monsignor. He was smart but he didn't understand things. Only God understood.

When I came out, the faces looked up. Several women stopped fingering their beads, eyes following me. Then they were back at prayer, whispering and whistling. Others glanced away, pretended a lack of interest. But I could tell they were guessing what I had been telling the priest.

The marble floor of the chapel was smooth and solid, and the light coming in the big stained glass window above the altar, especially the white and red bits, seemed glorious. Even the shine on the seat where I knelt – polished by generations of elbows – seemed joyful. So many different things working together to make the world gleam. I could almost feel God wrapping his arms around it and me, keeping us safe.

What I would like now was to be shot. If I could get my penance said and then be on my way out of the chapel, eyes on the door, and a gun fired from the balcony, say – a bullet shatter my skull – without me expecting it – that would be perfect. Hello, St Joseph, hello Our Lady, yes it's me, the one that had the bother with the bottle. Yes, dead lucky, considering. And after that, eternal bliss. It'd be like the thing you enjoyed doing most in the world, multiplied by a million, and another million on top of that. Whewwww.

Penance said I left the chapel, my soul nearly shining through my skin. The inner door was heavy and stiff, so I had to use two hands to get it open. Outside, the sounds and sights of life. Two women in head scarves near the entrance to Keenan the butcher's, talking as if their lives depended on it. A boy who used to be in my primary school class washing Wilman's shop window, using a bucket of suds and a brush with a long handle. When he had the suds cascading down the glass like a line of dancers, he took another pole with a flat strip of rubber on the end of it and scraped the window clean. From time to time he glanced towards where I stood but didn't speak. A dog came sprinting out of Keenan's with Dan Keenan behind him, roaring. Dan said something to the two women at the door and made them laugh, then went back in, wiping his palms on his striped apron.

I was ten yards past the Rat's Pad, almost at the bottom of Castle Street, when I heard a yodel. I looked back. Presumer stood at the entrance to the Rat's Pad, his hand on his Adam's apple. That's how he got the yodelling sound.

'Hi – Jim-jam!' he yelled. Came trotting down the hill towards me, put his arm round my shoulders, panted in my ear. 'Wednesday morning – see you here about ten, OK? Fail not our feast – vell-ee impoh-tann!' He strode back up the hill, turned halfway. Put his head back, put four fingers against his neck: 'O-dell-ay-eetee!' A final thumbs up and he'd vanished into the Rat's Pad again.

A couple of crows flapped against the wind, landed awkwardly on the cross on top of the chapel spire. Grrrcrawww. This time next year, I could find myself up in Belfast at the teacher training college, going out to dances and smoking whenever I liked. Or – hardly likely but possible – I could be looking at crows in Maynooth, saying prayers half the day, my life an arrow flying straight to God past the distractions of this life.

The catch with the Maynooth route was, I'd have to live my whole life with people like Francie talking about singsongs and never mentioning that in houses up and down the street and up and down the country, night after night, men and women were riding each other and still not committing sin, because they had got married and I hadn't. The crow cawed again and I felt my skin shiver.

Whenever I go on a journey/ Over the land or over the sea/ I always ask St Christopher/ To take good care of me/ And bring me safely home/ Wherever I may be.

CHAPTER 9

It was the second last day of 1959 – second last day of the Fabulous Fifties. On either side of the lane the grass in the fields had a fur of white. The cattle in the boiler house were all bawling at the same time, shifting and stumbling against each other in the confined space. Out in the field our own cattle lifted their heads from the feeding trough and listened to the boiler-house distress, plumes of mist puffing from their streaming noses.

I was halfway up Castle Street when Presumer emerged from the Rat's Pad. He was carrying a biscuit tin in his arms, which he placed carefully on the footpath beside him. Took a cigarette from behind his ear and broke it in two, passed me half. We stood and smoked in silence. Then he tilted his head towards the tin, which I now saw had holes in the lid.

'Carry that for us, OK?'

'What's in it?'

'A rat – here, don't drop the bugger! It's not a rat, it's a kitten – Jesus, think you were a wee girl.' He made sure I had a firm grip on the box and we headed down the hill and across the bridge. The frost made the banks of the river look white and hopeful. There was no sound from inside the biscuit tin but I could sense something alive in there.

'What way did you get over Christmas?'

'Quiet,' I said, trying not to think about Debbie Reynolds. 'What about you?'

'Sean drank nearly half the sherry that was to go in the trifle and started puking. Ma said it'd be useless putting in only half so she drank the rest herself. Tell you something – I hate Christmas Day. Supposed to be near the shortest day in the year. Fucking near the longest, I find.'

'What about that Mary O'Kane photograph – still putting it in the competition?'

'Haven't developed her yet.' He spat in the frozen gutter. 'Remember Neil's fingers sitting on Mary's back, like five tools at the end of his sleeve?' He closed his eyes and shuddered. Opened them. 'I'm going to get that bastard.'

We turned and walked back up Castle Street without speaking, our footsteps echoing across the street and back at us. Past the chapel and towards the next hill. You could have blown smoke rings with your breath.

'Some Tuesday night I'll do it. Him and Dickey play bridge. Four of them – Neil, Dickey, Dr Grant, and that woman has the horses. They play for matches – can you credit it? Money coming out their arse and they play for matches. Anyway. Some night that Neil and Dickey are staggering home late – boom!'

'What do you mean, boom?'

'Boom. The gruesome twosome get theirs.'

'Thought you were going to get just Neil.'

'Get them both.' He pushed his hands deep in his pocket and walked along, chin in his chest. 'Either that or a photo of Neil and Collette together, maybe. Take it and send it to Dickey, write on the back: "You're next, you big-arsed balls-merchant."'

'How do you mean, Neil and Collette together?'

'Well, say Collette called at his house and he answered the door. And then Collette, she sort of staggered and fell into his arms. And then I sort of jump out of the bushes and photograph them. What about that? Hot news – pheeeeeoooohhh.'

We passed Dan Keenan's, where he was hanging up chunks of pig with their ribs red and their backs white. I saw Collette's brown eyes staring up into Neil's face as she collapsed on top of him into the hallway of his big house.

'How would you get Collette to stumble?'

Presumer raised his first two fingers and thumb to eye-level and rubbed them together. 'Pay her.' He took the biscuit tin from me, peeped inside, handed it back. 'People will stumble till the cows come home if you pay them.'

'Have you money?'

He glanced quickly at me. 'No, but I know where some is. Same place there's record players.' Presumer put his finger to his lips. 'Kill two birds with one stone.'

'Dangerous,' I said. Inside I was thinking, 'Suicide. Madman.'

Presumer tapped the top of the biscuit tin. 'All you need's someone for a bodyguard. Somebody who can look after himself. And us. Rest is easy-peasy.' Presumer lifted a stone and tried to hit a lamp post ten yards ahead. He missed. Then lifted his arms to the sky, hands like claws. 'The scene: darkness. A lone woman knocks on Neil's door and asks for water. Neil brings a cup. Woman stumbles. Night sky is lit up with flash-click. "Town Councillor feels up circus hoor. Dirty brute shocks Omagh. See photograph below." Click-click.'

'I heard Neil has a brute of a dog,' I said. 'An Alsatian.'

'Can have a bucking crocodile for all I care. Won't save him.'

We turned into John Street, moved along its curve towards the New Hall. 'Although you never know. I might just forget about Neil. Dickey's the one I really want. Might just wait until Dickey's on night duty at the Brothers' house. Two in the morning, your woman Collette rings the bell. Dickey opens the door in his nightshirt, she grabs him, oooh darling Brother Dickey protect me, it's so daaaarrrkk. A rustle in the undergrowth, Livingstone of Omagh leps out. Click-click, job's a good one.'

'You take his photo?' Presumer nodded. 'Where does Paddy fit in?' I asked.

'He's a trained boxer.' Presumer dabbed at his nose with the thumb of his right hand, pretended to throw punches with his left. 'Fit as a fucking flea. Out of bed at six, runs four mile, knocks hell out of a punchball before even thinks about the breakfast.' He stopped to peer through a hole in the tin. A scrabbling and then a tiny miaow. 'It's orange with white paws. He'll be pleased with that.' Presumer straightened and shook his head. 'Or I could get Paddy just to help us knock hell out of Neil's fancy house – maybe that'd be better. When him and Almighty are away somewhere. Do that and forget the photo stuff.'

'It'll be locked with his Alsatian in the hall. You won't get in.'

Arms raised and left foot forward, Presumer pretended to fire an imaginary arrow from an imaginary bow. 'Doped meat through the letterbox. Then use that crowbar of ours on his back door. Soon see who doesn't get in.'

As we passed Andy Elliott's house, their dog rushed out. It had one eye brown and one eye grey.

Presumer swung his canvas-slippered foot in a wild kick and the dog lurched back. 'See that mouth? Soapsuds. Mad as a March hare. Here boy – fetch!' He sent the stone skimming down the road and the dog went skidding after it.

The Boys' Club was a green hut with a corrugated roof. Presumer stood at the door, one hand on the doorknob. From inside came a thudding sound: sometimes quick-fire, sometimes in single beats. Finger to his lips, Presumer opened the door.

The place smelt of sweat and embrocation. Along the walls, cardboard boxes, an old pair of boxing gloves with a stain of blood on the padded knuckle, a bucket and a brush. In the middle of the room, a punchball on a stand, bobbing from side to side; and his back to us, making it shake, Paddy O'Kane. His ginger hair was cropped to the skull except for a little tassel at the front that bobbed up and down over his three wrinkles. And he was wearing a singlet and shorts. In a chair at the far end of the hut, chewing gum and reading a comic, sat Tommy Harvey.

When he saw us, Tommy jumped to his feet, stuck his chewing gum under his nose and gave a Hitler salute. Paddy hit the ball a final tattoo of punches. Then stood, gloves hanging by his sides, sweat squirming down his neck.

'Look – will I show you the way to do it? Here's Freddie Gilroy.' Presumer steadied the punchball with both hands, drew back his fist and let go. '*Jesus. My hand.*'

Paddy smiled slowly. 'The gloves protect you. Sore without them.' Inside the box the kitten began to throw himself around. 'You've a kitten in there. That's a live kitten you've got, you bugger!'

'It's a rat,' I said.

Paddy crouched beside the box. 'You're even stupider than you look. It's a kitten. Take him out till we see.'

'He'll start skittering on everything and then run out and get killed by a lorry,' Presumer said. 'Hold your horses till you're home.'

'Mean I can keep him? Yippee-i-ay!' Paddy put the box down, swung round and thumped the punchball, once, twice, three times. Stood grinning. 'What colour?'

'Orange, with white feet.'

'Orange,' Paddy breathed. 'The colour of the sash me father wore.' Then he set the punchball going again until it became six vibrating balls. He was like a dancer, the ball responding to each fist in turn, right, now left, now right, as he shifted weight from foot to foot. Shoulder muscles caught shadow, flexed it out again, dimpled once more.

'Did you take a break from training at Christmas?' Presumer asked him.

Paddy wiped his forehead with his arm and picked up a skipping rope. 'Christmas Day and Boxing Day. Can't slacken – fighting in February in the Ulster Championships.'

'He's fighting in the championship,' Tommy explained. 'In February. Any of youse got a fag?'

When he'd finished, Paddy rubbed sweat from his face and neck with a towel, then rubbed embrocation on his legs and shoulders. Pulled the trousers of a grey suit over the top of his shorts, slipped a knotted red tie over his head. He stood panting quietly, his big nostrils round like a horse's.

Presumer produced a packet of cigarettes. 'Ma's in bed sick – can't smoke so she gave me these.' He offered to Paddy, who shook his head; then me; then took one himself. As an afterthought he flung one to Tommy. 'You're too bloody young, you skitter. That's your last.'

Three ribbons of blue smoke drifting behind us, we left the hut. Paddy put his kitten box on the ground, then carefully locked the hut door with a key he produced from his trouser pocket. We turned into John Street.

'Anything good coming to the Picture House?' Presumer asked.

Paddy took his eye from one of the air-holes. '*Ocean's Eleven*. Dean Martin is in it.'

'Jerry Lewis?'

Paddy shrugged. 'I never see half the pictures any more. Bloody boss makes me label films, lift papers, sweep the floor – everything but clean the lav. That bastard's asking for it, you know.'

'Asking for what?' Presumer said.

'Asking for me to get annoyed with him.'

'Any sign of that money was took from the Picture House?' I asked.

Paddy stared at me. 'How the hell would I know? It's gone – hid. Circus boys don't leave signs to where they've hid something.'

'Were you there when they came in and stole it?' Tommy asked. 'D'you see them?'

Paddy did a sudden skip and shouldered Tommy against the wall. 'Don't need to see them, Mr Smartarse. You weren't at the Battle of Waterloo, were you?'

Tommy stood rubbing his shoulder and grinning.

'Kiss my hardy – that's what your man Napoleon said at the Battle of Waterloo. I was right behind him, heard the whole thing. "*Embrassez mon hardie*." Swear to God.'

'That was Lord Nelson,' Presumer said.

'Will I tell you something? You saw fuck all,' Paddy told Tommy. 'That's what I'm saying. You weren't at Waterloo but you believe it happened. Blessed are those who have not seen but have believed.'

'I was just wondering,' Presumer said. 'Outside the ring. You ever fight outside the ring?'

Paddy peered into the box where the kitten was miaowing. 'I'll keep him in the kitchen until he's used to everything. A week or so. Especially Mary's bloody singing practice.'

'But did you?'

'What?'

'Ever take somebody on besides in the ring?'

Paddy's freckled hand ran over his skull. 'One time. Three boys at a dance.' He touched the bridge of his nose. 'One of them got me with a chair.'

'You should have got the police,' Tommy said. 'A chair and three of them – that's not fair.'

Paddy smiled. 'No need for cops. An ambulance was what your man needed when I was done with him.'

Presumer took out a bag of brandy balls, passed it round. Paddy took two. 'Know Neil Traynor?'

Paddy crunched the hard brown glass between his back teeth. Now he sounded like a horse as well. 'Skinny guy with a squint, played rugby?'

Presumer snorted. 'Councillor Neil wouldn't know a rugby ball if it got stuck in his hole. He's got a shop.'

'Oh, *him*,' Paddy said. 'No teeth, hardly any hair, drives a Volkswagen with the engine in the back?' Then

Tommy and him began staggering about the footpath, making farting laughs like the girls in the Picture House.

Presumer stared. 'Tell us the joke and we'll laugh.'

'He's—' Tommy pointed at Paddy – 'He's – his—'

Paddy stood there grinning. 'Shut your trap.'

'Neil Traynor. He's—' Tommy pointed at Paddy again – 'He's your man's sister's manager. Mary O'Kane's bloody manager! Paddy's. Sister! And you said. Does he know him!' Tommy went down on his knees laughing, then got up again and dusted himself off.

'You'll know where he lives, so,' Presumer said, unsmiling. 'And all about the "You are piss and we are princes" golf club he attends.'

Paddy looked puzzled. 'You're Princess Golf Club?'

Tommy Harvey had been forced into the gutter but now he skipped back on to the footpath. Tugged Paddy's sleeve and pointed at Presumer. 'Here,' he said. 'You should have seen the pasting Dickey gave him.'

'Who?'

'Brother Dickey near killed your man here for mixing me up in the operetta.'

Paddy beamed. 'You get beat up, Presumer?'

'One minute Dickey was telling me that apart from one wee slip, I was the best solo he could remember in a school show. And next thing, he's bounced across the stage and is pounding the stuffing out of your man. Weeeooooww. Skin and hair flying.'

Presumer blew a smoke ring and looked at the roof. 'He'd this idea I'd put you off your lines. Whoever gave him that idea.'

'He asked me what had put me off, that's all,' Tommy said. 'I told him it was talking to people and thinking and then getting myself all mixed up. That's all. And then the next thing, he went mad.'

'You said yourself he'd go off his head some day,' I reminded Presumer.

'Anyway, we weren't talking about Dickey. We were talking about Neil Traynor.'

'Did he beat you up too?' Paddy asked Presumer.

'Like to see him try.'

We walked on in silence. Inside the box, the kitten scratched and flung himself about.

'Neil's head buck in the golf club,' I explained to Paddy. 'Where Presumer's ma works.'

Paddy revolved his head one way, then the other. The muscles on his neck were like small ropes. 'So?'

'So that Fatso Neil gets on my nerves,' Presumer said. 'With his car a mile long and his arse a mile wide. Needs his teeth put down his throat.'

'Good idea,' Tommy said. 'Beat the bastard good-looking.'

'He's a fair size, mind you,' Paddy said.

Presumer punched the air a few times, dabbed the side of his nose with his thumb. 'Not so big after the first fifty punches. From a trained boxer.' He threw a flurry of uppercuts.

When we got to the Show Grounds the gate was shut, so we went round the side. Presumer and I helped Tommy up on the wall, then Paddy scrambled after him. And with the two of them in place, it was easy for Presumer and me to pull ourselves up. When we dropped on the other side, our shoes sank an inch or more into the soft ground. Presumer stopped at each footprint and scuffed it out, then rubbed his feet clean on the grass. A number of yellow geometric shapes on the grass showed where the circus tents and caravans had been.

'See that?' Tommy pointed. 'Buggers killed the grass with their foreign piss, then cleared off.'

'Who did?' Paddy asked.

'It was in the paper and everything,' Tommy said. 'Guy with the cut hand was summonsed and fined. Then they all had to pack up and leave. They should have gone on the run, like your man in the IRA. Wonder what they eat when they're on the run.'

'Spuds,' Paddy said. 'Nettles. Some of those circus hoors is worse than the IRA. Would cut your throat and eat your windpipe.'

'I heard there was a woman,' Tommy said. Presumer dug his hands deep in pockets, tucked in his chin. 'A sexy woman. Still here, staying in a certain person's house.'

'A mad woman, you mean.'

Paddy gave the box a little shake. The kitten miaowed. 'Is there a reward? Wouldn't mind a reward.'

'Maybe they'll put up posters,' Tommy said. 'Have you seen this woman? She's armed and legged and dangerous.'

'Shut your arse, would you,' Presumer told him. 'What time is it?'

'Nearly one o'clock.'

We left the Show Grounds again by a side door that somebody had forgotten to lock. We were on the Dublin Road now, walking away from the town. Cars passed us, most of them turning right to drone up the gravelled lane that led to the golf club.

'Can't stand that shower,' Presumer said, spitting over a hedge beside the road. 'What would you say if . . .' He was looking at Paddy but Paddy wasn't listening, because he had the box up to his eye trying to see into it, his tongue tip sticking from the corner of his mouth like a pink snail. We turned and walked back into the town.

Paddy took his kitten home and Tommy went with him. Presumer said he was going to the pitch-and-toss school in the Market Yard, was I coming? I told him I had to be home for my dinner by two o'clock. I didn't, but I didn't want to go to the Market Yard. I was on my way past Anderson's clothes and hardware shop when Mammy came out carrying a parcel.

'The very man. Hold that.' She pushed the box into my arms – the second box I'd been told to carry today. 'Don't let anybody touch it.'

'What is it?'

'Material for a skirt and an oilcloth for the kitchen table. I won't be two shakes of a lamb's tail.' She crossed the road and went carefully down the steps to the Ladies' Public Toilets, holding on to the brass banister.

Two girls in convent uniform chased each other up the steps, shrieking with laughter, and passed without a glance. A gypsy woman crossed the street to me, pushed her heavy face into mine, hand out. Her shawl smelt of turf. I shrugged to show I had nothing and turned away. A man in a bowler hat drove a pony and trap down the middle of Market Street, flicking his whip, staring straight ahead and calling 'Cck. Cck.'

Mammy was beside me again, buttoning her coat. 'That's a bit better. Now, we'll give ourselves a wee treat before heading for the bus.'

The Snack Bar was done up in pink and grey and was three-quarters full. Once we got a table, Mammy took off her head scarf, stirred her tea while looking round. 'A goldmine, that's what they have here,' she said. 'Eight pence for a bit of an oul' meringue.' A woman passed our table and Mammy reached out to tug her sleeve. 'Hello, Mrs Wenton. What way did you get over Christmas?'

The woman stopped and the boy and girl following her stopped as well. The boy, about eight, watched until his mother was busy talking to Mammy, then leaned forward and tried to pour the tea from my cup into its saucer. The girl grabbed his wrist and squeezed until he put the cup down. It was the red-coat girl.

'It's always something,' she said, gripping her brother by the neck. 'Last month it was boxes. He kept climbing into every trunk he could find and nearly suffocating himself. Speak I not the truth, O Malachy?' There was a lemony smell from her.

'Big fat liar,' Malachy declared, shaking his head and putting his fists against his ears. 'I was breathing the whole time. Liar bitchy Christy. Christy is a bucking liar bitchy,' he told me.

Christy gave his hair a tug. 'Cream meringues are a mug's game,' she said to me over his head. She had a round face and her teeth made her lips push forward.

'How d'you mean?'

'Wrecks your complexion.' She pointed. 'Look at the cut of your cheek.'

I could hear the blood beginning to thud inside my skull. 'Meringue didn't do that. Happened when I was five.'

'What? What happened?'

'Hotplate.'

'Hotplate?'

'On the cooker. When I was five.' A vein in my neck had begun to twitch as well. 'Mammy was out feeding the hens. I climbed up and put my cheek on the hotplate on the cooker. I was only five.'

She laughed. *Laughed*. 'What did you do that for?'

'To hear the wee man in the cooker make a speech. An uncle of mine said there was a wee Orangeman lived inside the cooker who gave a speech if you listened hard enough.'

She laughed again. 'You should put vanishing cream on it.'

Mrs Wenton moved her head closer to Mammy's. Spoke confidentially. 'The laugh of it was, it was a difficulty in my downstairs department the whole time. Not a thing to do with my heart. The doctors know nothing.'

'I saw you at that play,' I told Christy. 'Gawking round you during the singing.'

'Looking to see was there an exit some road. I was *desperate*.' Christy stuck out her lower lip and blew a strand of hair from her face. 'Trapped and my eardrums being assaulted by that Mary bloody O'Kane.'

Mary *bloody* O'Kane? 'She was at our operetta, sat right behind the Bishop. She's getting a record contract, you know.'

'If she sang "Blueberry Hill" or "Blue Suede Shoes" itself. But no chance.' Christy joined her hands under her chin and rolled her eyes like Jesus in the holy picture. '"Softly, softly, bee, bee-beeeeeee/ I swear to God I neeeeed a pee."' She stopped, looked at me with her head on one side. 'Are you going to the dance in the Foresters' Hall tomorrow night?'

'Not sure.'

'What about your chum – Consumption Livingstone?'

'Presumer. I wouldn't think he is.'

'You come, then, so. For all you know we could fall in love at midnight – undress each other with our eyes. That'd be crack, wouldn't it?' Her eyes were brown, with a black point in the middle that went back for ever. Now they looked past me to where her mother was already heading for the door. 'Chocks away, Biggles. See you over Hamburg. Cheerio.' She left, dragging Malachy by his jacket collar. Gave a little wave over her shoulder.

Mammy watched and dabbed crumbs from her plate with a moistened finger. 'That pair has their mother's heart broke.'

Maeve's face was at the kitchen window, watching as we came in the lane. She opened the door. 'Were you at the Snack Bar? Did you get me something nice?' When Mammy said she'd forgotten but she'd surely make it up another time, Maeve stuck out her lower lip.

Mammy ignored that and filled the kettle, put a packet of fig rolls on the table. 'It's sad to see the way they let that Wenton child run mad. Not half right.'

'He tried to bite me,' I told her.

'And the Christine one with brains to burn. But spends half her time working in Hutton's instead of studying her books. And now nothing will do her only going away to England to work in some office. Lord, thou art hard on mothers.'

'She told a girl in my class she was going to America to be a bareback rider,' Maeve said, pointing a bicycle lamp at the ceiling and switching it on and off.

'Put that away and don't be wasting the battery. Whereabouts is Our Father?'

'Out in the boiler house milking a cow.'

'We can make a fresh pot when he comes in, then.' She stood listening for a second. 'I don't believe it – the roaring and bawing is stopped. Did Isaac Norby come for his crowd of cows?'

'He did – two lorries. You should have brought me home a bun at least.'

I opened the *Irish News*, which had a big section about John Fitzgerald Kennedy. He and his brothers seized every opportunity to break off from politics and play touch football, it said. There was a photograph of him with a rugby ball beside his ear.

On the wireless in the back room Sam Costa was doing the hits of the year. 'This is one record I've enjoyed more than mucho, and so have you, going by sheet music sales, they are co-lossal, a certain Mr Emile Ford and his bosom buddies, the Checkmates, boo-da boo-da, boo-da boo-da bum, take it away, Emile.'

Emile and his buddies were halfway through 'Whaddya want to make those eyes at me for?' when there was a thumping at the door.

I turned down the wireless and tugged at the door, which was stiff. The minute it opened Maeve grabbed my arm and dragged me from the room. 'Come on quick! It's the roof!'

'What roof? What are you talking about?' I had to trot to keep up with her. We were out the back door now.

'The bu. The bub – boiler-house roof has fallen down on top of Daddy!' She stopped, head back, hands in the air. 'Oh why, God? *Why?*' I ran past her, thinking if I'd had a stick I definitely would have thumped her.

*

Two lorries had come for Isaac Norby's cattle a half-hour earlier, Maeve told us afterwards. Our Father had made her come out and stand in the lane to stop the cattle running out and on to the road. Then he'd gone round the back of the boiler house and somehow or other climbed in the window, shouting at the cattle and getting them to start going out the door and onto Norby's two cattle lorries. It'd taken a while because the cattle kept twisting around and banging into each other and into the walls. But in the end they were all hooshed out and on to the lorries. When they'd driven off Our Father brought our four cows from the meadow and chained them in their stalls in the boiler house. He must have been milking the second of them when the three big curved sheets of corrugated tin that formed the boiler-house roof came crashing down. The first sheet missed everything, just fell on the ground. But then came the second, and although it missed him it hit the cow he was milking, knocking it off its feet. Then instead of tumbling forward, the cow tumbled back on top of Our Father's legs and stomach, trapping him. And he'd no sooner been trapped than the third piece of corrugated tin fell on top of both him and the cow. He was lucky, though – it just trapped him a second time, without hurting him.

So there he was, with a cow and part of a roof on top of him. There was nothing he could do except lie still, white-faced and groaning. His cap had fallen off and his face looked waxy. Mammy and Maeve and me managed to tug the third bit of the roof off him, but even before we tried tugging the cow, we knew it was useless.

Our Father's lips looked sort of purple and moved slowly when he spoke. 'Is she dead?'

Maeve crouched beside him. 'Who, Daddy?'

'The cow, the cow.'

When we looked, its eyes rolled up in its head and there was blood leaking from the ear nearest us.

'Don't fret yourself about the danged cow,' Mammy said, picking some bits of straw away from his face. 'That's what brought this whole bother on, piling too many cattle in, putting a strain on walls were never made to stand it. I'm away to ring the doctor.'

'Get Gerry Connor,' Our Father whispered after her, his voice like sandpaper. 'Tell him bring a tractor and rope. Say he can have the cow for his bother.'

The doctor came out to the boiler house in his dark blue suit, wearing an old pair of Our Father's wellingtons in case he dirtied his shoes. He checked Our Father's pulse and felt his side and said he'd be as well to lie low for a while, in case he'd pulled or damaged something internal. 'Can you feel your legs?'

'Far too well,' Our Father groaned. 'A solicitor's letter – to cowboys built boiler house – soon fix them. Feel a load of the law on them.'

'You load sixteen tons,' Maeve whispered in my ear. I never let on I heard her.

Twenty minutes later Gerry Connor and his two sons arrived. They were younger than me but beefier and red-cheeked. Directed by Gerry, they shouted to each other and slipped a thick blue rope around the cow's rear legs and then round her middle and finally around her head and neck. The other end of the rope went out the door and over a small pulley on the back of Gerry's tractor, which had inched up as close as possible to the roofless building.

'Right, let her rip, Da!' the bigger boy called. The

tractor throbbed and inched forward and the cow began to slide free of Our Father. The two boys leaned into the cow's belly, pushing it up at the same time as their father pulled it clear. Our Father gave an extra loud groan and went grey.

When the cow had been winched up and tied on to the back of the tractor, the doctor eased a grey blanket under Our Father's head and gave him an injection in the bum. Then he got Gerry Connor and me and Gerry's two sons to lift Our Father very very carefully on to another grey blanket. And with each of us holding a corner, we carried him slowly into the house and up to his room. Our Father groaned at every step, and twice as loud when we were lifting him on to the bed.

When the doctor came back inside he went straight to the bathroom and Mammy brought him up a kettle of hot water and he scrubbed his hands. Then him and Mammy went into Our Father's room and stayed there for about twenty minutes. Maeve and I could hear them talking through the floorboards. First the doctor's voice rumbling, followed by Mammy's lighter tones, then the doctor again – like the priest and the altar boy at Mass. A couple of times we heard Our Father mutter something, or at least thought we did. Maeve said it could have been the floorboards creaking.

Then the doctor came downstairs and changed out of his wellingtons and into his shiny black shoes again. Ran a comb through his shiny black hair and washed his hands a second time and said he'd be back tomorrow to see how the Boss was getting on, that he'd given him something to help him sleep. After he'd gone Mammy took a brush and dustpan and cleaned the stairs carpet where Gerry Connor and his sons had left chunks of mud. Then she went over the spots again with a basin of water and a scrubbing brush, leaving patches of damp on nearly every stair all the way to the top. 'That's that itself,' she sighed, and brought tea and toast up the stairs to Our Father. But he was sleeping so she brought the tray down again and Maeve ate three of the slices and I ate one.

For the next hour after that Mammy said nothing. Went round wiping everything she could see with a damp cloth. The cooker, the table top, the picture of the Sacred Heart. Finally she set the dishcloth beside the sink and sat down heavily in Our Father's armchair. 'It's as well the people don't know what's round the corner. Where are you away?'

'Upstairs,' Maeve said from the door. 'To tidy my room.'

'Will he be all right?' My voice sounded high.

'Doctor says for him to rest, he can find nothing broke. But I don't like the look of him.' She pulled a comb from her bun, then jammed it back in. 'I don't like the look of him one wee bit.' Her neck was red maps under her chin to the V of her blouse.

A cold hot-water bottle had started to leak inside my chest. Why did the boiler-house roof have to fall on the cow? And why did Our Father have to be out there when the roof did fall? That time I had gone out the lane to Foxy's for the papers and had thought of Our Father with a slate stuck in his skull – maybe this was a punishment. Maybe this was God showing me up by hurting Our Father with a cow instead of a slate. Maybe the cow was a sign, to remind me of the Hound of Heaven and how if he was on your trail you'd be caught in the end. Or maybe God had shown me the dead cow so that any last thought of going to a seminary would die as well. Then I heard a voice speaking. Mine.

'There's a special New Year's Eve dance in the Foresters' Hall tomorrow night. Can I go?'

Mammy stared blindly over the top of the newspaper. 'Special dance?'

'For to usher in the new decade – the nineteen-sixties.' I clenched my fists inside my trouser pockets. 'Only two shillings.'

She reached into her apron pocket for a hanky and blew her nose. Pushed it out of sight again. 'The dear knows you might as well be dancing as moping. For there's not much to laugh at about this house.'

The doctor came the next day when we were still eating the rhubarb and custard Mammy had made for dessert. She brought him upstairs to examine Our Father. When he came down he stood in the kitchen and said Our Father might just have a touch of concussion, he'd have to think for a day about it. He wouldn't take him into the hospital except it was absolutely necessary. But meanwhile Mammy was to keep an eye on him. 'And these two tearaways will help you, I'm sure,' the doctor said, pointing at me and winking at Maeve. He washed his hands and waved away the towel Mammy brought him. Dipped two fingers into his breast pocket and used the big white hanky lodged there.

That was New Year's Eve morning. In the evening when Maeve saw me getting shaved and wearing a shirt and tie and putting a really straight part in my hair and Mammy told her where I was going, she was raging. That wasn't my fault. Our Father was upstairs and not well, so somebody had to stay behind and help Mammy.

And Maeve had always been far better at helping about the house than me.

Hail, holy queen, mother of mercy. Hail, our life, our sweetness and our hope.

CHAPTER 10

It was dark and windy riding the bicycle into town – the trees along the side of the lane sighed as I rode past: 'Fathersick, fathersick, faaaathersiiiiiick.' I lowered my head and pedalled harder. No good if I had stayed at home. Moping about. Using up oxygen. Being out of the house would leave more oxygen, make it easier for Our Father to breathe. A young person could use up a lot of oxygen, especially if they were worried and panting. When I went round the back of the Foresters' Hall there were about fifty bikes propped against the wall. Most of them were men's.

The sound of 'Heartaches by the Number' drifted from inside the hall, interrupted by the occasional screech from the microphone and a man's voice saying he wanted to see everybody on the floor, come on now boys and girls, the walls will hold themselves up, let's have everyone on their feet. When I pulled open the door, the noise poured over me, along with the smell of sweat and perfume. Beyond the table where they collected the money and gave you your ticket, javelins of light rotated, slicing the cigarette smoke. I had barely paid when Almighty came out of the crowd in brown drainpipe trousers, his hair in a quiff. 'I saw Christy Wenton coming out of the lavs,' he said, his neck stretched like a dog picking up a scent. 'She has black stockings and a red frock on.' There was a pause while we thought about this. 'Is that not a fellah's name? Like Christy Ring.'

'It's short,' I told him. 'For Christine.'

'Is that it? I was thinking of Christy Ring – he's a Christopher, isn't he? Not a Christine.'

I looked away. 'He's bald.'

'Who is?'

'Christy Ring.'

'I know that. Everybody knows that.'

I didn't reply. It seemed wrong that Almighty should be allowed to have her name in his mouth in any form. There was another pause. Then: 'Would you say?'

'Say what?'

'I might click.'

I looked at Almighty. The oil on his quiff, his bootlace tie, his wet mouth.

'Get off with Christy Wenton?' He nodded five, six times, eagerly. 'You could be lucky.'

'Let the dog see the rabbit, so.' One hand checking that his quiff was still in place, he slipped back into the crowd.

Then the music began to pound and the crowd surged forward. Suddenly, as if somebody was stage-managing things, there was Christy two feet away, standing arms folded, turned at an angle from me. Go on, *ask*. She hasn't a gun, she can't shoot you. I moved towards her, teeth clenched. Touched her bare arm. She turned, eyebrows raised, brown eyes round. And smiled, just like after *The Pirates of Penzance*. A Yes smile. We elbowed our way into the crowd of dancers.

It was like iron filings to a magnet. Her red dress and the parts of her inside it clamped themselves against me, from my jacket lapels all the way down to my knees. I tried not to breathe, tried to think of something else. Nettles, rolling in the snow at twenty degrees below, Matt Talbot rusty chains biting into my middle. How did people manage to get up in the morning and go to work, drive cars, eat food, when they could be having this kind of pleasure instead?

Hundreds of phrases were banging against each other inside my brain. I made a reckless grab at the nearest two. 'Brilliant band that. I mean, terrific.'

She pulled back, head on one side. 'Yeeees, I suppose it is. If you like a band that hits you over the head when it plays. Like a club.'

I couldn't think what to say after that. Any time I tried to string a few words together, they slipped loose and fell back into my brain. Then what she'd said about us undressing each other with our eyes started tiptoeing into my mind. Quick – get an image of me sliding down a banister made of cut-throat razors and hold it on the mental screen, sooore, soresoresore, that's it. But that was inside my head. Outside, the smell of her hair kept on drifting up and massaging the insides of my nostrils, and her front stayed attached to mine.

The music ended and she moved back a little bit, her hand like a bird on my shoulder. Then: 'Will I tell you the thing I want more than anything else in the world this minute?'

I swallowed. 'What?'

'A tinkle-pinkle in the wee girls' room. Back in a ticky-poo.' A blur of red dress and black stockings and she was gone.

Had she really said 'tinkle-pinkle'? Light a cigarette, try to look relaxed. Maybe she wanted to vamoose without hurting my feelings and that's why she'd said about the tinkle-pinkle. But feelings hadn't bothered her before. No feelings when she said that about being hit on the head with a club, or in the Snack Bar when she said about vanishing cream on my face and laughed. 'Ladies and gentlemen, your next dance is – a mixed grill!' the man at the microphone called, his voice ending in a half-shout. The crowd came heaving on to the floor again and couples locked their arms around each other.

Stop worrying. Nobody here knows that you're someone who had a girl say 'tinkle-pinkle' to him and then take off. How could they? Right, impossible. I climbed the stairs to the balcony. Below, a lake of heads bobbed as the band played 'Little Jimmy Brown'. 'Bom, bom, bom.' Leaves of light moved through the gloom, slid over heads and shoulders. 'All the chapel bells were ringing. Bommm.' Near the band where it was brighter, a cluster of people stood with their elbows on the edge of the stage. One of them was a girl with frizzy hair piled high on her head and held in place with combs a bit like Mammy's. Only it couldn't be. Except it was. I looked away and then back. Ohshiteshootmenow. Bernie.

Her dress was white with a blue sash round the middle, and the way she had her hair pinned up you could see all of her neck. There were several girls standing near her who weren't dancing either, but Bernie was easily the best-looking one. And while the others had that tired look girls wear when they haven't been asked to dance, Bernie's gaze was zipping around the hall, checking the dancers, peering at faces, on the look-out.

What was I waiting for? Pointless mooching around like a gom. Christy was gone. And even I did find her, she'd be sure to be dancing with some Tony-Curtis-hair bastard carrying a knuckle-duster in the pocket of his drainpipes. Only I didn't have to let that happen. I could change it this minute by going down and asking Bernie for the next dance. Go on, then. Kick Predestination in the arse – it's easy.

Except it wasn't. Bernie looked nicer than ever, in her white dress and her balancing hair and neat blue sash. But . . . It was like one of those films, where the fairy on the chocolate box comes to life and starts dancing to tinkly music. If I did go down and we were to start dancing and I was to be pushed up against her – there'd be no need for barbed wire or Matt Talbot chains. It'd be like dancing with the picture of St Bernadette. Although when I thought about it, in the pictures and even in the grotto, St Bernadette had a nice . . .

Bite hard on your thumbnail. This wasn't the way to think about a girl – much less a saint. What sort of good Catholic layman would do that? God wasn't going to be too impressed when I appeared before him on Judgement Day and his book said that on the last day of 1959 I'd thought about a saint with no clothes on and had danced with a girl who clamped herself to me. If I kept acting like this, he might change his mind and give me a vocation to be a priest after all. All right, he almost certainly probably wasn't going to, because that wasn't the kind God was, but I'd still better stop tempting him. 'You quarely tempt me, well,' Debbie Reynolds whispered. 'With your manly trunk.'

I closed my eyes and leaned my head briefly against the side of the pillar. Tried not to think about Debbie Reynolds and St Bernadette and the Last Judgement and crows perched on top of churches and small white coffins and pennies on people's eyes. When I opened them Bernie was turned my way, her smooth bright face smiling up to me in the balcony. At least I could have sworn she was. Except when I blinked she was turned away again. Maybe I was going mad. You couldn't get married if you were mad because you couldn't say 'I do' and mean it. And they wouldn't take you at Maynooth either, if you were mad or a convict or a bastard.

I went downstairs, found an empty bench along the wall. Sat with my elbow on my knees, stared at the floor. Occasionally the skirt of a dancer brushed past, touching my arm and hair. I smoked my three remaining Sweet Afton, lighting one from the other, dropping butt after butt on the yellow polished floor. Each fag-end left a comet tail of black where my foot had pulled away.

Someday, maybe some day during the 1960s, I'd be married. Sitting in my front room with a family of . . . right, five children. My wife in the kitchen, humming as she makes tea. Here she is now at the hatch between kitchen and living room, looking at me with the same smile she wore the day we were married. Now she's come into the room and is sitting on the floor at my feet, one elbow hooked over my knee and her armpits shaved so close you'd never guess there'd been hair there in the first place. Just the two of us, because the five children are asleep upstairs. 'Cigarette, pet?' she asks, reaching for the silver box on the mantelpiece. I nod, and she gets the heavy silver table lighter and holds it for me. Her brown eyes reflect the firelight as she smiles up at me.

'You by my side, that's how I see us,' the singer sang, and the dancers put their cheeks even closer together and swayed from side to side.

A hand on the back of my neck. Cool, smelling of cream. Christy.

'Mr Gypsy Rover – where did you go?'

'Nowhere. I was waiting—'

'Studying the talent, you bad bloody article. C'mon.'

On the floor, her hands link behind my neck. She puts her head on my chest and pulls my head lower. 'Are you sick of the nineteen-fifties?' Her voice sounds muffled. I nod, even though she can't see me. A blob of coloured light passes over her hair. It glistens red for a second, like blood in a dream. 'Me too,' she murmurs.

Then the music stops and the singer says that ladies and gentlemen, boys and girls, it is very very nearly time for our countdown, time for us to welcome 1960, a new year, a new decade as well! People unlocked from each other, looked around to find other people to hold hands with. The singer asked us to take our cue from him, were we ready, OK. And the drum rolls and we all go together, TEN, NINE, EIGHT . . .

And then the count was over and balloons had come drifting down in a squeaking cloud from the ceiling and people were grabbing them and trying to burst them, singing 'Auld Lang Syne' at the same time. Everybody kissing and laughing after they'd done it. A woman with a smell of stout kissed me and her lips were wet. A girl in a pink twinset kissed the man beside me, and when she saw me standing trying to smile she leaned forward and kissed me too, a little dry peck. There was a pimple at the side of her mouth.

'Hi, Mr Blue, woo-oo-ah-woo,' Christy sang, gripping my collar. Most of the others had finished kissing, but she didn't care. Her arms tightened round my neck like nutcrackers and her face pushed up tight against mine, her lips fatter and softer than I thought they'd be. For what seemed like a couple of minutes nothing existed except a lemony smell and a fizzing in my head. Miles away, the band sang 'Woo-oo-ah-woo, call me Mr Blue.'

'Jim!' For a minute I thought it was Christy speaking. Then her face pulled back and behind her stood Bernie. Her cardigan was buttoned across the front, her arms folded over it, her face tight as a priest's doorbell. 'How lovely to see you! Happy New Year.'

And before Christy could say anything or I could break free from Christy and run down the stairs and out into the night and home and into my bedroom and under the bedclothes, Bernie had elbowed past Christy and sort of banged her lips against the side of my face. On my good cheek. Then she stood in front of me, hands clenched and eyes glittery. 'Glad you're enjoying the nineteen-sixties so far, oh yes I can see that all right, I'm not blind thank you very much, but I'm afraid somebody is waiting for me and as I'm sure you know, it's bad manners to keep a gentleman waiting!'

I tried to think of something to say. 'A gentleman?'

Bernie's teeth clicked together in a smile. 'Oh yes – there is such a thing as a gentleman, thank you very much. And as a matter of fact he's waiting outside because he doesn't want to come in. I think you know him, too. As it happens.'

I waited for her to say who he was but she didn't. Instead she swung round, her white dress billowing out, and pushed her way into the crowd.

'Was that foam?' Christy asked. 'I could have sworn I saw foam on her lips.'

Afterwards, I don't remember asking Christy if I could leave her home, but I must have. Because next thing she was turning away to get her coat from the cloakroom, calling over her shoulder that she'd meet me out the front in ten minutes.

There was a line-up of girls for the cloakroom already, some of them scooping off one shoe to retrieve their ticket. I walked past and down the hall towards the men's toilets. People stood talking in twos and threes, reluctant to go out into the night. Near the entrance to the toilets a man sat, a girl in a yellow dress on his knee. She was patting his cheek with one hand. 'Oh baby, no,' she said as I passed.

Almighty was in the Gents, combing his hair.

'Such a wagon-load of heifers – ever see the like before? Asked three of them – *three* – one after the other, doh ray mee. Not one would dance. Twisting their faces and shaking their heads. Godalmighty.' He put his comb in his hip pocket and moved to one of the cubicles. 'And the thing is, they were *ugly*-looking ones. That's why I *picked* them. Trying to be *nice* to the hoors.' From inside the cubicle came the sound of a belt being loosened and Almighty muttering to himself between gasps.

I left by a side door and collected my bike, wheeled it round and took up position to the left of the main door where I could see people emerging without being noticed. Bernie descended the steps, her collar up, looking straight ahead. And there, moving out from a shop entrance and up the street to meet her, ohshiteshootme-now *Francie*, wearing a brown gaberdine coat instead of his black one, and not wearing his black hat or black tie either, but a twisted sort of smile on his face. What was he doing here – had he given up his vow of chastity? Maybe he hadn't taken one yet, which meant he was allowed to collect girls at dances but not go into the hall.

Bernie linked him and they moved off together into the darkness.

Then Christy was coming out, wearing a tight green coat and soft leather gloves. 'C'mere and warm us,' she said, pulling my arm round her. It was awkward pushing the bike with my left hand at the same time but it was worth it. We turned the corner of Bridge Street and headed up the hill past the Royal Arms and towards the Town Hall. The noise of people talking and laughing grew fainter behind us. The lamp posts formed pools of light.

'So now,' she said, narrowing her eyes as she looked up at me. 'End of the Fifties. What big thing do you want to happen in nineteen-sixty?'

'Not sure.' I was but I wasn't telling her.

'Bet the real you deep inside is sure. Give us your hand.' She held it, palm up, to the lamp post. 'Oh holy God in heaven. It's not possible.'

'What's not possible?'

'You're a flipping idealist. Should have known from looking at you. You have a generous nature, thoughtlessness hurts you, and you want the world to be a better place.'

'You can see all that in my hand?'

She nodded and we walked on. 'Sometimes – like on All Souls' Night – I see things I don't like seeing. Scary things. New Years aren't scary, though. They're just sad.'

'Though you said you liked it being nineteen-sixty. A new decade and everything.'

'I did – I do. But it's depressing at the same time. Especially for the likes of poor old Mumsy.'

'Who?'

'My mumsy. Stuck at home on her own at New Year's, with no Aloysius.'

'Who's Aloysius? And anyway what about Malachy your brother? Is he not at home?'

'My dad. Dadsy. He's Aloysius. He's in England. Malsy's worse than useless – goes around being stupid and hiding in boxes. All you have to do is listen to know where he is. Anyway, we've this press above the cooker, so this Saturday I climbed up and put my hand way, way in the back of it.'

'What for?'

'Looking for paints. I wanted to do a painting of a dead scaldy I got lying in a wee hidden place down at the river. Just listen, can't you?' Her voice sounded wobbly. 'I put my hand in and I could feel the tubes of paint and the brushes, the same as always. But there was something else. I could feel it – a bundle of something tied together. So I lifted it out. *Quel surprise*. Letters, with this faded blue ribbon round them. Two dozen or more. Do you know what they were about?' I shook my head. 'About her alabaster skin and her diamond eyes and the pearly sweetness of her smile. And all of them were signed "Your loving Wilbur".'

'That's . . . romantic.'

'*Wilbur*,' she repeated. 'I already told you – Dadsy's name is *Aloysius*. These letters were signed "*Wilbur*". Got it? About time too. And then New Year's Eve three years ago I came in and Mumsy was sitting by the dying embers, the bundle on her lap, and *weeping*. "*Wilbur*" she kept saying, the tears coursing down her face. "My lovely *Wilbur*." Like a parrot.'

I laughed out loud. 'Sorry,' I said. 'It's just that bit about the dying embers and a parrot. At New Year's Eve. It's hard to imagine.'

'Well don't strain your brain trying.' Her voice had

turned harder. 'You know nothing. About anything. Wait until you're trapped in a loveless marriage and your husband goes away on you. Put the smile on the other side of your face.'

I was going to say I would hardly have a husband, but then decided not to. We walked along saying nothing for a while. A loveless marriage. A priest on his own would be bad, but at least he would have peace when he got home in the evening.

'Your turn,' Christy said, sounding relaxed again. 'Spill the beans about someone close to you.' She took my arm and put it round her again.

Should I tell her about Debbie Reynolds? No. Women don't like you to talk about other women. The crowbar Presumer and I had hidden, then? I could take her there. We could walk down the road together, dig the crowbar up in the moonlight, restore it to its rightful owners. Then I thought of Presumer standing beside the trench with nothing in it, looking around, realising I had betrayed him. Forget it. Tell her about being in Neil's car? Forget that too. That'd mean involving Presumer even worse.

I took breath in through my nose, out through my mouth. Ohhhmmmm. 'I'm trying to make up my mind what to do with my life.'

She glanced at me and then practised a little skip-step. 'Are you not supposed to be going away to be a priest like your man Francie?'

It was like being kicked in the belly button by Jackie Taggart, the Tyrone midfielder. *Who the hell had told her that?* Had she read that in my palm too? In that case my palm was out of date. We walked on.

'It's just you have that priesty look to you. You know,

nervy and sort of worried-looking. And you go to the Snack Bar with your ma.'

Bloody cheek. 'You do the same thing, with your ma. That mean you're going to be a nun, then?' I could hear my voice edgy. 'Whoever told you I was going to be a priest needs their head examined.'

She linked my arm with her two hands and scratched her nose against my shoulder. 'Tut-tut-tut – testy, testy, testy. Just said what I thought, that's all. Anyway, if you ask me, you're the mad one if you *don't* go away and be a priest.'

'What'd be the point in that? Cut off from people and dances and . . . everything.'

'Hah. But what about in a hundred years? There'll be nothing left of either of us in a hundred years. Never think of that? Arms, legs, chest, guts and everything – nothing, only a bunch of squirmy maggots.' She paused, and stood there with her hand against her cheek. 'I *did* think about being a nun one time. A hermit nun. You haven't a clue what a hermit nun is, do you?'

'No.'

'They live on their own and pray all day and some-times all night, and people leave food outside their hut for them. And the birds and animals get so used to them living in the wilderness, they come right up. Terrific, eh? First thing in the morning, sun just come up, robins and willy wagtails perched all round the edge of a basin of meal, and the nun still holding it.'

I imagined Audrey Hepburn as a nun, with an enamel tray on her hip and a ring of birds bobbing on its edge.

'Nuns are called brides of Christ – did you know that?'

I nodded. 'Of course. That's why they wear a silver ring.'

'Hermit nuns are different. They're more like, what would you say, God's *lovers*. His *mistresses*.' Her brown eyes looked up from beneath a black fringe. 'This book I got out of the library was about Julie-Anne of Norwich. She was a hermit nun. Wrote about how God would come into her hut when she was in bed at night, and sort of, you know. She kept talking about that.'

Sort of? You know? What was she talking about?

'And I thought, that'd be good. Praying so hard you'd see God coming to you like, you know, a lover. Possessing you. The Julie-Anne one used to get so excited, she'd faint with happiness, and not wake up until the next morning. Only thing is, hermit nuns aren't allowed to paint or play music or have anything to do with things of the flesh, apart from imagining God coming. So I changed my mind.' She rubbed her nose against my shoulder again. 'Personally I'm glad the maggots are heading for us. You'd get sick looking at people for ever.'

I wasn't going to say it but then I did. Quickly, before there was time for second thoughts. 'Not everybody. I wouldn't get sick of everybody.'

She shook her head from side to side to emphasise each word. 'Everybody, everybody, everybody, everybody. Everybody.'

She was looking up at me, I could feel it, but I stared straight ahead. 'I don't think . . . people . . . would get sick of looking at you. Definitely. Know I wouldn't, anyway.'

'Beedee beedee bombom to San Fernando,' she said, bobbing her head again. 'What are you saying?'

My ears had begun to throb. 'Nothing.'

'Didn't sound like nothing. Sounded like Mumsy not saying a word but not needing to, because just the way she sweeps the floor and washes the dishes, it's as clear as anything I'm not to *dare* dream of going to England to work, because it's full of murderers and wife-beaters and sex maniacs. That's what it sounded like to me. But OK. Tell us this instead.'

'What?'

'Were you thinking of showering my upturned face with burning kisses when we get to my door?'

I looked at the toes of my shoes. Walking, walking. Debbie Reynolds wouldn't say the likes of that. Nor Audrey Hepburn. Nor the girl who got into Robert Jordan's sleeping bag. They'd just let the magic moment arrive. Maaa-gic. Moooo-ments.

'I'm asking because I want to be ready in case you get aroused. Sister Veronica at school says once boys are aroused, you can't stop them except you empty a bucket of cold water over the top of them. A girl asked Sister Veronica how she knew but she wouldn't say.' Our feet echoed along the emptiness of the street.

When we got to her door I didn't kiss her – she kissed me. Again. One minute she was leaning against the wall of her house, talking; the next she took my bike from me and propped it against a lamp post. Then her fists came up, gripped my lapels and swung me round against the wall. She was really strong, but her skin felt like Mammy's velvet collar. Her lips touched my left cheek. They were wet. 'That's for being nice.' Then my right. The bad one. 'And that's for not braining mad bitch Bernie.'

'She's not—'

'Sssh-shh. Be. Quiet.' Her hand came over my mouth 'And this is for what you'll be missing – the kissing you'll be missing, ba-doo ba-doo ba-doo – whenever you're a priest.'

It reminded me of lifting a load of clothes out of the hot press, the way she filled my arms and the fresh warm smell of her, except with Christy it was a lemony smell, but lemon without the sharp edge. Then she leaned back and took my hand and unbuttoned the top two buttons of her coat. 'Does Mr Fingers want to come inside?'

It was as if some of the cement in Monsignor's voice had stuck in my throat. Did she – what did she—?

'OK, OK. I never said that and you didn't hear me. When I count to three you will open your eyes and remember no-zzzziinnng. Onetwothree. Meantime, try vanishing cream on that pan of yours, OK? You never know.' She gave my right cheek a little rub. And then she was gone.

Bernie's light was still on as I passed Knockbeg Park. I remembered the way I'd stood there last Halloween, watching her combing her hair, longing for her to come out. Now she'd never speak to me again. And if we happened to meet on the street, she'd put on that spikey hating face and walk on by me with her head in the air.

But although it was sad in one way, in another it wasn't one bit. Because the truth was, I didn't care. Not really. A new decade had started and it was time to stop thinking what other people wanted me to do. In fact time to stop wondering and thinking altogether. Time to grab life before the maggots got started. Off with the old and on with the new. Nineteen-sixty, I . . . love . . . you!

I opened the back door quietly, easing down the bit of wood that was the latch so it didn't make noise. Took off my shoes and tiptoed into the kitchen. She was sitting in the armchair beside the Aga, the *Ulster Herald* in front of her. She lowered the paper slowly and at first I thought she was laughing, her face was so red and her lips pulled back so the gold filling shone.

'One o'clock. What kept you?'

'I was at the dance.'

'What kept you?'

I couldn't just turn round and say, 'I was chatting to some friends.' Or 'I lost my wallet.' Much less 'I was being kissed by a girl who asked if Mr Fingers wanted to come inside.' Only then before I could say anything she started to cry. Her voice was a kind of shout.

'The doctor said there was no need to worry, but he's not seeing what I'm seeing and listening to what I'm listening.' She took a hanky from her pinafore and dragged it down her face as if trying to rip the skin off. 'His whole side. I said to him, lift your leg, try like a decent man, but he couldn't. And then his eyes – there's a flashing in front of them, he kept saying. I said to the doctor, that's not a good sign, flashing, is it? But all he would go on about was not crossing our bridges before we came to them and the danger of hasty judgements and I don't know what more in that oul' lispy voice of his. And then he put ointment on his eyes and tied bandages over the top of them.' Mammy cleared her throat once, twice. 'For to rest his retinas and nervous system at the same time, he said. So now Our poor Father can't even see. With these bandages he has on.'

I wanted to tell her to be quiet, she'd waken Maeve. But it was too late. Maeve was standing at the door of the kitchen in her nightdress, shivering. She looked smaller than usual.

'Will I make some tea?' she said. Without waiting for an answer, she carried the kettle to the scullery and brought it in brimming. She'd filled it so full, she had to use two hands and it swung from side to side.

I didn't want to ask Mammy about Our Father. The thought of having to talk about him being sick made me feel sort of dizzy. The kettle on the Aga hissed. Why did people have to have parents? Buds on trees didn't have parents. Neither did flowers. They just grew.

'The doctor said we were to keep an eye on him and he'd think about whether it might be concussion. And for to watch out for any change and not let the light at his eyes.' She dabbed her own eye with the back of her hand.

'How – how would you know if there was a change?' Maeve's voice was croaky, as if she had the cold.

'My own poor father when he was nearing his end . . . There's no missing the change.'

'What change?' Maeve said. She just wouldn't stop asking questions in that shaky voice of hers, and yet I knew at the same time she didn't want the answer.

'Your poor grandfather – can see his face this minute. Turning the colour of brick. And . . .'

'What?'

'It doesn't matter,' I said loudly. 'It doesn't matter what. As long as we know what to look for.'

'And then an hour or two before he, he died, it turned white. And after that a sort of yellow,' Mammy said, and cleared her throat again.

Maeve wiped her nose on the sleeve of her nightdress and began to whimper.

'Sit down, child, near the heat. I'll pour a drop of tea.' Mammy pressed Maeve into the armchair near the Aga.

'And the rest of us will keep busy, that's the main thing. Won't'n we? Run up the stairs and put your head round the door, you Jim. See he's not looking something.'

Even knowing what was waiting up there, I felt relieved to get out of the room. Creak on the third step, creak on the seventh. I went on tiptoe round the corner of the landing until I came to their bedroom.

Held the doorknob tight in my fist and eased the door open.

Angel of God, my guardian dear/ To whom God's love commits me here/ Ever this night be at my side.

CHAPTER 11

'It's Jim.' His hand in mind felt fragile – like a skeleton wearing skin gloves, maybe come away in your grip if you didn't watch. 'Are you feeling any better?'

No reply. The only sound was the gasping coming out of his mouth, a sunken hole without the teeth. He had a bandage round where his forehead would have been if it was big enough. As it was the bandage covered the V-shaped chunk of stiff grey hair as well, with two strips coming down over his eyes, passing one another on the bridge of his nose. A crucifix with a bit of withered palm stuck behind it looked down from above the bed. I sat on the edge of the bed, making sure not to sit on his feet, and started talking. At least he couldn't answer back.

'In the *Reader's Digest* it said people who are unconscious sometimes hear people talking even though they can't show they hear. The article said people have even been buried alive; and the way they know is, they opened some coffins years later, and got the skeletons all twisted from pushing against the lid. That's nothing to do with you, except I want to let you know that I know you could be hearing everything I say.

'Did you hear Mammy crying? You probably did. Saying what would we do if something happened to you. But she always says the next life is the important one. Then shouldn't she be glad to see somebody getting out of this one? Not saying you are. Only you know what I mean.'

The rasp in his breathing seemed to get louder.

'Although helping too much would be murder. Euthanasia. So maybe it's better just letting things happen or not, whichever of the two it's fated to be. Foxy is always talking about that – how so many wee things can decide how things turn out, only you don't realise it at the time. I felt like telling him that maybe us lending him the pony was either going to be or not to be, and so there was no point in him asking us and no point in us answering. But I doubt if he'd have got the joke.'

Our Father made a noise in his throat and began breathing faster.

'Hold on, I'll get you water.'

I poured half a glass from the jug beside the bed. But when I lifted it to his mouth, I couldn't figure how to actually get him to drink. If I tried to tilt the glass, his mouth was so slack, the whole thing would spill.

Pour most of the water back into the jug, then. Now, with just a wee bit in the bottom, ease the glass towards the hole above the chin. At the last minute the lips moved.

'Mind don't spill on me.'

Maybe I hadn't been expecting him to speak. Or maybe I hadn't been expecting him to say what he said. Either way, I pulled the glass back suddenly and the water launched forward and drenched his lips and chin. He must have been breathing in because he began to gurgle, and then cough and wave his arms. One of his hands hit the edge of the glass and knocked the remainder of the water on to his pyjama top. A dark stain appeared, as if he was peeing through his chest.

'Jesus,' I said. His face had turned very red. 'Jesus, my Lord and my God.'

Maybe I should call for help. What if he died on me? On the other hand, if I called them and he didn't die, they'd say I'd made a fuss about nothing. Why did people always want to see someone dying anyway – rushing from halfway around the world, sometimes. Was it to make sure?

Finally the coughing eased. He sighed and settled back in the bed. I tried to think of something to say.

'Coughing like that's awful. A bit of carrot stuck in my throat once – I felt like somebody was strangling me from the inside.'

There was silence for moment, then he yawned. A huge yawn. It was as if his eyes and nose and the whole upper part of his face had been turned inside out and vanished. The yawn ended in a scrawking sound in the back of his throat.

On the bedside table were his rosary beads and a small statue of the Infant of Prague with a crack in its neck. That was because Maeve and I had knocked its head off once, wrestling around in the kitchen. I lifted the rosary beads. Maybe if he just held them, it would be a comfort. I put my hand on his arm.

'Keep a—' His hands on the sheet tightened and loosened, tightened again. His voice was like sandpaper. 'Keep—'

I leaned closer. 'Keep a bit of water in a jug – is that it?'

He sighed and moved his head wearily from side to side. 'Keep a, keep a—'

'No rush.' He was the helpless one now. I was in charge. 'Take it slowly.'

A deep breath, eyes closed. 'Keep away from me.'

The words tumbled over each other, rushing, confused, one sticking to the next. Afterwards his tongue lay peeping between his lips. Too tired to do anything, because when I listened hard he had. Stopped. Breathing.

No. He couldn't be. He must be just breathing quietly. Because if he'd stopped breathing, then . . .

I jumped up, my mouth open to yell. At the same moment he gave what seemed like a sigh, and two seconds later the bedroom door opened and Maeve's head came round it.

'What's up?'

'Nothing,' I said. 'I thought for a minute he was going to, to get worse. But he didn't. It's nothing.'

She put her thumb under the shoulder of her blouse and tugged a strap. 'Is he bad?'

I got up and came to the door. Put my face close to hers. 'You're not supposed to talk about people in a sick room. *They can hear you.*' Pushed her out of the room and shut the door behind us.

'D'you talk to him?'

'A bit.'

'What'd you say?'

'Nothing.'

'Big fat fibber, did so. I could hear you. And then I heard him start coughing—'

'Shut your damn trap!' I felt like whacking her one. 'I could hear you, big fat fibber, I could hear you, big fat fibber. Talk about childish!'

Mammy appeared at the top of the stairs and grabbed both of us by the shoulder, wicked witch claws through the clothes.

'Down. This instant,' she hissed. 'Squabbling there. Can't you see when a body needs their rest?'

'A body?' Maeve asked, looking back over her shoulder. 'Why did you say "a body"?'

For the next half-hour we sat huddled round the Aga drinking tea, with Mammy going over what the doctor had said and how Our Father would never take things easy but was always running and shouting, would listen to nobody, until it began to sound as if it was Our Father's own fault that he was lying upstairs with his mouth open and his tongue hanging out. But then she said how he was doing it all for us his family, we should be grateful to him, where would we all be today, in the Poorhouse probably. Eventually Maeve said she was going back to bed, she was tired.

It was exactly two o'clock, because the clock with the yellow face and Roman numerals was chiming, when Mammy put down her empty cup and reached into the cupboard above the cooker. After a couple of lucky-dip tries she came out with a tiny wooden box that had a brass clasp on the side of it. Inside was a glass bubble with a backing of either tin or silver.

'It's a relic,' Mammy explained, lifting it out reverently and putting it on top of the *Irish News*. 'Took from the frock Maria Goretti was wearing the day she got murdered for her purity. Say you a decade of the rosary and I'll slide this under Our Father's pillow.'

It was hard to pray – my mind kept slipping to other things. Like the way Christy's brown eyes looked straight at you as if they could see inside your skull and out the other side and then off into space, while at the same time her hand was at the back of my neck rubbing the hair and making a nice gristling sound. And then she had asked me if I wanted to put Mr Fingers inside. And she had said it the way you say something when you're used saying it, the way you say it when you've said it loads of times before . . . I must have dozed off because when I woke up Mammy was standing over me.

'Is he getting better?' My voice sounded like someone else's.

'Thanks be to God and his blessed saints and touch wood – I think he's on the mend. I went up with the relic and knelt down on the floor and said a decade of the rosary. And then I slipped Maria Goretti inside the top of his pyjamas, where his heart is, and against the skin. And herself and the rest of the good saints in heaven must have been listening, for before you could say cat, he's sitting up and asking about tea. They can keep their atomic bombs – there's nothing half as powerful as a good relic, if you ask me.'

It was just after nine the following morning when there was a knock on the back door. Nobody else seemed to have heard it, so I pulled on my trousers and went down. Presumer was pacing from side to side at the top of the yard, as if he was in too much of a hurry to stand at the door. He jerked his thumb over his shoulder.

'Sean – need help. For to search. He was with her yesterday evening – who the hell do you think, with my ma, *my ma*, of *course* my ma – she says he was in the house until after tea. She thought he'd gone to bed. And it wasn't until half-two this morning she looked in his bedroom and he wasn't there.'

'Wasn't in his bed?'

Presumer nodded. 'Searched the house, in case he'd

climbed into a press or a drawer or something. No Sean. Gone.'

I thought of Christy's brother Malachy getting into boxes. Him and Sean should get together. Presumer stood clenching and unclenching his fists.

'Did you tell the police?'

He nodded. 'Remember that gulpin I asked the time we were going down the street? Middle of the night, when I went into the police station – there he was, pencil behind his ear and ledger. Stared at me and said where was my ma. I told him she was bawling so much at home she wasn't fit to go anywhere, report anybody. So he stared for another five minutes and then said if Sean wasn't got by tonight, they'd start a police search. Tonight! What the hell's the good in tonight?' Presumer banged his fist on the doorframe. 'C'mon.'

'Where to?'

'I'm going to check a couple of places he sometimes goes to. Better than sitting on my arse.'

'I'd help you if I could, only we've had an accident ourselves.' I explained about the boiler house and Our Father.

'Seen that, coming in the lane,' Presumer said. 'Whole bloody roof away. But that's not a minor tragedy – that's nothing. He doesn't need you, your oul' fellah. He's got your ma and Maeve. And he's in his fucking comfortable bed, not like our wee Sean. C'mon.'

I went inside to Mammy, who was cleaning ashes out of the fireplace in the dining room. Could I help Presumer look for Sean?

'Be back inside an hour. Maybe helping out would bring us a bit of luck. Although I wouldn't want to be a wain in that house and lost.'

Presumer's mother was half-lying on their couch, with the coats and cats lying in a mound on the floor beside her. She had a hanky wrapped round her knuckles and pushed against her face.

'Oh Jesus, Mary and Joseph, the poor creature. Gerard son, what'll we do?'

'Jim and me's away to look a couple of places. We'll get him back.'

'Hail Mary, full of grace – it'll be all right, won't it, Gerard? They'll get him some road, won't they? Hail Mary, Mother of sinners, pray for us, God.'

'Shut your face, Ma, would you? Bound to find him.'

We walked to the other end of the Rat's Pad and round the back of the last house in the row. A small path between hedges took us to a wooden gate leading into a field.

We climbed it, broke two sticks and poked our way through the bushes at the end of the field. Nothing. Took the path that led behind the Rat's Pad houses, followed it up a slope until it came to a door in a high stone wall. Hamilton Estate.

'He wouldn't have been able to open that door,' I said. 'Handle's too high and too stiff.'

'Except some bugger opened it for him.'

We went through the door and into an overgrown area. Nettles and dock leaves and clumps of grass where broken glass glinted. Two twists of shite with flies on them. A dead pigeon. There was no pattern to our searching – sometimes we brushed against each other, other times we wandered out of earshot. Put a foot sideways into beds of nettles, eased the angry leaves aside to check. Nothing.

By the time we climbed back over the gate, my ankles

had a rash of stings, little white eyes spattered as high as my shins and across the back of both hands as well. We walked back along the path, feet crunching stones like at a beach. Down to the right you could see the river and sunlight glinting on it.

'Maybe he's met someone and is gone visiting with them,' I said.

Presumer spat. 'Six-year-olds don't go visiting. They're taken places.' He paused. 'I didn't tell Ma this but I'll tell you. Had a dream the other night about Sean. Was coming out of this building—'

'What building?'

'*A* building. How do I know what building? I'm not an architect – it was a fucking dream. He came out and his face all dirty from crying. And when I asked him what was up, all he'd do was close his eyes, like in slow motion. Cl-oo-oo-se ee-eee-ye-s – like that. Think a dream like that has some meaning?' I said I wasn't sure but I thought maybe it had.

When we got to Presumer's house half a dozen people, mostly women, stood outside. Ten yards up the street a policeman was pacing back and forward, hands behind his back. One of the women approached Presumer. His mother was in the back bedroom, she whispered. Word had come from Councillor Traynor at the golf club that she'd missed two days' cleaning when they'd been depending on her and she was to come and collect her cards before the end of the week. When she heard that, Mrs Livingstone had just lifted a bottle of whiskey from a drawer and gone into the bedroom and locked the door from the inside before anybody could stop her. There was talk of sending for the Monsignor to see could he get her to come out.

It was nearly dinnertime and Mammy would have a pot of stew and a saucepan of boiling spuds on the cooker, and maybe apple tart drowned in thick custard. I told Presumer I'd been told to be home inside an hour but I'd help him again tomorrow, maybe. He saluted as I left but he wasn't smiling.

Women of Omagh, weep not for me, but weep for yourselves and for your children.

CHAPTER 12

The next day, though, there was no chance to call on Presumer – I was kept going like a slave. Had to cycle to the town in the morning to get a prescription for him from the doctor and bring it straight home. Then pedal back in the afternoon to get the *Irish Press*; and when I brought it home, bring it up to his bedroom and sit reading out bits about prices at the Dublin cattle market two days earlier because he still had the bandages on.

When I went downstairs I complained to Mammy. Hadn't she said it was luckier to help people? And weren't we just looking for bad luck by not letting me help Presumer?

'You and Presumer,' she said. 'Charity begins at home, did you never hear. Not stuck up the Rat's Pad with a corner boy and his mother and her stocious half the time.' But in the afternoon she must have felt guilty, because she gave me two half-crowns and told me to ride into the town and get her a pound of bacon from Keenan's for tomorrow's dinner, and whatever bit of change there was to stop and get myself sweets or chips or whatever took my fancy.

The inside of Battisti's windows was wet with steam and every time Carlo emptied a shovelful of chips into the chrome bath, the fat would screech and a cloud of steam would hide him for a minute. Then things would settle and he'd emerge again, nose shiny, a strip of black hair tickling his eyebrows. Paddy was sitting in the corner booth, listening to Almighty. When he saw me he waved me over.

'There were six of them,' Almighty was saying. 'Shoulder to shoulder, marching up the street staring at their toes.'

'Six what?' I said.

'Saw them this morning when I was getting a bottle of milk of magnesia for my daddy. Going down Castle Street, looked into the Rat's Pad and there they were.'

Paddy produced a handful of change. 'I'm getting a fish supper.'

Almighty patted himself from neck to knees. 'Coulda swore I had a tanner with me.'

Paddy stared at him for a minute, then said, 'OK. I'll get chips for you.'

'Could you get us a bit of fish when you're at it? A wee bit of . . . OK, OK. Godalmighty, not complaining, chips is great, *said* they were great.'

I passed sixpence to Paddy. 'Chips for me.'

Carlo told Paddy to sit down, the waitress would bring the plates to the cubicle.

'Six cops?' Paddy asked, sliding back into the cubicle. 'And what were they looking at their feet for?'

'Searching for clues – every one of them, poking about with this stick. At first I thought it was guns maybe.'

'You thought sticks were guns?'

'So would you have. You weren't there, I saw them.' Almighty's voice was high and irritated. You'd never think Paddy had bought him chips a minute earlier.

'So did you tell the cops in charge you'd help them?' Paddy asked.

'What, and get a stick up my arse for my bother? Godalmighty, you're quare and simple.'

The waitress, who had pink fingernails, unloaded our plates. Almighty poured nearly quarter of the vinegar bottle on to his chips, shook salt over them, forward, back again, drizzle white forward a third time. When he took a mouthful he went 'Aah! Aah!' and panted, and you could see the squelched food at the back of his throat.

Paddy put three chips on his fork, then stopped halfway to his mouth and pointed at Almighty. 'Know what I think? That you're making this whole thing up.'

'What would I do that for? There were six of them, parading up and down. *And* they found something.'

Paddy stopped chewing. In the back kitchen Mario was yelling at somebody who was yelling back. Almighty lifted a really long chip, tilted his head back and swallowed it whole.

'What?' Paddy asked. 'What'd they find?'

The waitress passed our cubicle, carrying a tray. Almighty's eyes followed the backs of her legs. 'Six of them, poke poke poke down the street, looking for clues. And near the bottom of the Pad, just before Castle Street, they came on it.'

'What? What'd they find?'

'A piece of you know what.'

'What you know what?' Paddy asked. 'I don't know what. What the fuck are you talking about?'

'Dog's you know what,' Almighty said. 'A big chunk of cha-cha-cha poopies sitting at the side of the street.' He chuckled. 'And this one cop looks over at the sergeant and says, "Sir. Permission to circumvent."'

'Talk English, you humpy shite,' Paddy said, dipping

his last chip in a pool of vinegar. 'Bet you made half the whole thing up.'

Almighty shook his head. As he did so the door of the café opened and three men came in. Tight haircuts, English accents: soldiers. One of them went up to the counter while the other two leaned against a booth two down from us.

'It was hard, that's why,' Almighty continued, smiling. 'No smell off hard cha-cha-cha poopsie.' He lifted his plate and licked off some vinegar. 'But your man the sergeant wouldn't let up. "Insert stick into specimen," he says. "No telling what evidence we may now have to hand."'

Paddy started laughing and then began to cough, and that made Almighty and me start. And once you start laughing it's really hard to stop; Almighty would say, 'No telling what evidence we have to hand!' in a fancy accent and we'd be off again. I was wiping my eyes when a khaki sleeve appeared at the edge of our table.

He gripped the table with both hands and bent towards us. Little muscles in the side of his face moved as if he was chewing, only he wasn't. 'Me and my mate was wondering what you think's so funny.' He had a flat face with tiny holes in the forehead.

Almighty looked from Paddy to me and back again, blinking hard. 'No. Nothing. It was just . . . nothing.'

The second soldier pushed forward, arms folded. 'You laughing at nothing then?' His nose was like a beak and made a shadow on his face. 'You the village idiot or summat then?' Almighty looked down at his plate and shook his head. The soldier moved his gaze to Paddy. 'What about you, mate?'

Paddy raised his eyebrows. 'We were having a laugh.

Didn't mean to, you know, disturb you.' He began to stand up. 'Must get another plate of chips.'

The soldier's hand moved to Paddy's shoulder, pressed him down into his seat again. 'Sit on your arse, matey.' Then he bent his knees and put his elbows on the table so his face was level with ours. The hairs of his eyebrows met above the nose.

'Me and my mates ain't crazy about people as sit in corners doing the tee-hee-hee, begorrah, whisper-whisper, tee-hee-hee. We think people like that, maybe they're talking about us, Irish cunts 'at wants their arse kicked. Any of you lot cunts? Want your arse kicked?' We said nothing, tried desperately to think of something, but couldn't. ''At's good. You change your mind, get in touch, mind, OK? Top service, promise you.'

'OK,' Almighty whispered. Paddy and I nodded.

Then the soldier getting their fish suppers from Mario called 'Oy!' and the two at our table walked over to him, boots clicking on the floor, glancing back as they headed towards the exit. The beaky-nosed one said something and the other two laughed, the noise echoing into the afternoon street. We sat quiet, avoided each other's eyes.

Paddy cleared his throat. 'So anyway. Did those cops find anything after the clue?'

There was a brief pause. 'Shite all,' Almighty said at last. And the three of us smiled quietly, although we took a look towards the door before we started.

A few minutes later we buttoned our coats, turned the collar up the way Elvis did. Looked up and down the street.

'Those soldiers,' Paddy said. 'Good job they pushed off when they did.'

'I wouldn't mind,' Almighty said, 'if they were hard men or something. Only not half as hard as they think.' He looked up at Paddy and patted his right fist into the palm of his left. 'Or quarter. I'm away home.'

Five minutes later Paddy and I were going up the Courthouse hill when we met Presumer coming down. Where was he headed?

'Game of pitch-and-toss, Market Yard. Coming?' He seemed cheerful.

Paddy's voice had a clenched sound. 'No word on your brother?'

'Wee Sean? Oh aye – he was got an hour ago.' Presumer took out a butt and lit it. 'Neil found him. In his house.'

Neil had been going to leave the house, it seems, and was blessing himself from the holy water font inside the door when he heard what sounded like snoring. And then he went into a scullery back room he has, and there was Sean lying asleep on the floor, curled up like a dog. Must have got in an open window, Neil said. So naturally he rang the police, and they came and brought him home, and there was to be an article in the *Ulster Herald* about Neil the local hero and Sean the lost lamb that was found.

'See?' I said. 'Neil's OK in the end. Wait will Almighty hears about Omagh's town hero.' I stopped and thought for a minute. 'It's a wonder Almighty didn't say something about Sean being in his house, though.'

'Right,' Presumer said, and whistled the first few bars of 'Do Not Forsake Me, O My Darling'. 'Right enough, now. Anyway, I'm away to win a pile of money.' He strode off towards the Market Yard, giving the John Wayne salute without turning round.

Thou hast made mine enemies a footstool before me, O Lord, and the wicked thou hast crushed under thy heel.

CHAPTER 13

It was May – only three weeks of school left. It was like coming out after years stuck in a forest full of narrow paths and darkness – in the distance there were the yells of people having a good time in a clearing somewhere, maybe on a village green, but I still had to get through stumbling and scratching and poison ivy before I could join them. Teachers spent every class revising, giving little class tests, going over difficult bits on the blackboard, shouting if we showed signs of flagging. 'Say it over till you've it off like your what?' 'Like our prayers, sir.' Some teachers predicted topics for the Advanced Level exam – Fly Dolan claimed he'd guessed at least one right question every year for the last five. 'A record second to none, I don't mind admitting,' he said, buttoning and unbuttoning his jacket. Some teachers gave us questions to answer from old papers, and while we were writing they sat at the front reading *Time* magazine or the *Irish News*.

Then, with ten days to go and without giving me any hint of his plans, Presumer stopped coming to school. After he'd missed three days in a row the History teacher asked did anybody know what was the problem? We shrugged our shoulders and tried to avoid his eye. Then in English class Brother Dickey noticed.

'And where is the flower of the Livingstone line? Ill perhaps?' Silence. Eventually somebody at the back cleared their throat and said they thought so. 'How strange, Master Livingstone always impressed me as enjoying rude health. Most disappointing, to think he may after all be mortal.'

Eventually two or three people said they thought they'd heard somebody say he had the flu. They hadn't, of course, but you never knew when it'd be your turn and you'd need somebody to cover for you. I said I'd heard Presumer doing a lot of coughing, the last day he was at school.

Dickey stared at me, scratching under his chin with two fingers. 'From rude health to deathbed in a four-day period – an alarming decline. Perhaps we should petition that his organs be preserved for medical research. Or second thoughts: we send you, McGrath, down to his house to enquire in person about his condition. Mm? Tend the sick, comfort the dying, visit the prisoner – the corporal works of mercy. Who knows? Master Livingstone may one day leave the tending and comforting categories, to enter the third in the role of prisoner. The future is a mystery.'

I wasn't sure what he meant but I said I really didn't want to miss any class revision – could I call on Presumer after school?

'Very well,' Dickey said. 'Mind not to kick any empty bottles stacked inside the door.'

But when his mother opened the top half of the door about six inches that afternoon, her breath smelled more of medicine than booze. Just six inches, so all you could see were eyes and mouth against a dark background. Presumer was likely down at the Market Yard, the mouth said. Then there was a wail from the darkness behind her; the mouth swore and the door slammed shut.

When I tried again at lunchtime next day, Presumer himself opened the top and then the bottom. He looked as if he hadn't washed – hair spiked out at odd angles, eyes gummy, face pale. He waved me indoors.

'Revising at home makes far more sense than school,' he said. 'Hammering through the stuff morning to night. No distractions. Or not as many.' A sudden babble of talk came from the bedroom area, ending in Mrs Livingstone's voice saying something slow and serious that I couldn't make out. Presumer peered back at the darkness. 'She's half crackers fretting over Sean, you know.'

'But he's been back for months. He's OK, isn't he?'

'You bet. Only she's still got a rope tied round his leg with the other end tied to the bed. Once bitten, you see. Ask me something about the Industrial Revolution.'

So I did. I asked him about the Chartists, the Corn Laws, Sir Robert Peel. Everything we had revised at school plus a few more. He knew the lot.

'What'll I say to Dickey?'

'Say he can put his . . . no, better not.' Presumer looked cunning and thoughtful for a minute 'Tell him my ma said I'm sick.'

When I told Dickey he drummed a pencil on the desk. 'Well perhaps we should remind Master Livingstone's mother that failure to attend school on a regular basis can mean exclusion from Advanced Level examination registration. Would you say she is aware of this fact, McGrath?'

'I didn't ask her, Brother.'

'Perhaps then you will draw it to her attention,' Dickey said, reaching for *Vanity Fair*. 'Should your paths cross in the near future. Attendance is *not* optional.'

I told Presumer on the way home that day, what Dickey had said, and he said Dickey was a hairy-arsed rhino, but he came back to school the next day just the same. Dickey didn't speak to him during class. But then they hadn't exchanged a word, ever since the operetta. It was as if he wasn't in the class at all, didn't exist. But now, as the period ended and Presumer was passing his desk, Dickey's hand reached out and gripped his arm: 'A word, please.' I dawdled in the classroom doorway, then decided to wait at the bottom of the schoolyard until Presumer joined me.

'What happened?'

'He stood for about five minutes staring out the window, two big hands inside the soutane rubbing his arse as if he had Jane Russell in there. Then he swung round, the tail of it flying and the ould eyes popping, and said in this voice through his nose how he was inherently opposed to people that were slipshod about school attendance, especially with Advanced Level examinations now imminent. And he'd be scrutinising the regulations to ascertain my current standing. The fucker.'

When we reached Presumer's house he kept on walking. Out into Castle Street, down the hill, left into Brook Street, across wasteground towards the handball alley.

'What's up? Where are we for?'

'Something I want to show you.'

From the alley we could hear the sound of a ball pocking against the wall and the scuffle of feet. One pair of feet. We opened the door at the back. Tommy was crouched in the corner, playing dribblies against himself.

'How's the men?' he called. 'Any of youse fancy a game?'

Presumer closed the door, ignoring Tommy, and took a white paper bag from inside his shirt. It contained six photographs. Three of them were of Mary O'Kane performing on stage, taken from below, showing mainly her hands and the under part of her chin. The remaining three pictures were of a black cat perched, its tail in the air, on the bottom half of Presumer's door. All six pictures were partly obscured by a white balloon shape down the right-hand side.

'Bloody light leaking into the camera there,' Presumer said. 'Could have been good only for that.'

Tommy peered over our shoulders. 'Light leak right enough. Think somebody pee-ed on your pictures.'

'I think you should clear off,' Presumer said. 'While you can still walk.'

'Are you entering them for the *Herald* contest?' I asked.

Presumer rammed the photographs back into the bag. 'Shite like these? Not a complete eejit, you know.'

'Yeh, but don't forget potential,' Tommy said. 'The judges could decide your pictures have potential. If it wasn't for the light pee thing, they'd be good. Honest – I'm not just saying that.' Then just when it seemed that he really did mean it, Tommy started to laugh.

Presumer lunged forward and grabbed the handball from Tommy. Then he put down the pictures and chased him round the alley. Round it three times before he trapped him in one of the corners. Tommy sank to his knees, hands linked above his skull and Presumer hammered the ball against his head, his back, his hands. As hard as he was able, gasping and thumping. By the time he stopped Tommy was shouting, 'What did I do – hi, that hurt! What did I do?' and sounding as if he might start crying.

His chest going up and down with the exertion, Presumer walked back to where I was standing and took two cigarettes from a crumpled packet. Gave me one; then as an afterthought, tossed a half-cigarette over his shoulder towards Tommy.

'From the first day I got it,' Presumer said, squeezing the photographs back inside his jacket pocket, 'that camera was shite. Bloody Karsh of Ottawa couldn't take good pictures with it. And now it's shite *and* useless.'

Tommy struck a match on the alley floor and lit his half-cigarette, a safe distance from us. 'Where did you get it anyway?' he called. 'Buy it some road?'

'He won it,' I said. 'First in the mouth organ competition two Christmases ago.'

'A camera for winning a mouth organ competition?'

Presumer nodded. Tossed the ball gently from hand to hand. 'Neil was in charge of the concert that year, so the Monsignor gave him parish money for a prize and he said he'd buy a camera. Went up to Belfast and got this brilliant job: accordion movable lens, tripod – everything.'

'What's a tripod?' Tommy said.

'Only Neil kept it under wraps – hid the bugger. Then two days later, he went off and bought *another* camera – a Brownie – with his own money. Waited until I won, gave me this parcel wrapped in fancy paper with reindeers all over it, said it was a prize camera and when I took it everyone started clapping their fucking hands off and he stood there grinning. It was the Brownie the whole time. And he hung on to the good camera himself.'

'The stinking bastard did not,' Tommy said. 'Are you sure he did?'

Presumer ignored him and went on talking to me. 'What camera took photographs at the Brothers' Christmas dinner? The fancy one. Who took the photographs? Big-lip Neil. Same thing when Basil Brooke came here in his fancy car – they got Slobberchops to take the picture of him with the council ones grinning their arses off outside the Town Hall.'

'So he's a thief, then,' Tommy said. 'Can you believe it? Neil's a fucking cat burglar.'

Presumer nibbled on his thumbnail. 'He's more than a thief. A lot more.'

Maybe it was the way he said it – not loud and annoyed, but in a sort of growling noise. He lobbed the ball against the wall. Caught it and threw again. Tommy and I stood there, waited for him to speak. 'Sean hasn't been out of the house since he came back,' Presumer said over his shoulder. 'My ma has the front and back door locked, and the windows.'

'She doesn't want him lost again, that's why.' Tommy stepped in and caught the ball, started doing dribblies in the corner again. Right hand, left hand. 'He was lost and she doesn't want it happening again. What's that got to do with anything?'

'She keeps him under lock and key,' Presumer said, looking at me, 'because certain people did certain things to him.'

'What people? What things?'

Presumer crouched to tighten his laces. 'OK – what was the story? Neil says he found Sean in his house that morning, right? He did and his hole. It was the day before he found him, in the field behind his house. Brought him by the hand inside, with a load of nice soft chat; and once they got in the door, Neil locked him in a bedroom. That's what really happened. And guess who else was in the house at the time? Just a certain person who ruined a certain roll of film, that's all. In the bathroom, with all her clothes off, having a bubble bath.'

I was finding it difficult to breathe. Presumer lit another cigarette, took a pull and passed it to me.

'How do you know all this?' I said.

He ignored the question. 'After about half an hour Slobberchop took Sean in a glass of lemonade and two fig rolls. And then a half-hour after that, when Sean said he needed a pee, he took him to the lav. And that's where your woman Collette was.'

'Where?' Tommy said. 'On the lav?'

'In the bath. Leaning back in it, her hair all limp and floating behind her. And she had her big toe stuck in the nozzle of the cold tap – how do I know what for, suppose because she liked it – and her other foot in the air, where she could get at it with a bottle of red nail polish and a wee brush.'

'She was putting on nail polish in the bath?' Tommy said. 'Pheeeow.'

'Oil polish – doesn't come off in the water. Sean said the bath was full of bubbles.'

'Like Jane Russell in that picture,' Tommy said. 'Remember? Your man Randolph Scott comes into the ranch house and there's Jane and her big diddies, in the back room. Fu-fu-fucking marvellous— Who are you talking about?'

'She didn't look a bit like Jane Russell,' Presumer told

Tommy. 'You've got Jane Russell on the brain.'

'I meant the bubbles. The bubble bath was the same, that's all.' Tommy went back to the corner of the alley and began to head the ball against the wall.

'So then Neil went and got his fancy camera, tripod and everything, and set it up just inside the bathroom door. And every time your woman Collette moved in the bath, he would go fweeep, flash bang wallop, picture taken. Six different pictures of her nibs in the bath, lathering herself. And then finally she said she'd have to get out or she'd catch pew-monja. And she stood up and the soap bubbles all over her were bursting at a mile a minute.'

'Bursting?' Tommy whispered. He stood squeezing the ball as if he was trying to burst it. Presumer knocked it from his hands and threw it to the far end of the alley. Tommy scampered after it like a pup.

'And Neil, he gets a big white towel from the hot press. And puts it round her. And then when your woman has gone off with it wrapped round her big round bum and her big round diddies and all the rest, Neil looks at Sean and says, "You could do with a bath yourself."'

Tommy stopped playing and came back towards us.

'So he made Sean take a bath as well, only there was no more bubble stuff left. He gave him a big bar of Lifebuoy soap, told him to scrub every inch. And while he was doing it, Neil took photographs. "Do you not want to be famous?" he'd say when Sean would put his head down. "Think of the thousands will see your face. You'll be famous."'

'Thousands?' Tommy asked. 'What does he mean, thousands? Thousands of pounds?'

'He was talking about the photographs,' Presumer said. 'Thousands of people could see the photographs. He's planning for putting them in a dirty book or a magazine or something. It's obvious.'

'Did Sean tell you this?'

Presumer shook his head. 'Hardly spoke since he came back. Does drawings, though. Loads of drawings.'

Afterwards, up at his house, Presumer showed us some of them. They were crayon drawings, all very simple but clear and strong. The first showed a toilet, the second a plate of food, the third a bath, the fourth a man with a tripod camera.

'He's the best drawer in his class.' Mrs Livingstone took the drawings from us again and replaced them carefully under a cushion on the sofa. She stood with her arms half around herself, an old coat buttoned over her nightdress. 'Miles ahead of them. Not one of them could come near him at the drawing.' Her eyes moved restlessly from Presumer to Tommy to me and back again. 'Top scholar.'

Tommy said she was right, Sean really was a great drawer. Maybe the best drawer in Omagh, or the best drawer there had ever been in Omagh.

'Did he say anything, though?' I asked. 'Did he tell you that, you know, that Neil—'

Presumer raised his hand, stopped me. '"Man. Bath. Picture." That's what he says. "Man. Bath. Picture." But you know rightly what he means.'

'Leave the child alone,' Mrs Livingstone said, putting her hand on Tommy's chest and pushing us back. 'Youse have him tormented, and he's still not half at himself – sure you're not, pet?' And she turned towards Sean, who stood in the bedroom doorway.

'Sweet,' Sean said, and his mother produced a bag of them from her pocket and gave him one. Put the bag back without offering us any. Took him on her knee.

'Mammy,' Sean said. He put his head on her chest and his thumb in his mouth. 'Sing.'

'Name of God,' his mother told him. 'Have a titter of wit, child.' But then Presumer got his mouth organ from a drawer and began breathing into it. And Sean lay back looking up at her face and began to whimper. So she sang.

First 'Glasgow Belongs to Me'. And then 'The Black Hills of Dakota', although she got mixed up in the middle of it. And after that one that I hadn't heard before, a sad one about the foggy dew and Dublin town, sung in a breathless, tired sort of way. Sean kept smiling up at her as she sang, stretching his neck when she stretched hers, and moving his head from side to side. Then when she'd finished singing and Presumer had stopped playing, Mrs Livingstone poured orange juice into one cup and something else into another and her and Sean went back into the bedroom.

Presumer said he had *Palgrave's Golden Treasury* listed for revision the next day, only he'd lost his copy of it; so I said I'd lend him mine if he wanted to come out to the house and collect it. And as we started to head for the door Mrs Livingstone shouted for us to go out backways, so we could grab Sean if he broke free and tried to run out the door. But he didn't.

Tommy left us at the bottom of Castle Street and headed for his house round by Sedan Avenue. We passed a poster of a smiling soldier outside the Army barracks, with the words 'Join the Army and see the world' above it. Presumer said, 'You know the reason Sean's not talking much is, he's shell-shocked. Like soldiers in the war.' He cleared his throat and landed a gob of spit on the smiling soldier's face.

'Or he might just like drawing things,' I said. 'How come Almighty never said anything about Sean being in the house? Or Collette for that matter. Almighty would be bound to have seen them, wouldn't he?'

'He would. But he'd have been too scared of his da to say anything about anybody or any thing. Neil would kill him if he did. Anyway, you wouldn't tell on your da if he was up to something, would you?'

I thought for a minute. 'No, but Sean still might have had a gumboil. Doesn't have to be shell shock.'

'If somebody took off your clothes and started taking pictures you'd be shocked, wouldn't you?'

I thought about this. Switched things around in my head so Collette was taking the pictures instead of Neil. Better. Not as good as Debbie Reynolds or Christy taking pictures of me in the bath, or me taking pictures of them, but better than Neil. In or out of the bath.

'What would Neil want photographs of Sean for?' I asked.

Presumer looked at me for a minute without speaking. Cleared his throat again and spat over McCauley's castle-style garden wall. 'What did he want photographs of Collette for?'

'Yes but she's a woman. That's different.'

Presumer kicked a stone into the road. 'It is and it isn't. Neil likes photographs of nude women *and* photographs of nude boys – doesn't care. Hermaphrodites are like that. Do it with a hole in the wall if you didn't stick a bung in it first.' Presumer picked up the stone and threw it towards McCauley's pink barn. 'Know what I think? If Collette hadn't been there, and Almighty too probably, Neil would have had the suit off and into that bath with Sean.'

It was like a nightmare where people say mad things as if they were sensible things. I could hear my own breathing.

'Guys like Slobberchops, you see – they hate people standing up to them. Want the world population to line up and lick their arse, ask no questions. If somebody fights back – say, pops a couple of holes in their upholstery or something – they don't like that one bit. Do anything to get back at them. Photograph the person's wee brother in the bath, stick their tool into him. Anything.'

This was ridiculous. And disgusting. 'For God' sake,' I said. 'Neil's a councillor, he works with the priests, owns a shop. He wouldn't do that just to get back at you. You're annoyed because he won't let your mother work in the golf club any more – and earlier you were annoyed because she *was* working there. Anyway, what did you want to do that to his car for? There was no call for digging holes in the good seats.'

Presumer put his two hands on my shoulders and leaned in close, almost like the soldier had done. 'You're right – there wasn't. I shouldn't have stuck a knife in the seats. What I should have done was took a hacksaw to them. Put a sledgehammer through the windscreen, ripped every last fistful of stuffing out of every last fucking seat – that's what I should have done. Only I'm too soft.' He skipped in front of me and then, back-pedalling, pointed to his chest. 'But not any more. Because Neil. Has. Asked for it. And I.' He stopped in front of me so I had to stop as well. 'You. Me. We. Are going to give it to him in a way he won't forget. Right? Right-right-right-right-RIGHT!'

Vengeance is mine, saith the Lord.

CHAPTER 14

'Oh God,' Maeve said. 'Oh Mother of God.' She was standing at the hall window. 'It's not happening.'

Mammy looked up from where she was scrubbing the red tiles of the hall floor. 'I hope Our Lord isn't listening to you taking his holy name like a corner boy. Or he'll not be too pleased.'

'Look who's coming in the lane on his bicycle. The *cut* of him,' Maeve said, pointing. 'With his hairy nose.'

Sitting very straight on his boneshaker bike, with his chin in the air, was Foxy. As we watched he extended his right arm to signal he was about to slow down and park beside the outhouse, even though the only thing watching him was a couple of hens.

'I'm not going near him,' Maeve said, walking to the opposite end of the room from the window. 'Not even talking. Any time I go into that shop his eyes go running all over me.'

'Hold your tongue, you bad article,' Mammy said. 'Where's Our Father?'

But there wasn't time to find out, because Foxy came in the back door without knocking and stood in the scullery. 'I hope I'm not coming at a bad time, now.'

'Not at all – get a seat for yourself, Mr Johnston,' Mammy said, waving him into the kitchen. She lifted a couple of newspapers from Our Father's chair. 'You know you're always welcome.'

'No, no, no, no, no.' Foxy waved his arms as if trying to disperse smoke, then took two huge steps that left him seated on the bench along the wall. 'I'm powerful here, powerful. I suppose himself is no road handy?'

'That's him now,' Maeve said, as footsteps sounded in the back yard. 'He was out looking at the hens.' She gave Foxy a smile but he was too busy jumping to his feet to notice.

'Boys a boys.' Our Father leaned on his stick in the doorway and stared at Foxy. 'Quare to see you ceili-ing. I'd have thought you'd be in that shop of yours making money.'

Foxy gave a brief giggle. 'Well now, herself is over there working away. Whatever about the money-making.' He turned his cap between his two hands and stared at the label. 'Some boy said you had a near squeak a while back, and I thought I'd run over and see how you were keeping anyway. Dangerous contraptions, them ould outhouses.'

'I'm not one hair the worse, so now. Only lost a good cow and landed the expense of a new roof putting up, and I wasn't looking that. Double bad fortune.' Our Father took his place at the top of the table and Mammy put a plate of stew in front of him.

'Would you take a bite of dinner, Mr Johnston? I'd lay you a place in a minute.'

'No no no no, missus. Only here for to see the Boss here and get away from the smell of that oul' place of mine.'

'A cup in your hand itself, then.'

'From the shop?' Our Father said, a piece of stew halfway to his mouth. 'Smell from the shop?'

Foxy turned the cap over on his lap and shook his

head. 'Shop's grand – it's that oul' lav we have at the back. If the Health boys was to come on it, they'd murder us.'

Our Father shook salt on his potatoes and dropped a wedge of butter into the middle of his stew. 'Close you down – is that what you're saying?'

'See if I had transport? I'd have the place you could eat your dinner off it, if I had transport.'

'Transport.' Our Father put another forkful in his mouth and chewed slowly. 'Aye.'

'A pony and cart and I'd have the job soon done – shining like the Taj Mahal, it'd be. Thanks, missus.' He took a noisy sup from the cup of tea Mammy passed him.

Our Father put a half-sausage in his mouth. Chewed. 'How would it shine with all that poo about? You'll not make that vanish, tell you that much.'

'I have to go now,' I said, standing up. 'Meet someone.'

Foxy ignored me. 'Put it in the sewage works up behind youse, where do you think? Sure I'd only be bringing a drop to the ocean. That's some concrete headquarters they have built up on that corner of land.'

Our Father peeled a potato in his hand, then lifted one half to his mouth between finger and thumb. Shook his head as he chewed.

'Sure isn't the whole shebang at that plant processed. You couldn't be dropping your raw shite in a corner and walk away whistling.'

'Raw or cooked wouldn't bother me as long as it was away to hell from my wee shop.'

Our Father buttered a chunk of wheaten bread, pointed the knife at Foxy. 'Shite takes refining. If you were to start dumping your collection, we'd have every rat in the country nosing and squeaking about this place.' He chewed and swallowed the second half-potato. 'And there wouldn't be a fish alive between here and Derry.'

Foxy drained his cup, tried to smile. 'Half a day, that's all I'm looking. Have your pony and cart back before you could say sue-sue-sewage. The fish wouldn't so much as know I was near them.'

Our Father tapped his fork handle on the table. 'My wee pony would know, but. Kill a pony, hauling the likes of that around, if you weren't right and careful. Anyway, I'll be needing her myself.'

There was a pause as Foxy stood up and walked to the window through which Maeve had spotted him. 'Can't say I seen you working her a powerful lot before this, well,' he said as if to himself. Then pointed through the window towards his shop. 'We're at our wits' end over beyont, you know.'

I nodded. 'Mr Johnston's right, in a way. We don't use the pony that often. Not really.'

Our Father's knife and fork clattered on to his empty plate. 'So that's the next of it, eh? One day I'm near killed with boiler-house roofs. And the next I'm told what I can do with my own property. By Christ.'

'Sh-sh, now,' Mammy said. 'Nobody's telling you a thing. No call getting upset.'

I stood up. 'I can't stay, I must go,' I said.

Foxy jumped as if he'd been bitten. 'A gun!' he half-shouted. 'A gun to my ear and me bringing youse your newspapers week in and week out. Keeping my wee shop open half the night in case youse all might run out of milk or butter or some wee futtery thing like an ice lolly. And here's the thanks – a gun to my ear!'

'A gun to your arse,' Our Father said. 'We're the ones doing you the favour, buying the damn papers – not the other way round. You amadan you.'

Foxy shuffled forward until he was directly facing Our Father. The hairs in his nose seemed to curl and glint with irritation. 'That's all the thanks I get, then – sitting up there like a big man, like Lord Muck telling me I'm an eejit. Well by Christ two can play that game.'

'What game?' Maeve was in the kitchen doorway, eyes wide.

'The gun-to-the-ear game – the fish-on-the-hook game!' Foxy shouted at her. Then he stared at the floor for a few seconds, like someone trying to remember lines he had memorised. Finally looked up, small eyes blazing. 'Youse are all so smart. Well I've information'll put the smile on the other side of your faces.'

'Would you not sit instead and I'll pour you another half-cup, Mr Johnston?' Mammy asked, hovering with the teapot. Foxy swatted the invitation away with one hand and scratched his neck with the other.

Our Father pulled back from the table, walking stick in hand. 'What information? About the blaggards that stole the Picture House money – is that it?'

'What are you all talking about?' Maeve asked. 'What blackguards?'

'Shite,' I whispered.

'Mind you your manners!' Mammy mouthed at me behind Our Father's back.

Foxy's face seemed to be going several directions at once. 'To hell with Roy Rogers and Mickey Mouse – I'm talking about the real world. And certain boys that wreck certain property. And certain things buried certain places.'

'Excuse me,' I said, trying to get past Foxy. 'I need to go now if I'm—'

'Listen – do you know what you do?' Our Father prodded Foxy's leg with the rubber tip on his stick. 'Go and chat to the police if you're for accusing people. And give our heads peace.'

The number of little red veins in the whites of Foxy's eyes seemed to have doubled. 'Would you have peace if I told you the name of a burglar – would you have peace then?'

'Tell ten. Or a hundred.' Our Father stood up. 'But you'll still get no pony nor cart off me. For you're as twisted and knotted as a hangman's noose.'

Foxy looked from Our Father to me. His voice was a whisper. 'And if I told you one of the burglars was your son? Mooching about Stanley's place and breaking and entering. *And* damaging vehicles. Would I be a twisted noose then?'

There was silence for a couple of ticks of the clock and then Our Father began to laugh. 'By God you're a tryer, Foxy. First go you want to kill my pony. And now you want to make a burglar out of Jim here.' He wiped his eyes with the back of his hand. 'It's a circus you should be in.'

'Ask him, then,' Foxy said.

'Ask what?'

'Ask him did he do any burgling. Or property damage. He's standing there. Go on.'

Our Father didn't even glance at me. He stood, stick in hand, pointing at the door. 'You're trespassing on my property and you're slandering my family, Mr Johnston.

And if you don't shift your Orange arsehole out of my house this minute, I'll not be answerable for what happens to you.' He half-raised his stick.

Foxy shuffled to the door. Turned, one hand on the knob. 'Now it's coming out. The dirty talk, the bad attitudes that's hid away. But you ask him. That's all I'm saying. You. Ask. Him. And when he tells you, you might find your mind changed about that pony and cart.'

The door slammed after him and there was silence.

'The cheeky article,' Mammy said at last. 'There was a smell of drink off him, you know. Did you get it? Only I wouldn't have said that about Orange.'

Our Father sat down, picked up the newspaper and rattled it open. Breathed heavily through his nose. 'He'll get a solicitor's letter from me, see what way that smells till him. The lying wee hoor.'

Maeve stood with her back to the Aga, arms folded.

'Is he, but?' She was staring straight at me. 'Is he a lying wee hoor?'

'You bad article, hold your tongue!' Mammy snapped.

'I'm just saying what he said. So is he?'

Careful. Watch yourself. If you don't you'll get Presumer caught up in this. He's got enough to bother him with Sean and school *and* his war with Neil.

'No.'

'No what?' Maeve asked. 'No he's not a lying . . . all right, *person* – all right? Or no, you're not a thieving burglar? And property damager?'

I took a deep breath. 'No, he's not a lying . . . person. I was involved in a, a sort of burglary. And some damage. But it was months and months ago.'

Their yelps and shouts came piling over the top of me like a wave at Bundoran, bashing out any possibility of thought.

Our Father spent the next three days roaring about there having been many's a thing in the family but never a thief, wait until I was pulled up in front of the court and got two years' hard labour, I'd see what I thought of that then. But I still wouldn't tell him about the burglary or what property had got damaged. It wasn't a burglary anyway, it was more a preparation for a burglary, and it wasn't me burgled or damaged anyway, it was Presumer, only I wasn't going to tell him that either. And it wasn't even a burglary, it was only a damned frigging *fucking crowbar*. When I shook my head and kept my lips together Our Father would begin to shout again about disgrace and turning me in to the police, scratching the tiny wrinkled space between his hairline and his eyebrows as he yelled. And Mammy would start making tea and saying 'Och dear, dear, dear' and sighing. I looked out the window and thought what it would be like if Christy and I were running a clothes shop somewhere out in the country and we had a boat that we were able to row out on a lough for fishing, and in the evening we'd have trout fried in a black pan and buttermilk from a blue jug and go to bed tired and hot-cheeked from the fresh air. *Her hair was the golden brown of a grain field that has been burned dark in the sun.*

In the end, Our Father had to give in. For a day or so he struggled, slamming the car door and the door of the house, and if anyone spoke to him during a meal banging his knife and fork against the plate and shouting one-word answers. But on the Monday morning he drove over to Foxy's and told him to come and get the pony and cart when he was ready to use it. Mammy wanted him to say he was sorry about the Orange bit, but he wouldn't. That afternoon when he was sure Our Father was away at a cattle fair, Foxy came to the back door and told Mammy that he was a man that forgot many's a thing but never forgot a good turn, many's a thing got said in the heat of a row and sure sticks and stones and what harm, and a couple of hours' work and he'd have the place neat and clean as a new pin.

In fact it took more than a couple of hours. He had to work at night, because if he'd done it during the day, he said, the Health people might have seen him and if they did they'd be sure to close him down for not having had the business moved all along. That's what he called the shite – the 'business'. Only then Mammy began talking about him making money from his business, meaning his shop, and you could see from the way they were looking at each other that they were getting a bit mixed up.

So the red cart was set out for Foxy, and the pony was put in the fenced-off bit in the corner of the back field. For the next three nights, we could hear him going down the lane with the pony harnessed to the empty cart, the metal rims on the wheels and the loose boards making a good deal of rattle and the pony's hoofs going along the lane at a nice light clip-clop. Coming back, everything was slowed down. You could hear the pony snorting, and the cart wheels digging into the lane deeper and slower than the first time, and the harness creaking and groaning as they made their way up to the hill field and beyond it to the sewage plant near the river. 'Clck, clck' came Foxy's voice out of the darkness, encouraging the pony to greater effort. The second night he went up and down three times. Although maybe some of the trips were in my dream – I kept nodding off and then hearing the crunch of wheels and horse and the rasp of effort going up the lane once more.

He started on the Monday and he finished on the Thursday night. On Friday morning when Our Father went to the back of the byre, there was the red cart with its shafts in the air, and the pony in the small fenced-in bit, looking tired and his coat clumpy.

'Was it clean?' Mammy asked. 'He said he'd leave it like the Taj Mahal.'

'They're not wild fussy about the Taj McCall then,' Our Father said. 'Taj McCall and him would be right and sick if they ate their dinner off the likes of that.'

Our Father was well on the road to recovery from his boiler-house ordeal. He had a new walking stick with a brass bit on the handle, and he'd move across the yard and stand at the gate to the front field and stare down towards the river, where the cattle were grazing. Wouldn't move for maybe fifteen minutes at a time, so you didn't know whether he was looking at the cattle and thinking about what they'd make at a mart, or whether he was staring through the cattle and thinking about something completely different.

The morning after Foxy left back the cart I looked out the window and Our Father was standing beside the wired-off section where the hens were. Some of them were drinking from the tin trough and the rest were picking the ground and staring, as if expecting something to happen.

'Look at this one.' Mammy had come bustling out of the house and was standing with her shoulder nearly touching Our Father's. 'Gawking up at you, ready to conk out. Could you not see him?' She opened the gate and picked up a hen that was huddled against the wire. Its eyes seemed to have a crust of grey and its beak was pointing towards the ground. 'Distemper or I'm a Chinawoman.' Mammy pulled its two feet together and headed for the scullery. The hen gave a brief flap of its wings and then let its head hang. 'We'll put him in the carrier basket.' She tied the feet together with a piece of cord and crossed its wings behind its back to make it completely helpless.

Our Father watched, leaning on his stick. 'Mind you tie him in tight that he wouldn't jump out on the road.'

The basket on the back of my bike was lined with old copies of the *Tyrone Constitution* and the hen eased into it. Then she put more newspaper on top and knotted more string in place.

'Now – get that into Gracey's while it's still breathing.'

She put her hand on Our Father's back as she spoke. Pretended it was to steady herself but I knew it wasn't.

'Mind you don't hit a bump and fall off,' Our Father called. 'Could be the end of the pair of you.'

I pedalled a bit slower than normal. It wasn't likely to happen, the way the cord had been tied round the basket by Mammy, but I could see it in my mind – a stone in the road, a jolt, the hen suddenly exploding into life, skimming the nearest ditch like one of *The Dam Busters* planes, never to be seen again. And me never to hear the end of it from Our Father.

Gracey's was a huge grey barn halfway up Gallows Hill. Its front had two big doors that slid back on noisy rollers, one door open all the time to let air in.

When your eyes got used to the dark inside, you saw a bulb hanging from a rafter at the far end, with the wooden table and a couple of ordinary chairs and a big brown armchair with tears all over the material. Today there were about fifteen plucked hens laid out on the table. The floor was covered in white feathers. Seated in the armchair, feathers up to his mid-calf, was Joe Rolston.

'What's that you've got, cub?' he called to me, his eyes small and blinking in his big fat face. 'I hope to Christ it's healthy.'

I parked the bike against the tin wall and untied the basket. There was no movement from beneath the newspaper.

'Maybe she's having a wee rest to herself,' Joe said. 'Maybe she's a sleepy wee hen – you think?'

I said nothing – Mammy had always warned us to say as little as possible to people, in case you said the wrong thing.

Joe pushed aside the paper and held the hen at arm's length. It didn't struggle, just watched him from its crusty yellow eye.

'Mmmaaye,' Joe said, slowly turning it upside down and moving aside some dirty feathers to look at its arse. 'Aye. Well now.' He put it back in the basket. 'Put her over there. I'll give you one and six.'

'Mammy says it's worth half a crown.'

He stared at me, mouth open. 'Holy Jesus – a dealer like his da. Two bob, and if you don't like it you can kiss my arse. Have you a sweetheart at all?'

Joe liked to talk about sweethearts. He had never married, and at the end of each day he'd open a bottle of stout right there in the barn and drink it, with the corpses of hens mounted on the table and the feathers of hens lying around his feet and sometimes a loose feather or two drifting up and sticking to the wet outside of the bottle.

'I know one or two girls . . .' It sounded boastful and stupid when I said it, but it was all I could think of and there was no taking it back now.

'Christ – a bigamist. Give us that bag,' Joe said, pointing to where a leather purse like a bus conductor's hung from a nail in the wall. He counted out a shilling and two sixpences. 'Now. You'll be able to buy your sweethearts a pair of silk knickers each.'

I was outside tying the empty basket on to the carrier when I heard footsteps approaching. It was Francie. Home again. He stood with his two black shoes together and his black hat in place, the brim shadowing his face. His mother had sent him to buy a hen for the Sunday dinner, he said. Very good, I told him – there were at least a dozen inside. Probably more. Then he came closer and caught the sleeve of my jacket between his finger and thumb and drew me back towards the road, away from the open barn door. 'It's a sign, I'm sure it is. This morning in my prayers after Communion I asked God to let me meet you, and look what happened. I want to ask your forgiveness.'

'Hi, cub! Is that a customer?' Joe's voice echoed from the darkness of the barn.

Francie ignored him. 'Can you find it in your heart, Jim?'

I looked away, down the hill to where the chimneys from several dozen red-brick houses leaked a steady drizzle of smoke into the grey sky. I thought about Francie kneeling down to pray he would meet me, and about me kicking his arse until my foot was sore. 'Nothing to forgive.'

'There is, there is!' His voice seemed to have got deeper and I could smell his breath when he leaned closer. Cheese. 'I turned my back on our friendship and I turned my back on my vocation. Yes, only for one evening, I know, but I still feel . . . you know . . . stained.'

'Hi, cub! Are you deaf?' Joe shouted.

'You're not stained, Francie. You're as clean as a new pin.'

Francie shook his head, gave a little moan. 'No, no, no!' What had he got up to with Bernie on the way home? Murdered her? Committed adultery? 'I kept meeting her, you see, over and over. In the street or coming out of a shop or even the chapel. On her own.'

'Maybe it was God's will,' I said. 'Predestination.'

'HI!' Joe roared, appearing at the door of the barn. 'You in the hat – come in or fuck off, would you? What is it you're looking anyway?'

Francie blushed. 'I need a small hen for tomorrow's dinner. I'll be there in a tick.' He turned back to me, his face twisted as if he was going to cry. 'It was so easy talking to her – she was interested in everything about life in the seminary. And then out of the blue she asked me to take her home from the dance.'

'"Oh Rosemarie, I love you",' Joe sang from inside the barn. ' "I'd really like to ride you." '

Francie looked at his shoes. 'And even though I've been to confession and explained to Bernadette that I had made a grave error by putting myself – the two of us – in an occasion of sin . . . I still feel stained.' He pinched the top of his nose with his finger and thumb. There were definitely tears in his eyes.

'No need to feel stained. Told you that.'

'I was thinking maybe if I went to Lough Derg this summer – twice, maybe – that might make up for it. Bare feet and fasting and no sleep – they'd be bound to help me strip away the pride of life, wouldn't they? Our Spiritual Director warned us about the pride of life. Girls bring it out in people, he said. Only I forgot.'

Joe reappeared at the door. He had our half-plucked hen in one hand, its head limp like a deflated balloon. 'A hen did you say?'

Francie swallowed, nodded. 'Yes, please. Ready for cooking tomorrow.'

'Got the very article inside – hanging this two days. Have her parcelled before you can say brass balls.' He walked back into the darkness, singing a version of 'The Girl I Left Behind Me' that I hadn't heard before.

Francie began to follow him, then turned at the doorway. 'Bernie talked to me about it – she's very good. Says I shouldn't worry. But I do find it all quite . . . hard.'

I mounted my bike and freewheeled towards the road. 'What was that you said was hard?' I heard Joe shout as I rode away. 'Do you have a sweetheart at all?'

I propped my bike against the footpath outside Miller's Picture House. 'Gentlemen Prefer Blondes,' the poster said, with photographs of Marilyn Monroe and Jane Russell wearing sparkly bathing costumes. In Technicolor.

As I stood looking at Marilyn and Jane's legs, Willie Maguire came out of the entry carrying a bucket of paste, a brush and three rolled-up posters. He put the bucket on the ground, dipped his brush and began to slap paste on an empty bit of wall. When he had the space nice and damp he unrolled one of the posters, pressed it against the pasted space and slapped more paste on top. The poster was for Mary O'Kane.

'FAREWELL CONCERT,' it said in big letters at the top. 'Prior to her departure for England on recording contract, Omagh Star MARY O'KANE will make a final Appearance at Drumragh Parish New Hall (St Martin de Porres) at 7.30 pm on Saturday 4 June 1960. Top-class supporting acts in this Bumper Concert. Admission: 1/- Children: 6d.'

A hand gripped my shoulder. It was Presumer. 'What do you think?' he said, pointing at the poster but holding something behind his back with his other hand. 'Are you for going?'

'Not sure. What about you?'

He shook his head, spoke quietly. 'No chance. Business calls.' He watched Willie, who had moved further along the street and was pasting another poster on the wall outside Baldwin's Bicycles. Presumer turned back and showed me what he was carrying. A brown paper bag. Inside it, a can with a pump handle.

'What's that yoke for?'

'Used to be spraying flies. Now – decorating, maybe.' He pushed the handle gently and a tiny spray of red dots hissed out. 'Some modern art. A spot of Salvador Dali.'

'You for using that at Neil's?'

'Well now. Michelangelo did a powerful job on that Sistine Chapel. Neil could be lucky too.'

'You think he'll be pleased, do you? If you paint his house with that.'

'I'm not trying to please the bugger.'

'And you think he'll let you into his house to start cavorting around? Are you nuts?'

'Ah, that's where timing comes in, old partner. Because when I'm doing the Neil tour, he'll be attending – da-daaaaa!' He pointed to where Willie was putting up his third poster for Mary's concert. 'When she's singing "Softly, Softly" and he's in the wings gawking at her and thinking how much she'll earn for him and playing pocket billiards with himself, we'll be tiptoeing softly, softly up his stairs. And when she's hitting the high notes for him and he's getting a high mickey for her, we'll be hitting his home front. Psss-ssst. Gotta have timing, tick-a-tick-a-tick-a-timing.'

'For God's sake. Neil has a dog, you know. A brute of a thing. Almighty never tell you?'

'Here's the man'll take care of Mr Dog,' Presumer said. I turned to see Paddy emerge from the Picture House entry. His jacket collar was turned up and his shoulders hunched. 'I was just saying Neil's dog'll give us no bother with you around.'

'You betcha,' Paddy said, putting his thumbs in his belt and staring up the street. 'Dogs smell fear. Wasting your time going near them if you've the smell of fear off you.'

'That's where you're the lucky one,' Presumer said. 'Don't know what fear means. Right?' He touched Paddy's arm.

Paddy pulled away. 'See that cat you gave me after Christmas – that you said would be grand once I got it home? Damn sure you did, swore it would be no bother. Well the bugger spent four weeks shiting on everything it could find. Upstairs, downstairs, in my lady's chamber. And then just when we thought it'd settled – it had started eating scraps we threw out and sleeping on the kitchen window in the sun – here last month the bugger took off, no sight nor sound of him since. Grand when I got him home my arse.' Paddy ran the flat of his hand over his crew cut, making it hiss. 'Remind me what we're going to Neil's for.'

'Because he's the enemy,' Presumer said gently. 'For what he did to me and my ma – making her bow and scrape and slave for bloody peanuts for a year and a half, and then what happens? He says they've too many cleaners, sorry, and here's a day's extra wages to shut you up. And then look at that with your sister – way he keeps half the money she makes. And the way he wouldn't let you sing with her – you with a brilliant voice – anybody'd tell you that. Know what it is? It's time to turn the tide. Time the balance was righted. That's what we're going to Neil's for – to right some balances and turn some tides. And you're going to look after his dog.'

'So when are we for doing this?'

Presumer moved closer, spoke softly. 'Friday.' He guided Paddy to the poster. 'See? Everybody else will be in the hall, to hear your sister singing. Neil's her manager, so he'll have to be there. And Almighty'll be with him. Which means the only thing we have to worry about is this bloody Hound of the Baskervilles Neil's supposed to have. And like I say, you're the boy to handle that.'

'Of the what?'

'Baskervilles. It's a book.'

Paddy chewed his lower lip and frowned. 'But . . . what are we going to do?'

'Knock the fancy out of his fancy house,' Presumer said. 'Do a bit of decorating. Let him see the writing's on the wall as far as he's concerned.'

'Writing?' Paddy said in a voice far louder than I thought he should have. 'What's the good in writing? Wreck the place – that's what he needs. Sledgehammer his furniture. Put a match to his curtains. That's the only way to make a bastard like that listen to you.'

'I don't think we should go that far,' I said.

'Listen, listen, listen.' Presumer nudged me and, with his back to Paddy, gave a quick roll of the eyes. 'We just want to scare him. That's all. No need to knock his house down.'

'That bastard said I couldn't sing. Only for him I'd be on that tour in England. Knock more than his house down if he doesn't watch.'

'Yes, only if we do it the way I'm saying, it'll be twice as bad for him.' Presumer patted Paddy's arm again and Paddy again pulled back, this time half-raised his fist. 'Look, we scare him, OK? Leave him shivering in bed wondering "Will they be back tonight? Tomorrow night? And do something worse?" But if we burn his curtains and all that other stuff, he'll have nothing left to worry about. It'll be all over. See what I mean?'

Paddy nodded his head but didn't look convinced.

'I'm right, amn't I?' Presumer put his hand on my shoulder. 'Don't you need to keep people fretting so they think something worse is ready to happen?'

'Definitely.' I wasn't completely sure what he meant, but I knew I was supposed to say something like that.

Paddy muttered and headed towards the Dublin Road, hands in his trouser pockets and shoulders hunched. Presumer and I walked up the Courthouse hill, and as we passed the Belfast Bank, Presumer asked if I'd do a favour for him. 'Come to Neil's with us. Tell your ma and da you've the toothache, then sneak out.

You'll be back long before they come out of the concert.'

'But you'll have Paddy with you – muscle. I'd only be in the way. And the dog would smell my fear and everything as well.'

Presumer stopped and looked straight at me. 'Paddy'll look after the dog all right – but we need to be sure we can look after Paddy. Supposing he goes a bit nuts and wants to set fire to everything? You heard the way he went on there.' He gripped my arm. 'Listen – you're coming, OK? And bring a knife with you. Bread knife or carving or something. If he starts on again about burning the curtains, we'll let him give them a slash or two with the knife instead. Which'll really scare the shite out of Neil, because he'll see the curtains cut and think we're coming back to put some slashes in him. OK?'

And the veil of the temple was rent in two, and darkness descended upon the face of the earth.

CHAPTER 15

The night before the concert I mooched about down-stairs until the others had gone to bed. Sat in the dining room reading the bit in *For Whom The Bell Tolls* where Robert Jordan stopped holding hands with Maria and *held the length of her body tight to him and felt her breasts against his chest through the two khaki shirts, he felt them small and firm and he reached and undid the buttons on her shirt and bent and kissed her and she stood shivering, holding her head back, his arm behind her.* What was sinful about that? Married men and women did it every night. In five years' time I might well be married and doing it myself. I closed the book and thought about being married.

Ten minutes later when I could hear no sound upstairs I eased open the drawer in the sideboard. It came out with hardly a creak. There were two sets of knives and forks, laid out in blue velvet compartments. Along the right hand side some bigger stuff – a two-pronged fork for carving, two sets of nutcrackers, a soup ladle, and a long carving knife that swooped up to a point and had a little wavy pattern along its blade. The handle was white. I slid it carefully up the leg of my trousers, holding it against my thigh from inside my pocket. It meant walking slowly and carefully going up the stairs. Once in my room I hid it under the mattress.

During breakfast the following morning I ate only a

slice and a half of toast and pretended to not be very well.

'You sound like an elephant with the bum blocks,' Maeve said. 'Supposed to say excuse me when you make that noise.'

I spoke with my hand over my jaw: 'Shut your trap.'

Mammy said it was a shame to have the toothache, on the night of the Mary O'Kane concert too, we'd have to see about getting me to the dentist first thing tomorrow, and gave me two aspirins and a glass of water. At twenty to seven, with Maeve making faces at me behind her back, she asked me twice again if I'd come. I shook my head and closed my eyes wearily, and her and Maeve and Our Father went off in the car and left me on my own.

Be patient. Wait until the clock in the kitchen is at five to seven; by then anybody going to the concert will be bound to have gone. Sit still, count backways from three hundred. Then say the Our Father skipping every second word. Our who in hallowed thy thy come . . .

When five to finally came, I went up the stairs two at a time and got the knife from under the mattress. It seemed even more shiny and cruel in daylight. Several old socks from the back of a drawer fitted neatly over the blade and I tied them on with a bootlace. Once mounted on the bike I strapped the knife to my leg, then rolled down the trouser leg over it.

Riding was tricky. Each time I brought my right knee up, the handle pushed against the inside of the trousers, like some sort of swelling that ballooned up and then went down. It felt strange other ways as well – me, carrying a concealed weapon, heading to the scene of a crime. Uncle Father John had never done anything like this during his year walking the streets of Dublin. But then I wasn't him. The knife would only be used to slash a few curtains, Presumer had said, and if nothing else would keep Paddy happy.

I should have left the house five minutes earlier. If I had, I wouldn't have met her. Or if I hadn't been thinking about the knife I'd have seen her coming and been able to dodge her. But I left at five past seven, and at nearly ten minutes past I saw her at the bottom of the hill, walking towards me in her neat little coat with her neat little arms swinging. For a couple of seconds I thought of steering up a side lane and sheltering behind the hedge until she'd gone. But that would have been stupid; and besides she'd already seen me. Nothing for it but to keep riding.

'Hello,' I said as we drew level. The last time we'd spoken, she'd just finished giving me her Judas kiss and was tearing off to make Francie take her home. But now, as usual she didn't even look near me. Kept her chin in the air and her arms swinging and went straight past, her nyloned legs siss-hissing against each other and her little black shoes going pock-pock-pock on the footpath. Letting the bike freewheel, I twisted round in the saddle and glanced back. The calves of her legs were bulging with each step she took, just like those girls on the bicycle that day with the mud flicking up on to them. Well-fed little calves, full without being fat. Attractive calves. Getting big and then getting small again. The odd thing was, looking at the calves made me feel good but thinking about Bernie herself made me feel bad. Irritated. Annoyed. Odder still, not liking her was somehow related to the attractiveness of her calves, winking back at me in turn. The more I disliked her the better they looked.

Just like leaving the house later, if I'd turned facing the front on my bicycle a second earlier, I'd have been OK. But I didn't. I was only half-turned back when the impact came and the sky turned into a blur of clouds and tree branches and railings. Then there was a tearing sound, and I was lying on my back on the footpath with a hot pain in my shoulder and the bike on top of my right leg.

Lie completely still. Because if I move my head from the pavement it will start to hurt, and my knee will hurt even more when I lift the bike wheel, and my shoulder is probably broken.

'What happened?' She was standing with her hands on her hips, frowning down at me as if I'd done something deliberately stupid. 'You must have crashed into the railings or something. How did you manage that? Are you hurt?'

I was going to have to stand up and talk to her. Tell her how a bit of dust had flown into my eye and the pain had been so great I'd had to close it, and then lost control. Or else say I hadn't been looking where I was going because I'd been twisted round staring at her calves.

'It doesn't matter.' I struggled out from under the bike. 'I'm fine. Not a hair the worse.' Instead of helping me by lifting the bike from on top of me she stood there. With at least three bits of me throbbing, I pushed the wheel aside and staggered upright. She pointed behind me.

'What's that?'

On the ground, beside the grass verge, the carving knife. With only one sock still on it, its curved tip glinting in the yellow-butter sunshine.

'That's. It's. My mother's. It's, her. Birthday tomorrow and I was taking her, taking *it* into Baldwin's to get sharpened. As a surprise.'

I put the loose sock around it again and tied it to the bar of the bike.

'Must have come off,' I added.

'Are you hurt?'

My shoulder was aching now and I could feel a bump on my head and one of my toes had no feeling. 'Topper,' I said. Then added, 'Maybe that was punishment.'

No smile. 'Are you for the concert?'

'No, no, no. I told you, I'm taking the—'

'You can't be going to Baldwin's,' she said, her head on one side. 'Baldwin's shuts at half-five. It's quarter past seven now.'

Speak. 'Here, are you serious? I thought they stayed open later than that. God.' I tried to smile. 'So where are you headed?'

'Meeting Francie.' She stopped for several seconds after saying it, as if just saying his name was some sort of magic that would begin to work in a minute. Then: 'He's awfully unhappy, you know. You see, *he* thought that when I asked him to collect me from the dance that time I was, you know, asking him to take me *home*. In a way yes I was, but . . . I didn't mean it the way he thought I meant it, and that of course got him awfully upset. About his vocation. Which is worrying, and that's why I'm going to see him. Meet him.' She nodded several times, agreeing with herself.

'Great.' *What the fuck was great about it?*

She squeezed her lips together and shook her head. 'If it's the last thing I do – *seriously* – I'm going to talk some sense into that boy. I'm certainly not going to let a vocation get damaged, because of a *misunderstanding*! So if you'll excuse me. Bye-bye.'

Ten yards up the road she turned and smiled, gave me a wave. All was forgiven. Seeing me crash into the railings and nearly stab myself had changed everything.

Twenty past seven. I swept round Bridge Street, pedalling hard. Presumer had said we should meet no later than quarter past, or we wouldn't have time to do what we wanted to do and still get out of there in time.

He was waiting up the lane a hundred yards from Neil's house, with Paddy standing beside him. About two feet away and looking a bit white-faced was Tommy. I braked and dismounted.

'I'll stick this machine in the undergrowth,' I said. That's what people did in books. 'Won't be a minute.'

'No rush,' Paddy said in a low voice. 'We're going no road.'

'Yes we are,' Presumer said. 'Don't listen to him. We definitely are.'

Paddy's face went red. He took two steps towards Presumer, arms partly raised. 'He can listen to me if he wants!' he shouted. 'You're not the only one round here can decide what happens, I can tell you that. Mr Big Balls.' Then he turned and walked to the back of the tree where he sat down. 'If you're so smart, go ahead on your own,' he called over his shoulder. 'See how far you get.' Tommy produced two butts and they started smoking.

Presumer took me by the arm and led me away a bit.

'What's eating him?' I asked.

'He wants to bring Tommy with him, and I said that'd be too many.'

'We don't need either of them. We could do it ourselves.' What was I saying?

'And if somebody comes on us? Wise up. Paddy's our safety net. Mr Respectable Family. Buffer Boy Paddy, if someone comes on us.'

'So OK – bring Tommy as well then. He's a respectable family. Two buffer boys – two Mr Respectables.'

'Tommy's a yap. He'd have half the countryside told.'

'More likely to keep shut up if he comes with us. Then if he squeals on us, he'll be squealing on himself.'

In the end I got Presumer cheered up, or cheered up enough to tell Tommy that if there was a cheep out of him when we were on the job, he'd go straight home, no questions asked, was that understood? Tommy grinned and said fair enough. 'Only bags carrying this,' he added, untying the knife from my handlebar.

Presumer held his hand out: 'Give.' Tommy rolled his eyes but passed it over. Then we hid the bike and went through the hedge, so we could approach Neil's house from the left.

The side gate into Neil's made a chinking sound and a blackbird began to yell in the rhododendron bushes. Presumer gestured to the shrubbery.

'We'll go through those and work our way round the back. Quietly.'

'Thought you said he was at the concert,' Paddy said. 'Bloody Neil.'

'We still play safe.'

It was like one of those jungle films, the leaves hissing as we moved through them, bits of twig sticking in our hair. Eventually the greenery ran out, leaving ten yards of open ground between it and the back of the house.

'OK, in turn,' Presumer said. 'Me first.' He sprinted from the bushes and crouched, panting, against the wall of the house, like a soldier in a war picture. I went next and then Paddy and Tommy.

The house was silent; all we could hear was our breathing and the bleat of a sheep somewhere. The back door was locked, but directly above it on the first floor a window with frosted glass – the bathroom, presumably – was open.

Tommy nudged Paddy and pointed. 'You make a stirrup with your hands. I get a grip on that light thing in the wall. I pull myself up, get on the porch roof and over to that window. Then—'

Presumer put his finger to his lips and pointed to the other side of the back porch. We tiptoed round, one behind the other. A dining-room table with eight chairs could be seen through a window. The bottom of the window was open six inches.

'See?' Presumer said. 'Easy as you go.'

It took a bit of tugging before the window was loose enough to be pushed up and let the four of us crawl in. The room smelt of polish. I was starting to close the window behind us when Presumer grabbed my arm and pointed. 'Getaway,' he mouthed.

That was when the dog started barking. He was locked in the outhouse nearest the back door and he was barking as if he'd had a bag of pepper shoved up his arse. Presumer tapped Paddy and pointed. We watched as Paddy climbed out of the window again and crossed the yard.

There was a hole in the outhouse door, a diamond shape to let the air in. Paddy stood with his face up against this, calling 'Tk-tk-tk-tk-tk' and giving little whistles. It sounded like the gypsy communication with horses I'd read about in comics. Only it didn't work. The dog stopped for about ten seconds, then began barking louder than ever. Paddy reached into his jacket pocket, took out a brown bag, lifted what looked like a chunk of liver from it, and pushed the liver through the hole in the door. Almost immediately the barking stopped. No sound now except some grunting/gobbling, and the thump of the dog's tail against the door.

Paddy climbed back into the room and raised his clenched fists above his head. 'Good night, Irene,' he sang softly. Even Presumer smiled.

In the hallway there was a grandfather clock and behind it a miniature Traynor coat of arms. The walls were hung with photographs of groups of people, usually with a priest standing or sitting in the middle of them. The biggest picture showed a huge hall with twisty pillars and the Pope being carried through a crowd on a chair. Neil was probably in the crowd but we hadn't time to search for him.

There were three doors leading off the hall. The first led into a kitchen with an Aga like ours only nicer and bigger; the second opened on to a press full of sheets and blankets. The third was to a smaller room with a glass case full of books, three straight chairs and a roll-down desk. The bushes and trees outside shaded the room and cast shadows on the walls and ceiling.

Paddy opened the front of the desk, which rattled and creaked as it was rolled back. Then he and Tommy began to investigate the drawers on either side.

Presumer tapped both of them on the shoulder and put his finger to his lips; then gestured for me to follow him. The carpet on the stairs was yellow-brown and thick; we both kept our hands off the banisters to avoid fingerprints.

The upstairs landing was really gloomy and dark. There were four doors, two on either side.

The first room was a woman's, or had been. You could tell that the minute you opened the door. It smelt of perfume and powder, but perfume and powder that might have been bought a long time ago and let get damp. There was a brown coat and a hat with an artificial feather in it on the back of the door. In the corner was a bed with a brass headrail and a metal crucifix on the wall.

The next room was Neil's. There was a smell here too, of soap and socks. Beside the bed was a po with a yellow memory of pee in it. The bed was a double with a big wooden headboard and four pillows. Under one of the pillows was a pair of blue striped pyjamas. The chest of drawers had some shirts and four pairs of long johns. On top of the chest of drawers were two hairbrushes with silver backs, stuck into each other.

There was a sudden burst of talk from downstairs, then a shout from Tommy.

'C'mere to you see this. Quick!'

We hurried down. Paddy led us to a small room, almost a cupboard, off the kitchen. Its walls were lined with hammers and nails and saws. In the corner was a box with straw in it, a saucer of water beside it. On the straw lay the cat we had carried over to Paddy's on New Year's Day, the one he complained had run away. It was bigger than I remembered it, no longer a kitten but stretched out like a cat jumping from one place to another. Even though its eyes were open it was clearly dead.

'Can you credit that?' Paddy said, pointing. 'Look what the bastard did to the poor cat.'

'Must have caught a disease,' Tommy said. 'Leprosy or something.'

'Cats don't get leprosy,' Paddy said sharply.

'Could be a medical first. Look, its whiskers are coming off.' Tommy leaned down and prodded the corpse with his toe.

'I really liked that cat,' Paddy said.

'It's a wonder Neil didn't at least bury it,' I said.

Presumer nudged the stiff tail with his toe. 'Not dead long. Probably last night or today.'

The cat's eyes were glazed and his fur looked a bit sticky – the way your hair goes if you don't dry it after you've had a bath.

'Here,' said Paddy, looking cheerful for the first time that day. 'I know what to do with it.'

'You can't do that,' Presumer said again to Paddy.

'Why not?'

'Because it's not right – not civilised. Look – I have the paint spray yoke, all right? We'll put red paint on the kitchen wall, and some on the living-room wall as well, if you like. And Jim here has that knife, you can have it to slice up some of his fancy curtains. Right, Jim?' I nodded uneasily. 'That'll be enough. We haven't time for anything more. There's not more than . . .' He looked at his watch '. . . fifteen minutes to get out.'

Paddy turned to Tommy and pointed dramatically at Presumer. 'Listen to this. This is the man who was talking about breaking people's necks less than a year ago. Remember? You told me you'd like to take Brother Dickey and shove a billiard cue up his hole and then break his neck. I remember you saying that one time.'

'We're not talking about Dickey. This is a dumb animal that can't even protect itself.'

'Because it's dead!' Paddy stuck out his chin, as if inviting a punch. 'There's nothing to protect when you're dead.'

'Anyway, this is more a kitten than a cat,' Presumer said. 'Only six months old.'

'For a human being that'd be forty,' Tommy said.

'It would not,' I told him.

'Look,' Paddy said. 'The cat is dead. OK? Waste not, want not.'

'Yes, but cutting it up! How would you like somebody to start chopping you up?'

'There's a quare difference being chopped up, between if you're a live human being or a dead cat.'

'Jesus, Paddy – are you a Hottentot or something?'

Paddy leaned forward, beaming. 'That's exactly it – that bastard Neil'll think it was a Hottentot, a right madman or something. Scare the shite out of the bastard. Take us only five minutes, whole thing. Spread that newspaper.'

Tommy opened an old *Sunday Independent* on to the kitchen floor and Paddy laid the cat on top of it. Then Tommy was sent to explore the shelves and came back with a chisel and hammer. Paddy took them from him and very carefully, very gently, laid the chisel edge against the cat's neck.

'You're not taking its head off with that chisel!' I yelled.

Paddy stared. 'Not all of it. We'll use your knife for the stringy bits.'

I turned away and closed my eyes. I could hear him tapping on the top of the chisel, a delicate chink-chink that might have been bells in a Chinese temple. Then Paddy's voice telling Tommy to hold the cat's head back while he got the chisel lined up.

There was a clank of hammer hitting metal, then a mutter of voices. 'Slip the edge in there – no, over a bit – that's it, on the Adam's apple. Bang on. Here we go.' There was silence, then a loud metallic crack, followed by two small steadying clinks, followed by two final heavy cracks.

'Right,' Tommy said.

'Job's a good one,' Paddy said.

I turned and looked. The cat's head was sitting six inches from its body, mouth open, eyes unwinking, on the edge of the newspaper. There was surprisingly little blood and little black veins straggled out like worms at the top. The knife lay on the newspaper, its wavy edge coated in red.

Tommy leaned his face up close to me. 'When you look in its eyes, you'd think it was alive, wouldn't you? "Whaddya wanna make those eyes at me for?"'

'No you wouldn't,' I said.

'Where do you think it is now?' Paddy asked. 'I mean, it must be somewhere.'

'In cat heaven,' Tommy said. 'Eating a million mice and riding a million . . . what do you call she-cats? . . . Mares or whatever.'

'Vixen,' Paddy said. 'Now. Will we wrap it up in clean paper and put it on Neil's mantelpiece?'

But just as he spoke we heard the sound of car tyres crunching on gravel. A car was coming up the lane. We crouched, fists clenched, mouths open, unable to move. Outside, the car engine snorted for a moment, then stopped. Two car doors slammed. Voices.

'Oh my God,' Tommy said. 'Oh Jesus Mary and Joseph. Oh Mammy, Daddy.'

Presumer led the sprint towards the dining-room window. 'He was supposed to be at the concert!' he said over his shoulder. 'Until nearly eleven at least. Bastard. And guess who's with him.'

Behind us we heard the front door open, feet in the hallway, then the same feet fading and voices from the front of the house again.

Presumer pushed the window up. It creaked but not too bad.

'Should I go back and collect the cat bits?' Tommy whispered to Paddy.

Paddy held up what looked like a ball of newspaper. Except the bottom of it was wet and red.

'Is that them all?' Presumer asked anxiously.

Paddy nodded. 'Most of them anyway.'

Presumer clambered through the open window, landing lightly.

'Hurry, for God's sake. Out!'

Panting, I followed him. Then Paddy. We waited as Tommy took a run and tried to vault out. He would have managed it if his left foot hadn't been trailing. It caught on the sill and he fell heavily forward, landing on his back on the ground outside the window.

'Oh suffering Jesus!' Paddy said, tugging him to his feet. We ran for the shrubbery, ten yards away, Tommy being helped on one side by Paddy and the other by Presumer. Just before we plunged into it I looked back. Framed in the white rectangle of the window from which we'd jumped I saw a face. Collette's face, expressionless, staring after us.

*

As soon as we got to the lane I retrieved my bike from the long grass and nettles and jumped on to it.

'Didn't even get wrecking the bloody place,' Paddy kept complaining. 'That's what we get for wasting time on that bloody cat.'

Presumer called after me in a low voice, something about seeing me tomorrow, but I hadn't time to ask what about. I stood on the pedals and whirled towards home, my breath coming in hot spurts. Was Mary's concert over? It was only nine o'clock, it couldn't be. Then why was Neil back from the concert so early? Maybe something had happened. Mary had had a heart attack, she'd taken a fit of coughing, she'd fallen off the stage and broken her leg, the audience had demanded their money back. What's more, as I pedalled for home, our car would come up behind me and Our Father would yell out the window to know what the hell I was doing out on a bike when I was supposed to have the toothache.

I leaned over the handlebars and drove the pedals down and round, down and round. Get an answer ready, quick, quick. 'I was in trying to get a dentist to open'? No, they'd ask which one. 'I find breathing fast helps it, so the best way to keep breath fast is ride the bike.' Mmm. Didn't breathing fast make a toothache worse? All right then – try something nearer the truth. 'I found the toothache seemed to have cleared up, so I went for a spin on the bike to test it out.' Test the bike or the toothache? Both. But mainly the toothache. And how is it? It's gone. Completely. I have no more toothache. It must have been psychosomatic. What? Psycho – all in my head. What hell else would a tooth-ache be only in your head?

But nobody caught up with me. Our house was quiet when I got back to it. By the time the back door opened at half-past ten, I had another chapter of *For Whom The Bell Tolls* read.

'You're looking better too,' Mammy said when I told her the toothache was gone. Her hand on my forehead was cool. 'Only you missed the nicest concert.'

'It was bully,' Our Father said. 'The best singing in twenty years. Especially that one near the middle. She was a topper.'

Maeve sat on the bench and slouched forward across the table. 'Anybody could sing that. We learnt it at school.'

'Learnt what?'

'Joseph Mary Plunkett's poem.'

'It's a song, not a poem.'

'Well it was a poem when we learnt at school. Isn't that right?'

Our Father kicked off his boots and stretched back in his chair. 'Poem, surely to God.'

'Well, all I know is, we sing it. Our whole class.' She stood with her hands by her side, her chin in the air and sang: 'I see his blood upon the rose.' Her voice was soft and quavery.

'My bully girl,' Our Father said, tapping her toe with his stick. 'Sing the whole shooting match.'

So Maeve did. She probably knew Our Father would give her something when she got to the end. So she stood even straighter, fixed her eye on the Dalgan Missions calendar above the cooker, and sang.

'I see his blood upon the rose
And in the stars the glory of his eyes

His body gleams amid eternal snow
His tears fall from the skies.

I see his face in every flower
The thunder and the singing of the birds
Are but his voice and carven by his power
Rocks are his written words.

All pathways by his feet are worn
His strong heart stirs the ever-beating sea
His crown of thorns is twined with every thorn
His cross is every tree.'

'Bully girl,' Our Father said again. 'Twice as good as
Mary O'Kane.' Maeve blushed and made a face at me,
probably because she knew she wasn't quarter as good
as Mary O'Kane. 'Now,' Our Father said, and gave her
sixpence from his pocket. I nearly laughed out loud.

'Mind you, Mary O'Kane was good too.' Mammy
carried in the coke bucket and emptied it into the Aga,
to keep it going all night. There was a flicker of blue and
a gassy smell. 'It was nice in the hall, with all the people
listening, and her leaving first thing tomorrow. "I see his
blood upon the rose." More a prayer than a song.'

'"Little Smasher" is miles better,' Maeve said. 'On
sale in Traynor's.'

Lying in bed, the only sound a distant horn beeping, I
saw Mary O'Kane, a tiny figure in the spotlight on the
stage. The hall was packed with people, hundreds and
hundreds of men and women smiling and putting their
arms around each other. And God leaned down through
the ceiling and put his arms around them, because
people had finally learned to look for him everywhere

and were being good. It wasn't until I woke the next morning that I thought of the big sharp knife from the dining room. We'd left the bloody thing on top of the newspaper in the middle of Neil's kitchen floor.

Send forth thy spirit and they shall be created. And thou shalt renew the face of the earth.

CHAPTER 16

Next day was Sunday. Coming out of Mass I walked slowly and listened carefully, but no one seemed to be talking about a cat with its head cut off or a knife that belonged in the drawer of our dining-room sideboard being got in Neil's. Boyce's shop was full of people smoking an after-Mass cigarette and pushing each other to get first to the counter for the newspapers. It took me nearly five minutes to buy the *Sunday Independent* and the *Sunday Press* for Our Father. As I squeezed my way out again I felt a hard punch on the shoulder. Paddy O'Kane, wearing a suit, his ginger eyebrows pulled together and his face pushed close to mine. When he speaks he keeps his teeth together, like a ventriloquist. 'Jail Square, three o'clock today. Meeting.' Then he hurries away, fists in his jacket pockets and shoulders hunched.

'Presumer has a book of mine,' I told Mammy after dinner. 'I'm just nipping in to get it off him.'

'What kind of book?'

'An English book – what odds what kind? I need it for revision.'

'What way you can't hold on to your books and have them when they're needed, I. Do. Not. Know. Let him get his own books. And stop you hanging about the Rat's Pad wasting your good time.'

Our Father looked up over the top of the *Sunday*

Independent. 'Far too much time-wasting goes on, as far as I can see.' He tugged the waist of his trousers. 'And these trousers of mine would need letting out. Far too tight on me.'

'Three fars,' Maeve said quietly and put a spoonful of apple tart and custard into her mouth.

My bike had a flat back tyre, so I walked into the town. The sun was shining and a lot of people were out for an after-dinner stroll. Pierre Fontin, the Frenchman with the limp that worked in Nestlé's, on his own as usual, whistling and bobbing along. Presumer claimed the song he whistled was a French one about women in the *Folies Bergère*, and he whistled it so any woman who knew French would get his signal that he was looking for a ride. Fifty yards behind him Appleton the retired Church of Ireland minister, who carries a blackthorn stick and stops to stare after you when you pass him. And women pushing prams, their husband and maybe another youngster a couple of steps behind, the husband usually looking fed up. It must be a front, that long face. Maybe the minute they were sure nobody was around they'd go sprinting for home, taking corners on two wheels. Burst in the door, stuff the wains with food and sweets and into bed, then tiptoe into their own bedroom, breathing fast, and rip every stitch off each other. They were married couples, for God's sake. *How could they be fed up?*

The other three were already waiting in the top corner of the Jail Square, hidden from the houses overlooking the square by a turret. Presumer, hands in his pockets, was staring down into the Show Grounds below. Paddy was lobbing pebbles into the blue emptiness above the wall and leaning over to watch them land halfway down the slope to the Show Grounds. Tommy was walking along the top of the wall, arms spread for balance, repeating 'Above zee lions' cage she vaaalks, zee lions look up and feel zee lion 'orn, ooh la lah.' Presumer nodded to me and we joined Paddy.

Tommy stood on the wall above us, peering down. 'Any word? About the knife?'

Presumer shook his head. 'Not yet. Maybe they won't find it. Though if people had looked after whatever they were using, we'd have no bother. You take it in, you take it out. That's the rule.'

'Right,' Paddy said. 'Except we weren't the ones took it in. And tell you another thing – next one says, or even *hints*, it was my fault, is asking for it. I'm telling you. I'm getting fed up with smart remarks.'

'I hope you don't mean me,' Tommy said. He was sitting on the wall now and had to lean forward, his chin above his knees, to see us standing directly beneath him. 'Because if you do, Paddy, I'm telling you now, I'd nothing to do with it. Right, Jim?' I said nothing. 'You and Presumer work it out. Jim and me had nothing to do with it. Right, Jim?'

'We *all* had something to do with it,' Presumer said. 'The thing is, what we're going to do about it now.'

'I hadn't. It wasn't my knife – I didn't ask anybody to bring it. It wasn't my knife,' Paddy said.

'But you used it,' Presumer said quietly. 'You had it last.'

Tommy began to laugh hysterically and Paddy's jaw tightened as he swung round. 'Shut your yap, Tommy!' He turned to Presumer. 'Never mind who had it last. It was your knife, and it was your fucking hard luck for bringing it in.'

'Hard,' Tommy said. 'Your hard luck, your fucking hard.' And he began to laugh again, the sound bouncing off the turret back to us.

Paddy reached up and grabbed Tommy's leg. 'Last time – I mean it. We're all in this, so shut your face.'

Tommy pulled his leg clear and stood on the wall. Began to move carefully along it, arms out. 'No we're not. You are, I'm not. Nor Jim. You're the one cut up the cat. Your idea too – we said not to, you wouldn't listen. Admit it.'

'There's no point in saying who did what,' Presumer told him. 'The thing is, what should we do now.'

Tommy turned and moved back towards us. 'All I'm saying is, the ones that did it, they have to put it right, not start trying to involve people who didn't do it. Simple as fucking pie, the whole thing.'

'You're as simple as fucking pie,' Paddy told him, teeth clenched. 'Shut your face.'

'OK, OK, quiet down, everyone,' Presumer said. 'What I think we should do is, we should just go back and check for it. Neil will be out at bridge tonight. It might be just sitting there somewhere.'

'Playing bridge with the horsey woman and that doctor bastard,' Tommy said. He took six steps away from us along the wall again, then turned. 'See when I had appendicitis? That doctor bastard examined me. And know what he did? Stuck his finger up my arse. Swear to God.'

'Never mind your arse,' Presumer told him. 'We need to get organised here.'

Paddy stood in front of Presumer and began to give him little shoves in the chest. 'At it again, eh? Handing out orders to everybody, eh? Well here's what I think of you and your orders.' Presumer ducked as Paddy's right hand came towards him, but Paddy was expecting him to do that. His left fist, already cocked, caught Presumer hard on the mouth. He staggered backwards, kept staggering until the wall stopped him. Tommy scrambled into a sitting position directly above him.

'Fight, fight!' Tommy chanted. 'Ringside seats a bob!'

Paddy, boxer fists in front of his face, shuffled forward again. He hit Presumer with a hook, this time in the stomach; then swung his left fist, twice in quick succession, hard into the ribs. But the third time he swung Presumer jumped aside, grabbed Paddy's shirt-front and pulled him in against the wall. A bit like the way Christy had done with me, the time she kissed me outside her house. Now their positions were reversed, with Paddy's back to the wall and Tommy's feet dangling near his ear.

'Go get him, Paddy,' Tommy said, and giggled as he nudged Paddy's head with a sandalled foot. Paddy flinched but kept watching Presumer. 'Put his teeth down his throat,' Tommy urged and tapped Paddy's ear with the white-ribbed sole of his sandal. Tommy's mouth was still open laughing when Paddy dropped his fists, turned and grabbed Tommy's foot, and pushed upwards.

For a moment Tommy was lifted into the air, like a circus acrobat about to do a back flip. Then he began to scrabble with both hands and feet to get a grip on the top of the wall, but it was too late. His centre of balance tipped, his two sandalled soles did a quarter arc, just missing Paddy's face; then his feet and the rest of him were gone, out of sight behind the wall. It seemed quite a long time before we heard the thud.

'Jesus,' Presumer whispered, his face white. 'What'd you do that for?'

There were two exams on Monday and one every remaining day that week. Each day was worse than the one before. At quarter past seven Mammy would open the bedroom door, knocking on it at the same time and calling, 'Rise now if you don't want to be late for your exams!' I did want to be late – so late the school would be locked and there'd be a moon over it by the time I arrived. My wrist ached from writing, my shoulder blades were stiff from hunching over the answer-paper, and a kind of buzz seemed to be going through my body. Bmmmmmm-mmmm.

Each morning Our Father took me into school in the van, in case I got tired or was caught in the rain and had to sit in the exam hall all day in damp clothes. And because I was getting a lift, Maeve had to get one too. All the way in she kept saying I should have exams all year round, she hated walking to school. Our Father just cleared his throat and told me to sit away from the handle on the passenger door or I'd cope out on my head and get killed, and for Maeve not sit on his good trousers that he was taking in to Hutton's to get taken in. Maeve gave her yelp of a laugh and said the good thing about being killed was, I wouldn't have to do the exams. I ignored her and so did Our Father.

After each exam I walked down the schoolyard and as far as the Rat's Pad with Presumer. Sometimes we talked about the questions on the paper, how tricky, how *unfair* they had been. But mostly we just smoked and looked around at the buildings and walls and people that never had to bother with exams. The first day neither of us mentioned what had happened to Tommy in the Jail Square. But on the second day it couldn't be kept in any more.

'It's not as if he broke his back,' Presumer said. 'He could have wrecked his back falling that distance.'

'Almighty says his arm will have to be in plaster all summer. Your man Paddy's not right in the head. Tommy could easy have been killed.'

'Miracle. The thing now is, though, Paddy didn't do it.'

I could hardly believe he'd said it. 'Sure I saw him doing it. So did you.'

Presumer laughed. 'He says now he was nowhere near the Jail Square.'

'Who told you this?'

I tried asking him more but he shook his head, grabbed an imaginary guitar. 'Here comes summer, dwang-de-dwang-de-dwang-de-dwang.' He was right too. There was a heat in the air that got you between the shoulder blades. Birds were poking around looking for bread or insects or whatever stuff it was their young ate. The sun made the grass waxy-looking and my clothes sticky, the hedges gawky with growth.

But I didn't dare take my mind off exams for more than a few minutes. After tea each evening it was straight upstairs to look through my notes and books for the next day. Dates, names, plots, characters, three key points. Then at ten or half-ten a cup of tea and the rosary before falling into bed. Scenes from the novel re-enacted themselves, kings and prime ministers from history peered in my face and asked me was I asleep yet. Then after a short plunge into a pool of sleep, Mammy would be at the bedroom door calling for me to get up before I was late and be sure to splash plenty of cold water round my face and ears.

After the last exam on Friday there was no sign of Presumer. Dickey was at the bottom of the schoolyard, walking back and forward in the sun reading his prayer book. He glanced up and nodded as I passed. Was that an accusing look? A threatening glance? I did my best to smile.

At home Maeve was sitting sideways in Our Father's chair, her legs over the arm. Cait was seated at the table, her front slouched over it.

'A canary,' Maeve said, not looking at me. 'That's what I'd like. A wee yellow yoke. You can teach them tunes, you know.'

Cait put her right cheek on the oilcloth and spoke with her eyes closed. 'Mmm. Teach it to shout "Murder! Police!" if you were attacked. Guard bird.'

'Or a cat maybe,' Maeve said. 'All silky and you'd be able to feel the bony bits under its skin any time you stroked it. I'd like that.'

'Only you'd have a duty as its owner to protect your cat,' Cait said, opening her eyes and sitting up again. 'See if anybody tried doing anything to my cat? I'd get my daddy to them.'

'You don't have a cat.'

'*If* I had. *If*.' Cait stroked her chin as if she had a beard. 'Some people hate cats, you know. You get the vibes off them when they come into a room. Queer types.'

'What's vibes?'

'Vibrations. All shaky like a car that won't start. In fact' – Cait patted her right cheek and then her left, staring out the window as she did so – 'I think I feel the vibes this minute.'

Maeve glanced quickly at me, her cheeks red and bulging as she tried not to laugh. I wanted to lean down and shake her until her teeth rattled and her hair fell around her face.

'Know what I heard?' Cait asked Maeve, still talking as if I wasn't there. 'That a certain person took a cat and put a knife in its guts and killed it. And then he cut its head off, and tied it on a string, hung it from the ceiling like an apple at Halloween for biting into. That's what I heard. Swore I wouldn't say who told me, but I can believe it. Can't you?'

'Course I can.'

I'd begun to think about Cait's face and a hurley stick, only just as I started there was the sound of slow footsteps on the stairs. Maeve jumped up and sat beside Cait and waited as Our Father came into the kitchen. His hair was twisted, with hollows and spikes that would take ages of brushing and spitting to get out. Then Mammy came in the back door from feeding the hens and made him a mug of tea.

'You'd be as well to mind yourself,' he said to me, sitting back in his armchair with a cream cracker and cheese halfway to his mouth. 'If you were swimming and some Kyo-boy sinking, you'd steer clear of him, wouldn't you? For fear you'd be pulled down.'

'But sure Jim wouldn't be involved in any bad thing. With Kyo-boys or any other boys.' Mammy put another two cream crackers and a silver triangle of cheese on Our Father's plate.

'I can do the breaststroke and the overarm,' Cait said. 'I'd rescue him.'

Our Father didn't seem to hear her. 'If they tried to grab you you'd kick free.' He beat his chest briefly to knock some crumbs off. 'And if they tried to pull you down, you'd tell people who they were.'

Mammy began to sweep the kitchen floor, starting with the crumbs at Our Father's feet. Stopped and leant on the shaft. 'Everybody knows that Jim's no corner boy. So don't youse be making him out to be one.' She went on sweeping.

'But he wouldn't tell!' Maeve squeaked, leaning across the table. 'You asked him that time and he said he was involved in a thing and then he wouldn't tell who with.'

'Hold you your tongue!' Our Father said loudly.

Mammy picked Cait's coat off the hook by the door. 'Throw this on you, Cait dear – your mammy will be wondering what's happened. Maeve will walk the length of the lane with you and get me a loaf on the way back.' She produced her purse and gave Maeve a shilling. 'And buy Cait and yourself some wee thing with the change.'

When they had gone out, Mammy stood in front of the Aga with folded arms. Our Father stroked his eyebrows a couple of times and tapped his stick on the floor.

'This is a damn serious business. What kind of blurt are you, didn't tell us what you were up to, long before this?'

'What?'

'You knew we'd be worrying,' Mammy said. 'You knew we'd be tormented worrying.'

'Breaking into people's places like a gangster. Half-killing that young Tommy boy.' Our Father stood up and walked over to me. The sides of his mouth glistened with spittle. 'Who was with you? Eh? Don't think you're too big for a whaling. For you're not, I may tell you. Did you know the police was here today enquiring? Did you know that?'

Mammy came over and stood between us. 'Hold your tongue, for goodness' sake,' she told Our Father. 'Talking about hitting the child and him man big.' She went over to the press and took out a set of rosary beads – my old beads, that I used until I was about thirteen. 'Put you them in your pocket or round your neck. For to protect you from harm.' Her hand checked the hairpins in her bun. 'And from bad company of all sorts. It's the truth what the Almighty says – there's lions and tigers every road, seeking whom they may devour.'

Our Father had risen and was moving to the window, leaning heavily on his stick. Behind the shed two cats were fighting, their snarls and screeches coming in faint bursts.

Mammy looked up and seemed to address the picture of the Sacred Heart. 'It was that Livingstone creature, wasn't it? That's the one put you up to it.'

Say nothing. Make no sign. Sit there and think about Presumer searching for Sean, think about the crowbar we'd buried, think about the way he'd sung 'Davy Crockett' when we tried to get into the operetta.

'And don't sit there acting the smart buck – we know rightly what happened,' Our Father half-shouted. 'Don't we? Do you hear me talking to you?' But I still said nothing. If you have friends you have to stand by them.

Saturday and Sunday of that weekend were even worse than Friday. I wanted to ask them for money for the pictures but there was no point thinking about that if I still wouldn't tell them who was with me doing the cat thing. So instead I sat and let pictures of Christy and Collette float around in my mind. And then through the pictures, clear and hard, a thought hit me. Maybe Collette had told the police what she had seen, and who she had seen. And making matters worse and more complicated, Paddy was saying he was nowhere near the Jail Square and if Paddy was saying that, Tommy must be backing him up. So maybe keeping quiet was a waste of time.

It was half-nine on Monday and I was in the bathroom shaving, looking at a twist of blood worming down my chin, when I heard Mammy answer the phone: 'Hell-ooo?' Then 'Yes, Brother. Indeed, Brother. Yes. Yes, all right.' And then. 'Not at all. Right. Not at all, I'll tell him surely.'

It was a message from Brother Dickey, she called through the bathroom door. I was to report to him at eleven o'clock.

He was sitting at his table at the front of the empty classroom, filling in the roll-book. I couldn't tell if he was making up the little lines and circles in the squares as he went along or if he was copying it out from another book that I couldn't see. But his fingers seemed bigger and thicker than the nice fountain pen they were holding, and I could see little hairs sprouting on the back of his hand. He waved to a chair against the wall without looking up.

For the next fifteen minutes I just sat there. During that time he grunted when he saw something he didn't like, got up to pull a window closed with the help of a long pole, blew his nose into the white hanky he took from up his soutane sleeve, polished his glasses with a little light-brown cloth, put his hand in his soutane pocket and scratched his arse while leaning forward to read a sheet of paper on the table, tapped a tuning fork on the desk and held it to his ear before saying 'Mmmm', and then put all the papers and books on his desk into one neat pile at the top of the left-hand corner. When he'd all that done he pushed back his chair and looked at me over his glasses.

'Well then.'

Immediately I could feel my lips and eyes crinkling as if I was going to cry. What was going on? And was that my lip shaking? And of course my cheek had begun to throb. Dickey stood up, put his hands in his soutane pockets and then joined them behind his back. Started to walk up and down the room.

'Well, well, well. It's past time we had a talk. Mmmh?'

He opened a drawer in the cupboard, took out a tin box, removed a black cigarette with a gold strip at the mouth, lit it and exhaled a jet of grey smoke.

'These are Russian,' he said, holding the cigarette up and looking at it. 'Only right when you think of it. A Godless country producing black cigarettes. You don't smoke, do you?'

'No, Brother.'

'Glad to hear it. A bad habit, smoking.' He tapped his cigarette, then set it on the lid of the tin. Joined his fingertips and looked at me over the top of them.

'And bad habits, like bad companions, are easier taken on than got rid of. A damn sight easier. Some people, though, don't need bad companions to start up bad habits. For they've badness in their blood. You understand?' I nodded, even though I wasn't sure. 'Good.'

He resumed pacing, kicking a small piece of chalk under the cupboard as he passed it. His soutane flew out behind him, showing grey socks and a slice of turkey-white leg.

'Your own case, now, is different. By a long chalk. For you have the best of blood and the best of futures. And the best of parents, giving you nothing from Day One only quality example, Sunday Mass and the sacraments, the whole good and necessary spiritual diet. Anything that could be done for you, was done. That's what makes this whole thing such a damn shame.'

He turned away and stood staring out the window, as if expecting someone or something to come out of the bright morning air towards us both.

'This isn't betrayal. Let's get that out the way. If there's betrayal *at all*, it's a betrayal of *not* speaking up, rather than speaking. Not joining the ranks of those that are trying to put order and decency in the world. If you're looking for a betrayal that's where it is. If anywhere.'

He turned and came towards me until he was directly in front, blocking the view. Stood rocking his weight from one foot to the other, like Paddy bobbing and bouncing in front of the punchball, alert and relaxed at the same time. He even seemed to be smiling, although I couldn't be sure, because the window was so bright behind his head.

'The thing is, we know what happened. We know that only too well. There was at least one witness, although if . . .' He stopped and sighed. 'One witness, and what we now need is a voice added to that, saying "Yes that's right, I was there too and I can tell you that's exactly what happened." That's what we need – a corroborating voice. A good word for a good thing – corroborating. It's simply a matter of names – or name verification, rather. And I'm just a hundred per cent sure you're the boy can provide it.'

I stared at the floor between my knees and stayed that way. Collaborator? That sounded wrong. Brother Dickey began to walk up and down again. 'Names,' he said. 'Names, names, names. Words, words, words.'

I tried not to move. Kept my head steady, thought of it being held by a vice with padding on the inside so it didn't hurt, but holding me steady, steady as a rock so nothing in my head or my body or my face gave me away, or worse still, far worse, gave Presumer away. After what seemed a long time, Brother Dickey started walking again.

Watching his big shiny arse like a camel's hump moving away from me, the whole thing suddenly became clear. This was all a cod. Dickey was toying with me. He'd already talked to Collette and probably Neil, and God knows how many neighbours, so there were plenty of people – even Maeve and Cait, for God's sake – who knew what had happened. So he really had no right to be picking on me and asking me to say what had happened and who had been with me.

> *Tell the names of your companions,*
> *And other things we wish to know.*
> *Turn informer and we'll free you*
> *Kevin Barry answered, 'No'.*

Now Dickey was whistling quietly as he walked. It wasn't 'Kevin Barry' – it was some fiddly classical thing, notes going all over the place at different speeds. My toecaps when I stared down at them were well-polished for once, the little feathery scuffed bits plastered down into the black leather, like hair that's been well Brylcreemed.

'The danger is, something as ugly as this whole matter could end in a court of law.' Dickey's voice was deeper now. The judge in that film what was it, putting on the black cap and talking through his nose, the sound echoing round the high-ceilinged room, putting the fear of death on everyone. 'Because it's more than a question of breaking and entering, isn't it? It's violence. Not to mention that carry-on with that unfortunate animal. Takes the breath away a bit, that. Some might say . . . Black Mass tendencies, or next best thing. Not to mention the assault in the Jail Square. A potentially murderous assault.' He wheeled away as if frightened by his own words, and paced up and down between the desks. Then stopped opposite me again, nodding. 'Court cases nobody wants. People called on to give an account of their movements. Character witnesses. Boys' mothers and fathers – if they have fathers – dragged into the whole sorry business.' He tugged his Adam's apple. 'Pulling decent people, your own flesh and blood, through the mill. That'd be a shocking thing to do, wouldn't it?'

I could see what he was trying. A bright blob of sunlight lay on the window sill behind him, like the light the detectives used to shine in Mickey Rooney's eyes. Could I plead the Fifth Amendment? No, no. I *wouldn't* give up. Because this was temptation. I was Adam or maybe Eve, and Dickey was the snake. And he was offering me an apple, the kingdoms of the world or whatever. But I was no more going to slide into that trap than I was going to write Presumer's name in six-foot capital letters on a wall somewhere. Or Paddy's, or

Tommy's. It was like Kevin Barry, only now it was a spiritual thing. God was testing me, giving me a chance to resist the Evil One.

I must have closed my eyes for a second to think about that, because the next thing Dickey's face was inches from mine. He was down on his hunkers, so close I could hear his breathing, little whistles at the back of it, as if something was wrong with his lungs. And I remembered the way he'd panted when he'd thumped Presumer all around the stage that night, and I pulled back a bit in case he'd start swinging and knocking the tar out of me as well and I'd get sick in his wastepaper basket and the caretaker would find it in the morning.

But he wasn't going to hit me. He was smiling, leaning his face towards mine, so I could see the spittle shiny on his teeth, and the holes and red veins on his nose, and the little feathery hairs where the light hit his ears.

'Who was with you in Mr Traynor's?'

It jumped out, like a coughing tap, like the pup between my legs, before I could stop it. 'Livingstone.'

'Mmmyes.' It was as if he was pausing to write the name down, except he was still staring at me, his face closer than ever. If I got any closer I'd vanish into his eyes or up his nose. 'And who else?'

'Tommy. Paddy.'

'I see. And in the Jail Square? Just two of you, right? Livingstone was there, wasn't he? You and Livingstone and that poor young lad Tommy. Just the three of you?'

I nodded, felt tears springing in shame.

When I looked up he was nodding at me, the breath coming out of his nose in a little soft rasp of relief. In my guts a half-pound of butter had begun to melt, and all the parts of me that had been raw and dry and grating were now nicely lubricated by the melting butter with its little yellow bubbles.

Dickey straightened, one of his knees making a cracking sound.

'Good man. That's that. Now help me tidy up.'

And he made me lift boxes of exercise books that were piled up in cardboard boxes inside the door and carry them across to the other side of the room, where he put them neatly into presses ranged up to the ceiling. Then he got me to empty and wash all the inkwells. Some of them had bits of paper stuck inside them, that had to be got out with a little thin screwdriver he kept in a special locked drawer. And when I'd that done he got me to sweep half the classroom while he did the other half.

He didn't say a word all the time we were working except for orders, and he didn't really talk at the end either, except to tell me I could go now.

I was halfway out the road home again, with the sun still fresh and high in the sky, and the hedges pushing out big awkward shoots of thorn that tugged at my jacket as I walked past, before the peaceful feeling began to sour. At first it was a wrinkle, and then it turned into a crease, and before I got as far as McCauley's garden wall that had an up-and-down edge like a castle wall, it was a blade going in and out of my chest. It felt so rotten, if nobody had been around I might have lain down in the insecty grass at the side of the road and curled my knees up to my chest and groaned. But there were people about, men with their jackets off, women carrying their cardigans, children sucking ice lollies. So I gritted my teeth and kept walking.

'I don't care if they call you Lundy or not,' Debbie

Reynolds whispered, and she slipped her hand inside my trousers pocket and tickled my right ball. 'You only did it to protect your family. Didn't you?'

And Judas went forth and hanged himself.

CHAPTER 17

I really didn't go out much for the next week. Suddenly, after weeks of it, I didn't have to get up at seven in the morning to squeeze in another half-hour of revision. I didn't have to go in the car with Our Father and then sit in an exam hall driving my hand across the page, paragraph after paragraph. And I didn't need to hurry home and do more revision until, my head full of snakes, I crawled into bed. I had Nothing. To. Do. It felt good.

The morning after I'd spoken to Dickey, I woke at quarter past seven, force of habit I suppose. Groaned, pulled a wadge of sheet and blankets between my knees, rolled over, thought what Debbie Reynolds would look like if that little skirt thing in *Singing In The Rain* was taken off, and slept for another two and a half hours.

The days that followed were a half-awake dream. I wandered through the fields along by the river. Took the old football and kicked it against the side of the boiler-house wall. Ff-wump. Ff-wump. It felt good letting all the energy and strength in me transfer to the ball, and for it then to hammer itself against the whitewashed wall, lifting little flakes on impact. When I got fed up doing that I lay on top of my bed and re-read the last bit of *For Whom The Bell Tolls*, where Robert Jordan hid behind the tree with his gun and waited for the enemy soldiers. And then at night when I went to bed, I'd switch on Radio Luxembourg and listen to the Top

Twenty records, Little Richard and Adam Faith ('Wish you wanted my love – buy-bee!') and Cliff Richard and Connie Francis. Until it was one or even two in the morning, and the book in my hand began to sag or my eyes felt grainy . . .

It was good, but I couldn't keep the questions out of my head. What was happening? Had Presumer and Paddy and Tommy been arrested? Would I be arrested? And most of all I kept thinking: why had I told Dickey who was with me, in Neil's *and* the Jail Square?

I couldn't get an answer to that. It had just . . . happened. Like when you were small, and one minute you were in a dream and the next minute you'd peed the bed. It just . . . happened. But that didn't mean I didn't feel rotten about it, and dirty, and frightened even. That time I'd thought about taking Christy to see the crowbar Presumer had hidden – I hadn't done it. But now I'd practically told the police about him. And Tommy and Paddy. Maybe Paddy would come round and hammer the life out of me, the way he'd done with that punchball. Maybe I'd end up in court, in the dock beside them. I half-remembered a picture where the guy who told on the others got off, but then some others cornered him in an alley with water running down the walls and shot him dead.

The days drifted by like this until Wednesday of the next week. It was the middle of the afternoon and I was sitting on the second branch from the top of the big tree in the hill field. I could see right across the river, to where the Army had its soldiers training. They were doing some sort of exercises, wearing brown shirts and shorts and calling to each other. I could see the two spires of the chapel and the smaller spire of the

Protestant church – even our smaller spire was taller than their single spire. Some sheep were grazing on the sloping field on the other side of the river, and when I looked left I could see the Drumquin hills, blue and dreamy. To the right the hedges on either side of our lane ran like thin green streams down to the Derry Road. And as I looked, a figure on a racer bike swung at speed off the Derry Road, into our lane, and came pedalling fast towards me. Almighty.

'Goes like lightning,' he called up, one foot on the ground and the other on the right pedal. 'Only three minutes coming out here. Got it for my birthday.' He put the bike carefully against the trunk of the tree. 'Can I come up?'

It took him nearly five minutes to get high enough up to speak to me without shouting. Even then he was gripping the branch with both hands and talking in breathless bursts. I came down to his level and sat on a branch opposite him.

'It's dangerous, climbing these things, my daddy says,' he panted. 'A body could kill themselves.' I thought what it would be like to fall from a tree, bouncing off branches, crashing through some others, finally reaching the ground with a terrible thump, breaking my spine. Then Almighty said, 'Hear about Presumer?' and if I hadn't been holding on firmly, each hand gripping a separate branch, I might have started that fall.

Presumer, Almighty said, was going away. To England. 'He broke into our house when we were away, my daddy says, and killed three cats. Chopped them up and stuck bits of them into flowerpots all round the house. The smell on its own was ferocious, my daddy said, never mind the mess. Your woman Collette came on him doing it, planting one of the paws in a thing for geraniums. And then he kidnapped your man Tommy and took him up to the Jail Square and threw him over the wall – you not hear about that? Could have killed him, only broke his arm, lucky enough, but God-almighty. Mad, he is. Never done threatening people. The police were going to arrest him, only my daddy said because his mother was, you know, sick sort of, and because of his wee brother being lost and everything, they should go easy and be merciful. So he has a week to pack and go to England.'

I stared out between the branches, breathed the tangy green smell of the leaves. The hills were still dreamy and blue, the soldiers were still yelling and rushing around dismantling guns, the blackbird in the hedge below us was still sending notes wobbling out like floating ribbons. Inside a week. This day next week he'd be miles from Omagh.

'Was anybody with him? Anybody else . . . involved?'

It came our jerky and nervous, even though I'd tried to sound casual. Almighty looked up at me for a minute without speaking.

'If I tell you what my daddy said, do you swear never to say? I mean, Godalmighty, if he knew I told you he'd murder me.'

My word is my bond. I nodded to Almighty.

'Well, my daddy says there might have been a couple of others, but the police said if there were, they weren't to blame, because Presumer is a born ringleader and troublemaker, you'd know to look at him even. So he's the one has to clear off. Any other boys that might have been involved would have been decent boys really, my daddy says. He knows their families.'

After that Almighty gave me a couple of goes on his bike, in and out the lane. The tyres were thin like greyhounds and the handlebars shiny and light, and when I bent my head and pedalled, the wind whistled round my ears and sometimes bungled into them.

'It's brilliant.'

'I know.' He stood looking at me. 'Presumer says it was probably Foxy tipped them off he was in Neil's.'

I nodded. 'Our Maeve says his eyes roll all over her every time she goes into his shop. So I wouldn't put it past him.'

Almighty tucked his trouser-ends carefully into his socks and mounted the bike. 'All over her?' I nodded and he sucked in his breath. Then he leaned back in the saddle and lifted the front wheel so the pedal was in the right position for starting. 'Fixed front wheel on her,' he said, pointing.

I plucked a blade of grass and chewed the juicy end. 'When's Presumer for away?'

Almighty lowered the front wheel and went wobbling along the lane, picking up speed. 'Tomorrow after dinnertime,' he called over his shoulder. 'Bus for Larne and then the boat for England.' I was turning into the house when his shout came faintly after me: 'And remember, I never told you nothing!'

When I told them Presumer was going away, Maeve said nothing, just bent over her nails and began to paint them with varnish from a bottle. Mammy said good riddance to bad rubbish, and Our Father said long runs the fox. I went down to the room with the wireless in it and listened to Workers' Playtime and thought hard about what to do and in the end decided the best thing to do was let fate unfold. Let tomorrow come and then tomorrow pass, because every day came and went anyway, no matter how much you were mad about it or frightened by it or having a good time. So wouldn't tomorrow do the same?

But next morning, instead of being at home setting snares or kicking a ball, I was standing outside Presumer's house. Didn't have to think about it – just found myself there as if I was a robot that had been wound up and sent there. The Rat's Pad was quiet but I saw the odd curtain move, the odd head pull back into the darkness again. Knock. No sound for a while, then suddenly the top half of the door pulled open and there was Presumer cradling a gun, the barrel pointed at my chest.

I shouted something and cowered back, my fists against my chest, as if that might save me. Presumer lowered the gun and laughed. 'Not even loaded. Useless even if it was – giving it to Paddy for a going-away present. With a bit of luck he'll end up shooting Tommy *and* himself. And if we're *really* lucky that bastard Foxy too.'

He propped the gun against the dresser and waved me indoors. His hair looked longer, with a parting at the side, and he was wearing a shirt and tie.

'You look – like somebody else.'

'Ma made me wear the tie.' He closed the door after us. 'Said people would give out about her not looking after me, if I didn't.'

He bustled around whistling, mixing the tunes together, sometimes sliding from 'The Gypsy Rover' to 'She Wears Red Feathers'. As he whistled he repositioned items in the suitcase, squeezed in another pair of socks and a towel.

I cleared my throat. 'I'm sorry.'

He turned slowly, a pair of socks, one tucked into the other, in his right hand. 'What for?'

'The – the way things have worked out.'

He laughed, continued packing. 'It's not how they worked out – it's the way things are, that's all. If it hadn't been this, it'd have been Dickey stopping me doing the exams. Or something.' He turned and pushed his neck forward, stuck out his lower lip and made his eyes bulge like Almighty. 'That wee shite, though. Eh? You couldn't be up to him.' He continued cramming clothes into the suitcase. Then: 'Hear about Collette? Left yesterday for England.'

'Maybe you'll catch up with her.'

'Maybe. She's going to join Fossett's Circus.' He went into his bedroom and came back with a razor and shaving brush.

'What time's the bus?'

'Ten to eleven. Sean and my ma are away buying me polish and *Time* magazine. I'm to meet them at the bus depot.'

He put the suitcase on the floor, leant his fists on its lid. The case creaked and closed, the catches looking as if they might burst open any minute. On the sofa he had a brown parcel tied with cord, his name on the side. He picked up the parcel, which left me the suitcase. It felt as if it had a block of cement inside.

Half-doors opened as we made our way down the Rat's Pad, women leaned forward, arms folded, eyes watchful. 'Away, are you, son? Mind yourself, now.' An upstairs window opened and a girl's head appeared.

'Yoo-hoo, Gerard!' she yelled, before being replaced by another head with pigtails and a waving arm. 'Yoo-hoo!'

Presumer gave a little sigh. 'Yoo-hoo now. When I was here they wouldn't look near me.' But he still waved up, blew kisses towards them.

As we approached the chapel Father Breen emerged from the darkness of the porch, stood waiting for us with folded arms.

'What's this I see – not another emigrant son?'

'Surely to God, Father – on the boat for England,' Presumer said, smiling and blinking faster than usual. 'The tears near sprouting already.'

Father Breen looked serious. 'Not at all, not at all. Sure England's a powerful country. The best people you'd meet, the English – better than our own, a lot of them. Worked there for three years myself.'

'Is that a fact, Father. How many of them would you say were better?'

'Well, now, that's just what's called a figure of speech. A lot. So. Have you got a spot to stay itself?'

'My Auntie Clarissa,' Presumer said. 'Widow woman on her own. Glad to take me in.'

Father Breen nodded. 'That's the way. Blood thicker than water again, you see. Clarissa. A widow. Right now. And what part did you say you were headed for?'

'Didn't say, Father. But I'm headed for the part called Blackpool.'

'Couldn't have picked a nicer place. A chum of mine, Father Doherty, is stationed there. The pair of us soldiered together in Maynooth. In fact . . .' He rooted in an inside pocket, took out a small leather-backed notebook. 'His address here some road if I'm not mistaken. Doherty.' He flicked through the pages, frowning. 'Dougan, Donaghy . . . There now. Father Tony Doherty, PP – they make them PPs a lot younger there, you'll find. Address and all. A sound man, Father Doherty.' He wrote out the address and gave it to Presumer.

'Powerful stuff, Father. I'll be up hammering on his door first thing tomorrow.'

'The afternoon might be better, I dare say. Don't forget your Mass and sacraments now, whatever else. First things first.' He shook hands and patted Presumer's shoulder.

Presumer's mother was coming up the steps from the Ladies' Public toilets, a shopping bag in one hand and Sean by the other.

'Divine Diarrhoea,' Presumer said. 'Jesus meets his blessed mother.'

Mrs Livingstone said nothing. Just passed a tin of polish and *Time* magazine to Presumer, who put them in his overcoat pocket. Then fell into step beside Presumer, her head down, Sean's hand still gripped. When people saw the four of us coming – Presumer, Mrs Livingstone, Sean and me – they stood back into shop doorways and stared. It was like *High Noon*.

At the junction with Bridge Street, a figure scurried across the road.

'I guessed you'd be coming for this bus,' Almighty panted. 'Had this feeling. Was in the kitchen playing patience when something inside said to me, "He'll be going on the next bus." So ran down here, and I was right. It's a gift, my daddy says. A sixth sense.'

'Any sense is better than none,' Presumer said.

'You're a lucky duck, ask me,' Almighty told him.

'The rivers in Scotland are the best in the world for fishing, my daddy says. He says my granda took him fishing in Scotland and some day he's going to take me.'

'I don't fish.'

'And Blackpool's near as anything to Scotland. Only you have to have a licence. How long do you think you'll stay in England?'

'Three years is the arrangement,' Presumer said. 'More or less. Although your da could probably tell you better than me. Mother MacCree here is coming to visit me – aren't you, MM?' Mrs Livingstone looked towards him briefly but didn't speak. We crossed the road and went through the gate saying 'Omagh Bus Depot'.

Almighty pointed. 'Dee-pott. It's a French word but you're supposed to pronounce it the English way. Dee-pott. Like garridge.'

'Who told you that?' Presumer asked.

'Don't need telling things like that – you just *know*. Dee-pott. There's a right and a wrong way of doing everything.'

I prodded his ribs with my elbow: 'Almighty, Presumer's going to England. Shut your trap.'

'I know where he's going. That's why I'm saying stuff about depots. Dee-potts. To cheer him up.'

'How's that supposed to cheer him up? Snap your trap for once, would you.'

'Well, that's where you and me is different. At least I try to help people.' He put one hand on his stomach and the other in the air and began to sing like Mario Lanza. '"Eeef I can help somebod-eee as I pass along/Then my lee-e-eving. Weeel not. Be in vai-in." Is that the Larne bus maybe?'

There was a smattering of people on board – a

middle-aged man in the back seat, a younger man two seats forward, a fat woman with a child in her arms just inside the door. Mrs Livingstone got on to the bus, moving down the aisle until she came to a seat five from the back. We followed her, Almighty bringing up the rear.

'Sit here,' she told Presumer, pointing. 'You'll see the scenery from here.'

'Me go too, Mammy. See scenery,' Sean said, tugging her coat.

'Scenery my arse,' Presumer declared. 'I'll be reading *Time* magazine. Look – that's your man Monkey-jaw on the front of it. Richard Nixon.'

'Well, look up every so often, then. Say goodbye to the countryside.'

'Where'll I put this?' I asked Presumer.

'All cases here inside the door,' the bus conductor called from the front of the bus. 'Stack your cases in here.'

'To let some wee bugger lift and walk off? I'll be damned apt,' Mrs Livingstone said in a loud voice. 'Don't heed a word out of him. We're not that soft!' she called up to the conductor.

'Ma, lay off,' Presumer told her. 'I'll keep it here but you button your lip.' Mrs Livingstone said nothing, just sat down in the seat behind Presumer's, with Sean squashed between her and the window. 'And don't bother getting settled either – we'll be leaving any minute.'

Presumer's mother ignored this, as did Almighty, who slipped into the seat beside her. 'Hear about the man whose wife ran away with another man?' Almighty paused, eyebrows raised. Then, 'He chased her by bus, by train and then by helicopter. Get it? Hell-He-Copped-Her.' Nobody responded. 'Djou know there's three ways to tell people something is happening – telephone, telegram, tell a woman.' He looked out the window of the bus. 'Or sometimes they just have their own way of discovering what's going on.'

Outside the bus, arms linked, Cait and Maeve stood giggling. When they saw us watching them they turned away, clutching each other.

'Just this man travelling?' the conductor called from the front. 'The rest of youse better skedaddle – we're for away.'

'See?' Presumer said.

'How'll you leave with no driver?' Almighty called.

The conductor moved down the aisle towards us. 'He'll be here in a minute. He's doing something right now but he'll be here in a minute. He's making a phone call. Take him no time.'

'He must be some man if he can make a phone call from that dee-pott,' Almighty said.

'The what?'

'That dee-pott. It's an English word now. Because there *is* no phone in there. My daddy's always giving out about it. Your man's in the lav, isn't he?' Almighty said. 'The driver. Nothing wrong with that. All you have to do is say it.'

I looked out the window. Maeve and Cait were staring up, their faces intent, trying to figure out what was going on.

The conductor raised his voice and his arm at the same time. 'Off, the pack of you. Or do you want me to get the inspector?'

'Don't forget the priest,' Mrs Livingstone said.

'What priest? There is no priest.' The conductor looked worried.

'Soon as you get the length, go to his house and have a chat with him,' Presumer's ma told him. 'He'll put you on the right road. Get you started.' Her voice was hoarse.

'Couldn't I get a start with Auntie Eileen?' She'd stopped being Clarissa but it didn't seem to matter now.

'She could be busy at Christ only knows,' Mrs Livingstone said. 'And even she wasn't, she'd still not have the pull of the priest when it comes to jobs.'

'I *told* you, I've got a job lined up already. I *told* you.'

'The priest'll give you a free dinner, wait till you see. Tons of meat and cabbage.'

I glanced out the window. Maeve and Cait had their arms around each other and were whispering. Maeve glanced up and along the bus to where Presumer sat.

Then the driver was hurrying across the car park, rubbing his hands. 'Right, ladies and gentlemen, adjust your drawers for action!' He clambered into the driving seat, checked some sheets of paper. Then the starter was tugged once, twice, and the bus rattled into life.

'OK – off. Off off off off off!' the conductor shouted, shooing us down the aisle. Presumer knelt on the seat and opened the window and put his face to the space.

'Bye-bye, girls!' he called. Maeve and Cait both waved, eyes wide, grinning. Cait looked almost pretty.

And then Christy came trotting across the bus depot, carrying a big flat parcel. She jumped on to the platform of the bus as it began to reverse.

'Can I – give this – to him?' she asked, her shoulders and chest inside the light grey sweater going up and down.

'Give to who? – Say you who and I'll give them it,' the conductor told her, sort of panting too.

Presumer hurried down the aisle to the bus platform. 'You did it!' he said to her. He sounded like Paddy that time he'd received the kitten.

'I only got it finished there now.' Christy's brown eyes roamed over his face, looking for a reaction. 'And then I had to wait for the paint to dry. Look at it on the boat. You'll have plenty of time to look then.'

'Brilliant,' Presumer said. 'Brilliant.'

They stood there on the bus platform, Christy's shoulders still heaving slightly, her mouth open.

'We're away,' the bus conductor said. Christy hopped off. Presumer went back to his seat, knelt at the open window as the bus reversed across the middle of the depot.

Almighty shouted something to me above the grinding of gears. I shrugged to show I couldn't hear him and he pointed at the bus.

'Three hundred horse power! Swear to Godalmighty!'

Christy stood, one hand to her mouth, watching the bus nose towards the Belfast Road. Ten feet away, Maeve had begun to cry.

'Did I hurt your arm?' Cait asked. 'Didn't mean to. Honest.'

''S OK.' Maeve pulled a hankie from the strap of her watch.

'You can keep that Pat Boone record if you want,' Cait told her. 'I'll tell my daddy I lost it.'

'That Pat Boone's a homo or I'm Donald Duck,' Debbie Reynolds whispered in my ear. 'You should see the cut of some of the ones goes in and out of his apartment.'

Maeve put the hankie against her mouth and spoke through it. 'I don't know why I'm crying.'

'Hip hip hooray,' said Mrs Livingstone. 'She's away.' The bus pulled out and went rattling up the Belfast Road, round the corner past Torney's garage and out of sight. A blue tangle of exhaust fumes hung in the air.

Her eyes still on the Belfast Road, Christy touched my arm. 'Your daddy's trousers are ready at the shop. I'm going up there – get them for you if you want.'

We moved through the town, not speaking. When I glanced back, Maeve and Cait were following us, twenty yards behind. Halfway across the bridge, Christy put both elbows on to the low protecting wall and stared into the water. I stood, waited, thought. Christy washing herself in a pool in the Rockies. On a hill overlooking the pool where I'm finished eating a tin of beans and starting to play the guitar.

'I know what you're thinking,' she said. 'You're wondering what was in the parcel I gave Presumer.' I felt my guts go watery. 'It was a painting I did. He gave me a photograph and I did a painting. That's all.'

'What was the photograph of?'

'Him. Took me half the night getting it done – my eyes feel stewed now.' She spat into the brown water, slowly and awkwardly, the spit a little bubbly dot of grey. 'Paintings are better than snaps – they show you the hidden bits of people – that's what Vincent Van Gogh said. The bits they hide under the skin.' Beneath us the water plopped. A brown trout showed for an instant and was gone again. 'What would you say Paddy O'Kane tries to hide?'

I hesitated. 'Not sure. That he's a bit jealous of his sister, maybe.'

Christy squeezed my arm. 'Top marks. Jealous is it exactly. It can drive people mad, you know.'

'Probably does,' I told her. You could see the stony bed of the river from here. 'Paddy sees Mary doing things and going places and that makes him feel it. Jealousy.' Don't think about the parcel Christy had given to Presumer. Don't think about her fingers holding the brush, her eyes moving from photograph to painting, a smudge of red on the front of her overall. Don't think about the beauty spot on her neck.

Christy turned towards me, leant her back against the wall. 'I'm going to tell you something – OK?' I put my hands on the bridge wall to stop them shaking. 'Remember Miller's Picture House where the fifty pounds was gone? And they figured the circus ones had broke in?' I nodded. 'I know who really took it.' She had a strand of hair lying along her right cheek and the end of one of the hairs was stuck in the corner of her mouth. 'It was Paddy.'

The water was full of dark shadows and little swirls and twitches. As if the river was anxious, not sure how to respond to people who leaned over its edge. People who spat into it, threw cigarette butts and car tyres and even old bikes into it.

'He took the fifty quid and hid it in his drawers. Then broke the window and spilt a thing of blood he had, to throw them off the trail.'

'A thing of blood? How do you mean?'

'The cops found blood inside the window, right? They got this pile of broken glass and this pool of blood, and they thought it was a man from the circus. All it was, was blood Paddy had brought in.'

Christy's face with her brown eyes and her teeth

slightly stuck out. The gurgle of the river below. Maeve and Cait a dot on the edge of my vision, watching us.

'He had it saved from his daddy killed a pig before Christmas. All he had to do then was break the window, splash the blood and next thing the cops were round at the circus, searching.'

'But Paddy's family have a big house. Music lessons and everything. He's not going to do something like that. What would he want money for?'

'Badness.' She looked down into the river again. Gave another little creamy spit that came out slowly, hanging to her lips as if reluctant to leave them. 'Pure badness.'

'Who told you all this?'

'Presumer,' she said without looking up. 'When we were out the Hospital Road for a walk last week.'

I could have asked how *he* knew but I didn't trust myself to speak. Had she promised to do the painting for him then? Had she told him that she liked the way he didn't care about things no matter what they were, the way people like Dickey thumped him or the way people like Neil got him sent to England, but he still didn't care and wouldn't give any of them the satisfaction of thinking they'd upset him? What else did he tell her? And what else did she tell him?

Maeve and Cait were walking away now. Probably decided that Christy and I were getting on like a house on fire.

'Mind you,' Christy said. 'I'd be bad myself if I had Little Miss Sunshine for a sister. Put a saint up the walls, that one.'

We left the bridge, moved round the curve on to the Hospital Road. A little way down the road was a wooden fence with steps built over it, to let you climb into the field and down a path to the river. As Christy climbed them, small dimples of fat on her legs winked back at me. Then she was over and I was hurrying down the path after her. Where was she going? What about her work and Our Father's trousers?

'In here.'

The voice came from behind a line of thick shrubbery and overgrown grass. I squeezed through to find Christy sitting in a clear space, her arms around her knees. She patted the ground beside her and I sat, our shoulders touching. *How are you feeling yourself?* The river gurgled past, brown moving lines glimpsed through the greenery.

'The womb,' Christy said, putting her chin on her knees and staring straight ahead. 'That's what Presumer called this place.' There was silence for a moment. 'There's this man called Sigmund Freud who thinks everything is wombs. We don't know they are but they are.'

I gripped my knees and stared at my shoes. The right toecap was scuffed, paler than the rest, as if it was trying to grow a beard. A few yards up the river a plopping sound. Another fish rising. Or a rat going in.

'It's great being in here with somebody, because it lets you talk to them and hear them breathing. But even you're on your own, it's good. Like the Garden of Eden. Do you find that?' Her left hand fluttered on to my shoulder and sat there. Warm. Like at the dance. 'I keep telling myself I won't miss this when I go but I will.'

A bird flew up the river in little swoops, skimming the surface, gulping invisible flies.

'I didn't know you were going.' My voice sounded as if someone else was speaking a few yards behind me.

Her fingers moved from my shoulder to my right cheek. Traced the furrows in it as if she were removing dust. 'He's not going to Blackpool, you know. Presumer. He's for Huntingdon. Nowhere near Blackpool – miles further down England. No football teams down there at all. But guess who's from it? From Huntingdon?' She stared at me, little teeth nibbling on her lower lip. 'Oliver Cromwell.' The name hung in the air like a rattle of thunder. 'I read about him. Know what he used to get his soldiers to do when they were in Ireland? Throw babies in the air, see who could catch them on their swords coming down. One bad bugger, Cromwell.' She tugged a blade of grass and put it in her mouth.

Blood on the face and hair of the man beneath, like Presumer's blood flicking on to Dickey. The sword being lowered under the weight of the small body.

'Are you going to England yourself?'

She turned and looked at me, her eyes brown and steady. 'Couple of weeks' time.' Her hand moved from my cheek to my back, slipped under my shirt. When I shivered she laughed. 'Like an electric shock, isn't it? Only a nice shock, not a bad one.' She leaned over and kissed my face. Her tongue wet and warm. 'Poor little cheek. Now. Do you think your cheek will go to hell for that? Burning for ever?'

Then her face was laughing closer to me, so close I could see a loose black eyelash on her cheek and feel her breath against my eyelid, and then we were lying side by side. *Holy Mary Mother of God, pray for us sinners.* One minute I had been waving goodbye to Presumer, who I had betrayed only he didn't know it. Now I was here lying on a river bank with his girlfriend wobbling with laughter and pretending to bite my chin.

The time I had nearly shown Christy where we had buried the crowbar. The time I had thought about Jesus as my brother. The time in bed on Christmas night and the pup going throb, throb, throb and Debbie Reynolds going up the chimney. But now this wasn't thinking or imagining, it was all real. Christy kissing my left cheek and telling me I was a brave little man to have come through an accident to my poor face like that and never to go talking about it or looking for pity. And there was no need to be shaking or blushing the way I was doing, the whole thing was just a bit of fun, pure and simple, to cheer the pair of us up after Presumer leaving, if I didn't stop taking everything so personal and serious I'd land myself in the Asylum. *Oh my God I am heartily sorry that I am offending thee.*

Afterwards, I couldn't stop myself. As she stood up and began to brush bits of grass off her skirt and from her hair, I looked at the space where the river showed and blurted it out. I was the one had told Dickey about who had broken into Neil's. And who'd been at the Jail Square. 'It was me,' I said, staring at the ground. 'Not Foxy.'

'Presumer thought it was both of you.'

I stared at her. 'You mean he knew I'd – I'd said, all along? You knew?'

She leaned down and patted my cheek. 'For God's sake. Presumer was going to go to England anyway – it's no big deal. Don't start that craw-thumping routine again, whatever you do.'

She headed up the path towards the Hospital Road, little red weals on the back of her legs from where she'd been lying on the grass.

CHAPTER 18

When I was ten I got chicken pox and dreamed about meeting a tiger. It had a body the shape of a torpedo, striped legs with razor nails, and it was coming down a cliff path towards me. When I turned to run my body felt awkward, out of control, drifting from side to side on the cliff path. Coming in the road with Christy that afternoon the tiger kept rolling about in my head, its claws scraping red lines inside my skull.

Christy was OK, though. Even though she had been up half the night she didn't seem a bit tired. She whistled 'One Night With You'. Did little tapdance steps, arms out to balance herself as she walked along the footpath's brick edge. Bent to pluck dandelion clocks, calling in Irish as she blew them: '*A h-aon a chlog* (puff), *a dó a chlog* (puff), *a trí a chlog* (puff).' Tiny parachutes floated in front of her, some of them, lucky bastards, lodging in her hair. Safe and happy, like the time I'd imagined climbing in with the jewellery, waiting for Bernie outside the Picture House.

'Come in – I'll get your trousers in a tick. Only say nothing.' T-ting! went the shop bell. Her boss sat behind the counter, his bald head bent over pound notes and columns of coins. When he saw us he scooped everything into a drawer and rose, his mouth puckering into little wrinkles and smoothing again as Christy hurried towards him.

'Oh Mr Hutton, you must be raging, all my fault, except that Jim here had to ask his mammy if he should collect his daddy's trousers, and she was out a back field with a calving cow and we had to use the sound of the cow, you know the way they go when they're calving, awful I know, like a cry for help, to guide us, and I'm awful sorry.' She stood biting her lip and twisting her finger.

Mr Hutton, when he moved out from behind the counter, was at least six inches smaller than her. It was hard to tell what he was thinking as he looked at her face and down at her twisting fingers.

He might have been thinking about how he could teach her a lesson by grabbing her and giving her six of the best on the bare b-t-m. Or maybe he was imagining chasing around the shop after her, their shoes squeaking on the linoleum, their breath hot, until she gasped and collapsed at his feet. I have no idea. Except that with his little twitching mouth and moving-up-and-down eyes, he looked as if something agitated was definitely going on in his head.

'Well, you know, calving or no calving, rules are rules. A shop can't run if people – even part-time people like you, miss – do whatever comes in their head. Rules and reliability come first and that's the size of it.'

Christy shook her bent heat and her hair fell in little black curtains on either side of her face, the way it had done when she had kissed me a half-hour earlier. 'No repetition – understood?' Mr Hutton tapped Christy's fringe with a nicotined finger. 'No repetition.' When he turned away Christy crossed her eyes and pretended she was going to scrab the face off him.

T-tching! the bell went as the door closed behind me

and I stepped on to the street. 'That is one two-faced wee fat tart,' Debbie whispered, falling into step beside me. 'Mocking her boss and opening buttons for every Tom, Dick and Harry.'

Past the Courthouse, along in front of the chapel and down Castle Street. In the gutter beside Gormley's, a toffee-apple. Some wasps had made a hole in it and were crawling in and out, little striped bellows throbbing and jerky with the effort, around and over and under each other. The edge of the hole was brown and the centre black, like the darkness up a person's nose. At the back of my head the tiger began again, hanh, hanh, hanh.

Then something thudded against my shoulder and I was staggering into the street, landing on my knees with the grit stinging through a tear in one leg. From behind me came laughter, and when I straightened Paddy and Tommy were standing in front of Gormley's shop window. Tommy's right arm was in a sling, with a plaster from his elbow to near his fingertips. The side of his face and upper neck was bruised purple.

'He was going to pick that apple up, wasn't he?' he said to Paddy, pointing with his left hand at me. 'If you hadn't shoved him he was going to eat a rotten toffee-apple off the street. Like a fucking beggar or something.'

Paddy stood with his legs apart and emptied a packet of Wrigley's chewing gum into his mouth. 'Hear your friend has buggered off to England,' he said. Chewed for a minute. 'Mr Know-It-All.'

'Couldn't take his fucking oil,' Tommy said. He took the two portions of chewing gum Paddy gave him and started to chew.

'Yes he could,' I said, pointing back at Tommy. 'Shut your trap.'

'Shut you *your* trap – never mind me, shut you *your* trap. Standing there with a gob like a half-ploughed field.' He wouldn't have said that if his arm hadn't been in a sling. And if Paddy hadn't been with him.

Paddy pulled his gum out in a string and lowered it back into his mouth. Chewed. 'Your chum Presumer. He was a great man for blaming other people. Went and told the cops it was me organised that thing at Neil's, you know.'

'Lying bugger,' Tommy said.

'If my daddy hadn't lived in the house next to the police inspector one time,' Paddy went on, 'I could have been a goner. Up in court, in jail even.'

'And me, don't forget,' Tommy said. 'Accomplice to the felony at Traynor's. Paddy's da saved our hides, goldarn it.'

My tongue seemed to have swollen to three times its normal size. Behind me panting: hanh, hanh. 'What did he do, then?' I asked carefully. 'Your daddy.'

'What do you think? Told the inspector what really happened, that's all. The way Presumer was the one was all for it, come on and we'll wreck the car, come on and we'll break into the house, come on and we'll cut up the cat. He's been in trouble with the police since the day he was born, the inspector told daddy. Was going to break into Foxy Johnston's too, only the police had a tip-off. Typical Presumer. Loves doing things and then loves blaming other people. Not all there in the upstairs department.' Paddy pulled another grey string of gum from his mouth, tilted his head. Chewed. 'A wonder he didn't blame you when he was at it.'

'What would he do that for?' I said. 'There's nothing to blame me for. What could he blame me for?'

'Anything came in his head. Breaking and entering, killing the cat, cutting it up – anything.'

Tommy came up close to me and tapped my chest with his left hand. 'Know what the stupid bugger was going around saying? That *we* cut up the cat. Me and him.' He nodded his head towards Paddy. 'And that Paddy pushed me off the wall in the Jail Square. You believe it?'

'But he did!' I said. 'It was you. And you were the ones did that stuff to the cat. Cut it up and all.' Hanh, hanh.

'This is the latest,' Paddy said. 'Listen to this now.'

'Lying bastard, that's all you are,' Tommy said, his left hand tapping my chest, pointing at my face. 'A crinkly-kissered lying bastard.'

Paddy gripped Tommy by the shoulder and eased him aside. 'Know what you tell Presumer?' he said to me. 'On the phone or whatever? Tell him he's for it. He comes back here again, he's a definite hundred per cent for it. I've started training.' Paddy took his wad of wet chewing gum from his mouth, looked at it, put it back in.

'Father Breen was the one asked him to come back and train,' Tommy said. 'He's going to build up the boxing club.'

Paddy said: 'Father Breen's OK when you get to know him. Have to know him first to know, that's the thing. He's going to get us six new punchbags from the Army. Ones they don't need.'

'And he knows about singing,' Tommy said. 'He said when my arm's better, I can get my voice trained. And if I practise hard, scales and all that, I could be touring same as Paddy's sister. Look what the cat brought in.' The last remark was directed at Almighty, who had appeared from the shop eating a toffee-apple. 'Hungry fucking Horace himself.'

'Or Hungry Horace fucking himself,' Paddy said. He and Tommy laughed.

Almighty lowered the toffee-apple and started to say something, but the sound of a horn interrupted. Uncle Father John's car was coming slowly up Castle Street. Uncle Father John behind the wheel, Our Father and Mammy in the back seat.

'He was a bossy bastard, Presumer,' Paddy whispered quickly and spat out his gum. 'England's too good for him.'

Tommy leaned in to me: 'Big shite. Squealing on other people to get himself off.'

The two of them moved down the street, Tommy glancing back over his shoulder. Almighty leaned his back against Gormley's window and went on eating his toffee-apple.

Uncle Father John opened the driver's door and stood, one elbow resting on the car roof. 'Nearly missed you there. Lucky your mammy spotted you or we could have driven past and paid you no heed. We're heading for a bite in the Silver Birches Hotel.' He looked past me to where Almighty loitered. 'Would you like to come yourself?'

I remembered the parcel under my arm. 'Need to bring these trousers home. They were being fixed.'

Mammy leaned forward from the back seat and called through the window. 'I left Maeve and Cait in charge of cooking operations – tell them to see you're looked after. Is that a tear you have in the knee of those good trousers?'

Our Father leaned past her from the back seat. 'Mind

and not drop that parcel. Trousers cost money, I may tell you.'

Uncle Father John started to get back into the car, then bobbed up again. 'I was talking to Brother Dickey a while earlier. He'll be in the Brothers' House from four o'clock, in case somebody like yourself would be looking to have a chat or something.'

I nodded. Uncle Father John slapped the top of the car, got in and they went droning up Castle Street, wisps of exhaust smoke drifting slowly towards the sunny side of the street behind them.

'Four o'clock,' Almighty said, sucking his toffee-apple stick. 'That's a full hour. Wait in my house if you want. My daddy's gone to the Graan for a confession. Listen to records.'

As we walked back up Castle Street and past the chapel, Almighty told me Neil went to the monastery in Enniskillen once a month in his car. 'He says the monks in the Graan get you more grace in confession than the Omagh priests, but I asked Father Breen and he said there's no difference. I always go to Father Breen.'

God. Somewhere in the centre of darkness. Whose sins you shall forgive they are forgiven.

The sun went in as Almighty opened the gate at the bottom of the path up to their house. Then we were in the hallway with the photographs, darker than I remembered it. Through to the room with the Aga. I sat in a big armchair while Almighty went to the table in the corner on which the record player sat. Through the window I could see the clouds, one behind the other, gathering above the Courthouse. A smell of polish came from the linoleum floor. Didn't remember that either.

The first record Almighty put on was Lonnie Donegan

singing 'The Sloop John B'. While it was playing he poured two glasses of Lucozade.

'You're not supposed to drink this except you're sick but I like it so my daddy gets it. My uncle says he shouldn't, that he's only spoiling me.' What the hand and what the eye. 'See when I was wee? My daddy and mammy lost me one time in Bundoran. I didn't even know. I was just wandering along the beach looking at the height of the waves, like big white walls collapsing on swimmers, when my mammy grabs me from behind and starts crying and saying she thought I'd gone away for ever. And my daddy looked as if he was going to cry too, but he didn't. My mammy sat in the back of the car with me the whole way home, going on about how she thought I was maybe drowned or knocked down or murdered. Bet you that's what Presumer's ma was thinking that time Sean was lost – wouldn't you say? It'd be nice, though, having a, a, a, a family. Wouldn't it?' I wanted to tell him to shut his bloody gob so I could hear Lonnie Donegan, but I couldn't. 'Say if you were buying them Christmas presents and measuring their feet for shoes and that. My daddy says I'll inherit his shop, be running it myself some day, so I should pay attention and find out where everything is. But it'll be OK, because my uncle says he'll help me out if I don't know where something is kept. If he's still alive then.' I nodded. Framed thy fearful symmetry. 'The Sloop John B' ended and Almighty jumped up. 'I've a Buddy Holly record in my bedroom. Won't be a tick.' He trotted from the kitchen before I could say anything. Came back, holding the record in its brown paper cover above his head.

'They found it after Buddy died, Pete Murray says.

His wife who was his widow by that time, you know, Buddy Holly's widow I mean, she said, OK, he'd have wanted people to hear it, because he'd recorded it before he died. And so the people that did his records, they listened and said Godalmighty, we'll do it surely, these are great. Does your Maeve like Buddy Holly?' I didn't answer. Whistling, he crossed to the record player and took Lonnie Donegan off. The smell of the tiger's breath, blood on its lips. 'It's called "Think It Over".'

The volume was up so high, you could hear the hiss of the needle. Then the first down-thrashing chords sounded, and Buddy's little back-of-throat voice was singing, 'Think it over and think of me/ Think it over and you will see.' Da-ding da-ding da-dingdedingding-dingding.

I got Almighty to play that song twice more, really loud, so the words and the music filled the room. Especially the last bit: 'For my heart grows cold and old.' Da-ding da-ding da-dingdingdingdingding. Once or twice Almighty looked at his watch, and three times he said he had Mary O'Kane's record, 'Little Smasher'. But I didn't want to hear 'Little Smasher'. I wanted to hear 'Think It Over', the big strong chords at the end of each verse – da-dung-da, da-dung-da, dadungadadungada-dungggg – and then the Crickets singing 'Over and over, over and over' and the guitars jangling and deerumpa-pumpapumping again. Think it over, think it over. For my heart grows cold and old.

'It's five past four,' Almighty said, twisting his arm round to show me his watch. 'You'll be late.'

'It's all right.'

The Courthouse clock was chiming quarter past four by the time I left. Outside a breeze was pushing up the street, and the layered clouds had been replaced by big dirty blanket-bundle ones. Outside the chapel gates I lit a cigarette. The paint had been put on so thick, little green tears of paint had solidified down the side of the bars. The tiger stretched flat on the cliff path, head on razor paws, waiting.

Then the rain began – drops slicing into my face, gusts of wind behind them. Even though all it was was rain, not tears or anything, I could feel my shoulders shaking and my nose running and I had to swallow before I could manage a pull on the cigarette. Did he who made the lamb make thee?

A hand on my elbow. Francie, the other hand clamping his black hat on his head. 'Jim! What are you up to?' Girls' calves. Mud. Weals. 'I was on my way inside here for a visit.' Behind him was the dark mouth of the chapel. 'Were you heading the same place yourself?'

'No!' Hadn't meant to shout. Only wanted him to hear me above the wind and rain.

But now he had jumped back, embarrassed. 'Sorry, Jim. Just thought—'

'I have to see somebody!' I shouted. Then repeated it quieter. 'Need to see somebody. And then when I've seen him, I'll see you.'

'Ah, I see. Well now. Good man. That's grand.' Francie patted my shoulder before heading through the chapel gate.

Hurry along the path past the chapel and up the hill to the Brothers' House. In her grotto on the left Our Lady is being drenched but she doesn't seem to mind, just goes on standing there with her flat chest, arms out, smiling. That was good. Our Lady in the rain, Francie kneeling in the chapel, Brother Dickey in his room with the holy pictures. 'Jesus, such an amount of praying,' Debbie whispered.

Slow and cumbersome, like a 78 record being played at 45, the bell of the Christian Brothers clangs along some dark corridor. A silence; then strong firm footsteps. 'He's coming!' Debbie hisses. 'Could you not run like that night? There's still *time*.' But there is no time. Because the door is opening, Dickey is standing with the hall light behind him, a black cigarette trailing smoke, the cuff of his soutane frayed. He doesn't say anything, just gestures me inside, the hint of a smile looking down at me. Then the door thuds shut behind us, closing out the wind and rain.